NIGHT THUNDER

"[*Night Thunder*] gallops out of the starting gate . . .
Gregory expertly weaves the various plot threads
together, creating a tight, well-balanced story that packs
an emotional punch." —*Publishers Weekly*

THUNDER CREEK

"A transfixing blend of fiery romance and spine-tingling
suspense." —*Booklist*

"For tales of romance and adventure that keep you reading into the night, look no further than Jill Gregory."
—Nora Roberts

"A compelling tale that works on two levels, as a well-
structured mystery and a first rate romance. Gregory . . .
writes the stuff that romance readers yearn for. If you
haven't yet read her, you're missing out on a great treat."
—*Oakland Press*

"Fans . . . will be pleased by her treatment of the protago-
nists' relationship and drawn in by the book's cozy, small-
town setting . . . Once the action revs up, readers will
gladly sit back and enjoy the journey."
—*Publishers Weekly*

ONCE AN OUTLAW

"Gregory's sensitive characterizations . . . will drive a
herd of new readers to pick up this heartfelt family
drama . . . The story escalates with fast-paced action,
romance and several surprises as the fiery attraction
between Clint and Emily hits fever pitch."
—*Publishers Weekly*

NEVER LOVE A COWBOY

"A western version of Romeo and Juliet . . . This is a who-done-it with strong elements of suspense . . . but the emphasis is definitely on the romance. This book has wonderful, tender scenes . . . Jill Gregory creates not only a very human hero and a likeable heroine but also very evil villains with interesting motivations."
—*The Romance Reader*

"Sensual . . . Enjoy *Never Love a Cowboy* . . . A western, a suspenseful mystery, and a good book. Combining grit, sensuality and a cleverly plotted mystery takes talent."
—*Romantic Times*

JUST THIS ONCE

"Refreshing characters, witty dialogue and adventure . . . *Just This Once* enthralls, delights, and captivates, winning readers' hearts along the way."
—*Romantic Times*

"Here is another unforgettable story that will keep you captivated. She has combined the Old West and the elegance of England into this brilliantly glorious tale. The characters are undeniably wonderful. Their pains and joys will reach through the pages and touch your heart."
—*Rendezvous*

ALWAYS YOU

"*Always You* has it all . . . Jill Gregory's inventive imagination and sprightly prose combine for another bellringer." —*Rendezvous*

"Compelling . . . definitely a winner!"
—*Affaire de Coeur*

Also by Jill Gregory

NIGHT THUNDER

THUNDER CREEK

ONCE AN OUTLAW

ROUGH WRANGLER, TENDER KISSES

NEVER LOVE A COWBOY

JUST THIS ONCE

ALWAYS YOU

DAISIES IN THE WIND

FOREVER AFTER

CHERISHED

WHEN THE HEART BECKONS

JILL GREGORY

Thunder at Dawn

A DELL BOOK

THUNDER AT DAWN
A Dell Book / August 2005

Published by
Bantam Dell
A Division of Random House, Inc.
New York, New York

Dell is a registered trademark of Random House, Inc., and the
colophon is a trademark of Random House, Inc.

ISBN 0-440-24178-2

Printed in the United States of America
Published simultaneously in Canada

www.bantamdell.com

OPM 10 9 8 7 6 5 4 3 2 1

In memory of Scamper, who always kept me company and slept beside my chair as I wrote, who brought our family so much joy and love for fifteen years, and whose sweet memory will live every day in our hearts

Thunder
at Dawn

Chapter 1

Thunder Creek, Wyoming

"HOLD IT RIGHT THERE, LADY. STEP AWAY FROM the car. I happen to know it belongs to our sheriff—you're under arrest."

Faith Barclay straightened from placing two sacks of groceries in the backseat of the silver Explorer and smiled at the man bearing down on her on Thunder Creek's main street. Her cousin Roy Hewett wore the same shit-eating grin on his face she'd seen a hundred times when they were kids—right after he'd slipped a frog down the back of her T-shirt or challenged her and her brothers to a race through the cemetery under a full moon.

"Good to see you too, Roy—I think." She had to laugh as he scooped her into a bear hug, then swung her around in the air like she weighed no more than she had when she was ten.

"Ty told me you'd be arriving today." He set her down on her feet and bussed her cheek. "Nice he could leave Josy's car at the airport for you to use while you're here, but too bad he and Josy were headed to New York right when you finally got your butt out here for a visit. Don't worry, though, big cousin Roy is here to keep an eye on you. You need anything, you know who to call."

Faith laughed, shoving her windblown, toffee-colored curls out of her eyes and giving him a hug. She was touched by Roy's concern. And at the same time she fought down a twinge of irritation.

What had her mom and brothers been telling him . . . telling everyone? Did half the town know she was "going through a rough spell," as her father so delicately put it?

"Thanks for the thought, Roy, but I don't need a babysitter. I'm more than able to take care of myself."

"You always have been, Faith. Hell, we know that." He gently tugged one of her curls. "Still . . . you're family. And me and Corinne are here for you."

"How is Corinne? Excited about the baby?" Faith was more than happy to change the subject from herself to Roy's wife. He and Corinne had gotten married just over a year ago and now they were expecting their first child in March. *Much more pleasant,* she thought, *to discuss babies and nurseries and small-town life than the train wreck of my own life.*

"Excited?" Roy smacked himself in the forehead. "She can't talk about anything else. Names. Girl names, boy names. Do I like *Cassandra,* she asks me. How about *Viveca*? If it's a boy, *Roy Jr.* and we'd call him *RJ*—or how about *Caleb*? I swear, she must have that book *A Million and One Baby Names* down cold."

"So which ones *do* you like?" Faith asked.

Roy threw up his hands. "Don't you start too. How about a cup of coffee? Bessie's Diner, right now. I'm buying. Then you should come on home with me—Corinne always has plenty for dinner. Might as well have a home-cooked meal your first night here—"

"How about a rain check, Roy? I'm beat," Faith lied.

She ignored the guilt snapping through her at her cousin's disappointed expression.

"I'm worn out from the flight and the drive in from Casper." She spoke rapidly, apologetically. "I just want to get out to Blue Moon Mesa and settle in."

That part, at least, was true.

"Sure, but you gotta eat—" he began, and she interrupted him with a forced grin.

"I've survived twenty-nine years without you or my brothers spoon-feeding me, Roy. I'm pretty sure I can survive a monthlong stay in Thunder Creek too."

"But—"

"Kiss Corinne for me. Tell her I'll come by and see her soon."

Without giving him a chance to argue further, Faith gave him a quick hug and stepped up into the Explorer.

"You always were a damned stubborn snip of a thing," Roy called as she put the SUV into gear and started forward.

"You bet your ass," Faith murmured to herself, waving, yet her faint smile of amusement faded as she left the sun-dappled bustling town behind and headed west toward Blue Moon Mesa.

She knew Roy and the rest of her family meant well, but their concern only made her feel all the more pathetic. Just because her job and her love life had both gone south in the past six months, and sleep was little more than a distant memory, it didn't mean she was falling apart. True, she'd forgotten to eat a few times lately, hadn't had a manicure since last Christmas, and had spent 90 percent of her time at the office the entire summer, but she was fine. *Fine.*

But deep inside, Faith wondered if they could be right. She was losing her equilibrium, filled with self-doubt. She badly needed this break. In the end, that's why she'd decided to chuck it all for a precious four weeks and see if a good long vacation at her family's Thunder Creek cabin would help her get her head together.

There was no better place to unwind than the Barclay cabin on Blue Moon Mesa, smack in the middle of land that had been in their family for generations. She'd been coming here a few times a year ever since she was a baby.

Usually Faith drove slowly through the grassy foothills leading to Shadow Point and eventually up to the rocky heights of Blue Moon Mesa. She liked to savor the green tall pines, the deep wild ravines, the rich open silence, letting the wild grandeur of Wyoming's open spaces soothe her the way nothing else could.

But today she was still tense from her morning in court and from the three cups of coffee she'd gulped before ditching her ringing phone and her office and the gritty streets of Philadelphia for the flight to Casper. Still in her professional uniform of black suit jacket over a gray silk blouse, knee-length black skirt, discreet gold shell earrings, and her trademark black stiletto heels, she couldn't wait to strip off the trappings of Faith Barclay, assistant district attorney, and pull on sweats. Tension still knotted her neck muscles and she drove faster, her gaze glued to the road, her foot pressing relentlessly on the accelerator as the glorious grass, scrub, aspen, and juniper trees blurred by.

Only another ten miles, she realized, shooting past Antelope Rock, and she'd be at the cabin.

The thought sent a surge of relief through her.

For too long she'd resisted the idea of taking time off, preferring to hunker down and work through her problems, diving into her caseload and blocking everything else out, the way she had after she and Kevin called off their engagement. But when the damaging courtroom events of the past few months had hit on top of her unraveling personal life, work had no longer been a refuge—it had become another huge source of stress.

What do you expect? Two major cases got screwed up on your watch.

The burden of that weighed on her slender shoulders like a set of barbells double her weight.

And she'd known she needed to take some time to figure out what she wanted to do with the rest of her so-called life.

Until recently, Faith had been the golden girl of the district attorney's office, the shining star who'd surged through the ranks of prosecuting attorneys like an ascending comet. All of the lawyers and judges and support staff of Philadelphia's Court of Common Pleas for the First Judicial District had her pegged to make deputy DA by the time she was thirty.

She had a way of leaping over obstacles, brainstorming her way out of tight corners, and shining like eighteen-karat gold in the courtroom. The best defense attorneys in the state of Pennsylvania considered her a ball-breaker, which was just fine with Faith. She prided herself on her fairness, attention to detail, and dedication to the law, on vigorous prosecutions all carried out stringently by the book.

If her adversaries couldn't keep up, so much the better.

But both the Clement and Bayman cases had hit her hard. Her staff was still reeling, the newspapers were churning out investigations into how the system failed, and Faith had spent the past three weeks being grilled by an oversight committee and personally reviewing every shred of evidence in the Clement case, every interrogation, every file, with a fine-toothed comb.

Because now she not only had a stalker out on the streets when he should have been behind bars, she also had an innocent dead man on her conscience.

And no matter how she tried to justify it, both of those horrible miscarriages of justice could be laid, unofficially, at her door.

Technically, she wasn't responsible for Jimmy Clement's death—or for that monster Hank Bayman getting probation.

But that didn't help Faith sleep at night.

"A few weeks at the cabin will get this in perspective," her father had told her when he called last night while she was packing. She hoped to hell he was right. Slowing down slightly, she tightened her grip on the steering wheel as the Explorer plunged around a curve on Badman's Road, then she sped up again as the road evened out and blue sky and black-smudged mountains rose straight ahead.

It would be impossible not to sleep at the cabin, she told herself. Impossible not to be lulled by pine-laced mountain air, the immense silence of the Wyoming night, the sky spangled with a thousand gleaming stars.

Maybe it would only take a week or two, instead of the four she'd planned, before she felt restored and ready again to face the frenzy of work awaiting her, the pressure of the high-stakes cases flowing steadily to her desk. Before she was no longer worried about Susan Bayman and her kids, and furious every moment of the day because Hank Bayman was stalking the streets again, searching for his wife and children.

Her throat closed every time she thought about what

would happen if Bayman found Susan and the kids. The man was certifiable. And he was relentless.

And she was pretty certain that he was the one who'd been calling her cell phone lately and hanging up without saying a word. He believed she knew where Susan had gone, where she was hiding, trying to start over.

And he was right.

But she'd be damned before she'd tell him anything other than to go to hell.

If he thought calling her in the middle of the night and breathing into the phone would scare her, he was as big a fool as he was a bully.

Suddenly, as the road curved abruptly, Faith's mind was jerked back to the present. The sight of a black Ford pickup hurtling toward her from the opposite direction had her slamming on her brakes, jerking the wheel to the right, perilously close to the edge.

The pickup veered left at the same instant and missed ramming into her by a nose. Her heart pounding, she dragged the Explorer to a screeching stop. The front end was angled awkwardly less than five feet from the drop into the ravine.

Taking gulps of air to calm herself, she heard oaths coming from the other vehicle, then a strapping male catapulted from the pickup and stalked toward her.

Still catching her breath, Faith shoved open her door. Fury had her usually dreamy blue eyes snapping. She was outside, hands on her hips, glaring as the other driver approached.

The sun burned in her eyes and she squinted, trying to make out the face of the tall, muscular cowboy bearing down on her, but all she could see was a black Stetson shading his eyes and a white T-shirt and jeans encasing a body buff enough to model for Powerhouse Gym.

"Going sixty on a road like this, mister? That'll get you killed," she began blisteringly.

Then he was closer and the sun passed between the clouds and she saw his face. That handsome, hard, and angry face. He looked dangerous as sin and older now than the last time she'd seen him, ten years older, but her heart fell to her knees anyway and her mouth went dry as dust.

"You." The word came out in a breathless gasp. It sounded nothing like anyone who worked with Faith Barclay in the DA's office would ever recognize coming from her lips.

"You," she said again, harder, stronger.

Rage curled in her belly. She controlled it. She ignored the stupid ancient pain that seemed to still have power to stab her heart.

"You got a death wish, Faith?" Zach McCallum's eyes were silver slits. "Never mind, cancel that. You haven't changed, have you?"

Zach McCallum, no longer the lanky nineteen-year-old who for one glorious secret summer had laid claim to her heart, shook his head with the darkly sexy amusement she remembered so well.

For a moment time stood still. Faith might have been nineteen again too—and in love. Foolishly, stupidly in love with the bad boy from Texas who had raised hell that summer in Thunder Creek and had left boot marks all over her heart.

She hadn't seen him in ten years. Which was fifty years too soon.

"What are you doing back here, Zach? Besides driving on the wrong side of the road? You still make up all the rules as you go along, don't you?"

"Hey, don't blame him, Faith. You were speeding!" A

female voice piped up from behind Zach, and Faith's gaze flew to Candy Merck, as the blonde she'd known since high school stamped over from the pickup, her orchid-blue eyes as round and darkly lined as ever.

Great. Candy'd always had her eye on Zach. Well, she could have him. Unless his wife objected, of course.

Faith ignored Candy and focused on Zach. "You were driving recklessly. As usual." Good, she sounded cold as ice now—the tone she used in court when the opposing attorney made a particularly weak point. She met his gaze steadily, forcing herself to return the stare of those hard indifferent eyes and not to focus on the sensuous slant of his mouth, or the broad slope of those powerful shoulders.

He was in even better shape than he'd been as a teenager, she noticed with a sinking heart. There were attractive creases at the corners of those penetrating silvergray eyes, and a hard cynical wisdom in his face, a face that was still dark and beautiful all at once.

If anything he was even more impossibly handsome than before.

"I wasn't the only one being reckless," Zach said in a low tone. "You must have been going sixty, minimum."

"At least I was on the right side of the road."

"No one got hurt, Faith. I guess that's all that matters."

"Since when do you care who gets hurt?" The words flew out before she could stop them. All these years as a lawyer, in control, disciplined, weighing her words while shooting with both barrels, and yet that came out as if ten days had passed since Zach had broken her heart and not ten years.

She flushed, the warm color surging through her cheeks. *Get a grip,* she ordered herself.

"I hope you were speeding out of town, back wherever

you came from." The words were cool now, almost light. "Don't let me keep you."

As if I ever could.

For a moment he stared at her, his eyes shuttered.

Faith willed her own gaze to appear equally unreadable, equally detached.

Damn it, why couldn't he have looked slovenly, fat, decrepit? She felt prim and stuffy and dull in her dark suit and tailored silk blouse. Especially since the last time she'd seen Zach McCallum she'd been wearing a scoopnecked purple T-shirt and tight jeans. Her hair had streamed well past her shoulders, halfway down her back, and she'd been wearing too much eyeshadow and Love's Baby Soft perfume. That was before she'd graduated high school, or gone to Yale, or interned for Judge Cobb.

And before she'd become the woman who could tell Zach McCallum to go to hell and mean it, she thought, her lips compressing.

Zach was studying her in a most discomfiting way. There was something in his eyes, something deep and quiet that drove a stake through her heart.

It better not be pity, she thought desperately.

"I can't believe you're still pissed off at him after all these years," Candy muttered. She tugged on Zach's arm.

"Sweetie, I have to get back. I have another meeting at my office at four. If you want me to redo those contracts for you—"

"Right." Zach tore his gaze from Faith's pale, rigid face, forcing himself to focus on Candy. "Let's go. We're done here."

"Contracts?" Faith kept her voice level, though anger and dismay were flickering through her. "Don't tell me you're buying property through her—property in Thunder Creek?"

"No." He flicked her another glance. "I have enough property in Thunder Creek already. But another party is interested in leasing some of it from me."

"Since when do you have . . ." Her voice trailed off as she remembered. *The Last Trail ranch.* Zach had inherited all of it, the ranch, land, cattle, oil company—everything—from his aunt's estate, one of the largest properties in Wyoming. Ty had mentioned it once, casually, but she'd blocked it out, never imagining that he'd do more than sell it off to the highest bidder. So now the rich Texas boy who'd prided himself on his Lone Star roots had a foothold in Thunder Creek real estate—big time.

But it didn't matter to her, she reminded herself. She was only staying four weeks. And Zach was probably winding up this lease deal and leaving town. Back to Texas. *Yeeee-haw.*

She wouldn't have to see him again. This meeting was just a fluke.

"Anything else you want to know about my property or business, Faith?"

"I know more than I care to already. Don't let me keep you."

Candy Merck fixed her with an exasperated glance. "Honestly, Faith, you don't have to be so rude."

Her glance swiveled to the curvy woman in high-heeled boots, jeans, and a yellow blazer. She and Candy had never been the best of friends, but they hadn't been enemies either.

"No offense intended, Candy. This just . . . threw me a little. It's not every day someone nearly drives me off the road. But you and I are fine." She tossed out a quick smile and climbed back into the Explorer.

"I don't suppose you need any help backing away from here?" Zach said, eyeing the nose of her car perched perilously close to the edge.

"Damn straight." Her mouth curled into a tight grimace and he got the message.

Without another word, Zach and Candy headed back to the pickup. She deliberately waited until they had rolled past her and disappeared down the road before she put the SUV into reverse.

Damn. Running into Zach McCallum after all these years is not a promising way to kick off a vacation.

But he'll surely be gone by tomorrow, she told herself. *You'll never have to see him again.*

Yet as she backed the SUV onto the narrow road, she realized her hands were trembling. *Come on, grow up. You were all shaken up seeing Zach again when the truth is you were over him years ago. Damn it, you were engaged to Kevin. You would have gotten married . . .*

But you didn't. You aren't.

That's because I'm a loser at love, she thought grimly. *Or I'm jinxed. First Bayman goes free, then Zach roars back into Thunder Creek.*

Look on the bright side. What else could possibly go wrong? The rest of this vacation will have to be a breeze.

Her cell phone rang at that moment and she reached for it as she eased back onto the road. It could be her assistant, Liz Cooper, calling with a question, or the deputy DA, Ben Waverly, with an update on the Russell appeal.

But she didn't hear Liz's or Ben's voice on the phone.

She heard only silence.

Bayman again, she thought, her tension spiking. Susan

had told her how he'd often called, not saying a word, just breathing hard. And then she'd wake up in the middle of the night, and he'd be standing over her bed, looking down at her with a baseball bat or a Swiss Army knife in his hand.

"Who is this?" she demanded, her fingers clenched around the phone.

Silence. And she could picture him then, with that macho smirk on his face, imagining she was afraid of him.

But unlike Susan, she wasn't.

"Go to hell." Faith disconnected, tossing the phone down on the passenger seat.

Bastard. At least Susan was safe. Bayman had no way to find her. And Faith was determined to keep it that way.

She fixed her gaze on the road, forcing herself to forget about Zach and Bayman and Kevin, her own personal fiancé from hell. And about everything else in her life.

Faith thought about the upcoming winter here in Wyoming. She'd never been here in the autumn before, when the weather was changing, the wind carrying with it the tang of snow and the land taking on shades of taupe and rust and gold. She thought of how wonderful it would be to stay up in the cabin all winter long—alone, peaceful, snowed in and cozy with nothing but a fire, a few months' worth of pizza and steak and frozen lasagna, and a half dozen novels and jigsaw puzzles to occupy her time.

Life felt simpler here in Thunder Creek. A helluva lot simpler than the mess of failure she'd left behind.

Chapter 2

"SUPPER'LL BE READY DIRECTLY. IF I WAS YOU, I'd start rounding that boy up now," Neely Day said darkly. "If you *can,* that is."

Standing in the glossy oak-floored hall of the Last Trail's gracious ranch house, Zach glanced up from his perusal of the day's mail.

Having gotten his attention, Neely gave a sniff, her iron-colored brows drawing together. "He's in the barn," she muttered. "And it's not good news."

Zach studied the plump, gloomy face of the woman who'd cooked and cleaned in his father's ranch house south of Houston ever since he could remember. And he didn't need to wonder if she'd ever complained so gloomily about him and his brother when *they* were growing up.

Neely Day had been widowed at the age of thirty-two, and had spent the next thirty years working full-time for his father, spurning any attempts to coax her into having a life of her own. She'd turned her back on the world and devoted herself to the McCallum family, all of whom had learned to take her grumpiness and complaints in stride. Optimism was not in Neely Day's character, but she was softhearted as a lamb underneath the bushy gray hair and stout figure, and she also happened to be the best ranch cook in the western United States.

"What'd Dillon do now? It can't be as bad as the tricks I played on you when I was his age." Zach regarded her with his most soothing smile.

But Neely was in no mood to be mollified. "Hmmph. *Tricks* I can handle," she retorted, shaking her head so the Brillo pad of gray hair flew about her bulldog face. "This boy is different. He and his animals'll be the death of me."

"Uh-oh. What now?"

"The Olsons' barn cat had kittens a few weeks ago. And now Dillon's brought one home."

"Only one, Neely? That's a first."

"Thank the good Lord. You going to let him keep it?"

Zach grinned. "What do you think?"

Neely shook a fist in the air, her mouth turning down in a scowl. "Lord help me. I think this place is turning into a regular zoo. One of these days that boy's going to come home with a bobcat cub and that's the day I walk out that door."

"Neely, you know we couldn't get by without you."

"Hmmph. Sweet talk don't work for me, mister. A body can only take so much, and all of these critters running around this fine house is going to be the death of me one day."

She shot him a dour glance and stomped back into the kitchen, where Zach could hear and smell the sizzle of fried chicken.

Dillon's favorite. There'd be mashed potatoes, corn on the cob, and watermelon slices too, he knew. Neely's menus were predictable, but there was no better food on the planet.

Neely Day might be no Mary Poppins, but she'd been

the only mother figure in Dillon's life since Alicia had abandoned the boy, abandoned both of them. And Zach knew she'd no sooner quit than cut off her ears. The bond between his son and the housekeeper who'd helped raise him was as solid as this house his aunt Ardelle had left to him. And for all Neely's peevishness and threats, she was a pushover, a sour-faced Pillsbury Doughboy of a woman with a heart as big and mushy as a cinnamon bun.

Still, she had a point about Dillon. The boy never met a creature he didn't like—and didn't want to adopt.

Tossing the mail down on the oak table in the hall, Zach took himself off to the barn.

"Dad, look! Her name's Zena and you have to let me keep her!" Dillon's eyes were shining with excitement. At nine, he was small for his age—he took after Alicia in that department, at least for now. He was smaller-boned than Zach had ever been, and he had Alicia's fine, sandy blond hair, as well as her elegant, perfectly balanced patrician features. But his eyes were Zach's—quicksilver and changeable—like gray smoke sometimes and the misty silver of a winter sea at others.

Every day Zach thanked God that Alicia's high-strung moodiness hadn't been passed down to their son. At least no signs of it had appeared yet. Dillon was a boisterous, energetic, talkative child, a boy who loved to take in strays, eat spaghetti with his fingers, and try to beat his dad at every video game he could get his hands on.

The only thing he didn't like was going to bed early. Dillon was a night owl, just like Zach, and sometimes midnight would find the two of them alone in the kitchen, drinking milk shakes and playing gin rummy.

Zach knew that most of his business associates and employees would be astonished at the thought of him sipping milk shakes from a straw in the night with his little boy.

They only knew the tough-minded businessman who made a dozen deals a day, didn't accept tardiness or excuses, and rarely took more than ten minutes away from his desk for lunch.

Zach kept his private life separate from his work—and aside from two hours in his study every night, working at the computer or on the phone, he kept his work time at the house to a minimum.

"You really want this ugly critter?" Zach asked, crossing to the corner of the barn where Dillon crouched on the floor beside a crate. A tiny gray-and-white ball of fluff was cuddled up against his shoulder. "You're going to take care of it?"

"It's not an *it,* Dad. It's a *she.* A girl kitten. And you know I'll take care of her, just like I take care of Batman and Jelly and Tigger."

From the bench where he was stitching up a saddle, Gabe Hawthorn, Zach's sixty-year-old ranch foreman, guffawed. "Might as well just say yes to him now, boss. There's no way you're getting that cat away from the boy."

"He's right, Dad. Just look at her. She's the best cat ever!"

Zach didn't bother trying to suppress a smile.

He met Gabe's shrewd, amused gaze for a moment and the foreman shook his head with mock dismay. Gabe, who'd worked for Zach's father for decades before jumping ship and going to work for Caleb McCallum's youngest son, knew him too well.

It wasn't that Zach believed in spoiling his son, but he also didn't believe in depriving him. Not of pets, or of time just to be himself—or of praise and patience and love.

"That settles it then. She's part of the family." Zach reached out and tousled his son's pale hair. He smiled as Dillon's eyes lit up like it was Christmas morning. "You hungry?"

"Yes, but—"

"Better wash up for supper. Neely's expecting us pronto. Afterward we'll move this little lady up to the house and fix up a bed for her in your room. There's a clean crate in the storage shed, and I'm betting Neely will come up with a few spare towels she can sleep on."

"In my room? Awesome!" Dillon slapped him a high five before setting the kitten back in the crate. "You're the best, Dad."

When Zach and Gabe were alone in the barn, the foreman set down the saddle and peered over at the younger man. Zach had stooped down, reached into the crate, and was absently stroking the kitten. With Dillon gone, his face had settled into grim lines bordering on a frown. Gabe had known him for too many years not to recognize that expression.

"Something bothering you, boss? You look like you've got more on your mind than this here cat."

"Hell, no." Zach set the kitten back in the crate and stood up, his thumbs hooked in his belt. "You're imagining things, Gabe."

"Ahuh. If you say so." The foreman shot him a skeptical glance and Zach met his gaze in annoyance.

"Everything is coming along on schedule," he said shortly. "The lease deal for the land bordering the creek is almost wrapped up. Candy's redoing the contracts to add another two hundred acres. That way, the Skye Blue group can build a swimming pool for the kids."

"Well, that's good, right?"

"Yes, it's good. Though some folks won't like it—especially those who don't want too many new developments in Thunder Creek." Zach snorted. "Unless they're headed by Wood Morgan."

"Everyone's sure happy about the corporate branch office you're building," Gabe pointed out. "Lots of jobs there. Money flowing into town."

"Yep, everybody likes money. They'll welcome Tex-Corp, but this other land deal . . . well, we'll have to see. Might not be too popular."

"So why'd you do it?" Gabe knew the answer. He also knew that Zach needed to remember it.

"I'm not interested in winning popularity contests. Never have been."

Boy, he could say that again. But that wasn't the answer Gabe was looking for. He raised his brows. "Now you sound like your old man."

Zach shot him a frown, but Gabe met his stare and held it. There weren't many men who could sustain eye contact with Zach McCallum when that ice-cold gaze, reminiscent of an Old West gunfighter's stare, was fixed relentlessly on them.

But Gabe was an old-time Texan who'd known the McCallums since he'd been not much older than Dillon, and he was one of the few who'd never backed down before any of them.

"If I do, so be it," Zach said in irritation. "I come by it naturally."

"You're not like Caleb though. Not in most of the ways that count."

"You looking for a raise, Gabe? All this flattery."

The foreman chuckled. "You know damn well you're leasing that land because you think it's a good thing to do.

A good cause. You just don't want to give yourself any credit."

"What are you now? My shrink?"

Gabe laughed. "Why the hell not? I got me a degree, a real good one—from the school of hard knocks. Taught me all I know about human nature, cattle, weather, and everything else." Gabe eyed him shrewdly. "And something tells me your guts are in a knot over something. And if it's not that land deal, it's something else. What happened today?"

Scowling, Zach shrugged. "I just . . . ran into a ghost."

"You don't say."

But as Gabe waited for more, Zach shook his head. "It's not important." He clapped the older man on the shoulder. "Neely fixed fried chicken for dinner tonight. Why don't you stick around and join us?"

Gabe accepted. He was still concerned about that brooding look he'd seen in Zach's eyes, but knew better than to ask a second time. Zach didn't like anyone messing in his business. Even an old friend.

And Gabe, who made a religion of keeping pretty much to himself as well, couldn't say he blamed him.

Zach went into his study at the Last Trail ranch and tossed the mail on his desk. Then he drew the curtains wide and, ignoring the comfortable brown leather armchair, crossed to the window, staring out at the topaz sun sinking in a splash of rose light over the Laramie Mountains.

He'd been Texas born and bred, and his heart would always belong to the Lone Star State, but this Wyoming majesty was pretty damned hard to resist. It had impressed him in his younger days and it still held him in its spell. Especially at dawn, and again at sunset.

He enjoyed the pure magnificence of this land. It was

wild, vast, and rugged, a place that possessed a beauty so fierce it grabbed a man by the throat and never let go. It called out to anyone with eyes—flaunting its crystal-clear mountain streams and dizzying waterfalls, its array of elk deer and cougars and coyotes. Wyoming was chock-full of nature at its grandest, with deep canyons and red buttes and twisting ravines, with endless prairie and plains, and foothills that in the spring and summer glowed with wildflowers.

He couldn't imagine ever tiring of the vista spread before him from every window of this sprawling house.

Yet, strangely, he still missed Texas. Despite all the bad memories of growing up there in his father's house, the tough hard plains of his boyhood still called to him, to something deep inside him.

He knew he'd never go back, at least not to live. For business, yes. But to work and reside full-time in Buffalo Springs, where his father had ruled the town, the county, half the damned state—no, those days were gone. He'd broken away from Caleb McCallum and his oil and cattle empire years ago to make his own mark in the world. Eventually, he'd become CEO of a rival conglomerate that had offered him the sun and moon to come onboard, and he'd amassed his own fortune totally independent of his father's wealth.

He hadn't done it for the money though. He'd done it for himself.

That had been in the days when Caleb McCallum thought Jock, Zach's brother, could do no wrong. That Jock was everything Zach wasn't . . . that he was everything Caleb wanted him to be . . .

He caught himself thinking about the past and wheeled from the window, crossing to his desk. He made it a habit

not to look back. It was a waste of time. Looking ahead
had gotten him where he was today. As the successor to his
father at TexCorp Oil, he ran a business with nearly thirty
thousand employees and offices all over the world. Many
people depended on him, above all his son.

Looking back wasn't going to take care of any of them.
The future was ahead of him and it could be whatever he
wanted to make of it.

He didn't want much for himself, but for Dillon, he
wanted a whole lot more. Like a loving home, a solid foun-
dation, and the freedom to choose his own path. That's
what he planned to give him in Thunder Creek. A future
where he could be more than Caleb McCallum's grandson
and Jock McCallum's nephew.

And Zach McCallum's son.

Dillon would have the opportunity to become his own
man—just as Zach had managed to do—on his own terms
and in his own way.

Picking up the mail once more, his gaze fell on a save-
the-date card with midnight-blue lettering.

He studied it thoughtfully. *Autumn Auction and Dinner
Dance: a benefit fund-raiser for the new pediatric wing of
the Thunder Creek Hospital.*

It was being held September 1 at the Crystal Horseshoe
Dude Ranch, owned by Wood and Tammie Morgan.

He noted that Patti Maxwell was the chairman of the
event.

Patti Maxwell. Another name out of the past, that distant past when he was nineteen and had spent one summer
in Thunder Creek visiting Aunt Ardelle and her husband,
Sheriff Stan Harvey. Patti Maxwell had been Patti Reese at
the time, and had been best friends with Faith Barclay
back in those days. He wondered if they still were close.

And he also wondered if Faith would be attending the auction and the dance.

Then he dropped the card onto the desk. *What difference does it make?* he asked himself in irritation. It wasn't exactly pleasant to run into Faith after all these years, but they were both adults. In a town this small, they were bound to see each other now and again. So what?

Yet he grimaced, wondering if she'd be back in Philadelphia, or wherever she'd come from, before the benefit took place. She was a big-time prosecutor now—that's what Ty Barclay had told him the one time he'd asked about Faith. A career woman with a full and successful life.

So chances were slim that she'd be sticking around for the next few weeks. Not that it mattered to him one way or the other.

Frowning, he folded his long frame into his chair and pulled up a spreadsheet on the computer.

Yet Faith Barclay's face still lingered in his mind.

What the hell is wrong with you? he asked himself. *You survived all those years growing up in Jock's shadow, and under Caleb's thumb, and married to Alicia, and now you're bent out of shape about a summer girlfriend you made out with ten years ago?*

But this wasn't just any summer girlfriend, and he knew it.

It was Faith.

Seeing her today had affected him more than he'd ever expected. It had hurtled him back in time for one overwhelming moment, and he'd been stunned both by the emotions that had flooded him and by how little she'd changed.

She was still slender, sleek, delicately built. But her

body had ripened, her breasts were fuller, her cheekbones sharply, almost exotically defined. And she still had the sexiest fluff of riotous curls spiraling down to her shoulders that he'd ever seen.

After ten long years, the slim tomboy beauty who'd sparked his heart the first time he met her was still a firecracker, a spitfire of a girl who didn't take crap from anyone.

But now she wasn't that slightly lanky, slightly gawky girl with the wide, breezy smile. She was a woman, a long-legged, beautiful woman, powerful in that elegant black suit, devastatingly self-contained and tough as a cop in the way she'd raked him over the coals for speeding.

Damn, he'd nearly killed her. They'd nearly killed each other.

Just goes to prove my point, Zach thought as he heard Dillon burst into the house. *You're no good for each other. You never were. If ever there was a moment, a blink in time where Faith Barclay belonged in your life, it was ten years ago. Ancient history. That time, that moment, is gone.*

So don't look back.

He sure as hell didn't want to *go* back.

And from the way Faith had lit into him this afternoon, she didn't want to either.

Faith's bags were completely unpacked by 7 P.M. and finally, she felt herself starting to unwind.

She had grilled herself a cheese sandwich and had zapped a cup of tomato soup in the microwave—thanks to the fresh groceries her sister-in-law Josy had thoughtfully left for her before Josy and Ty headed to New York.

Ty had definitely picked a winner when he found Josy. She was the best sister-in-law in the world. A successful, down-to-earth fashion designer, she'd been orphaned at a young age and had grown up in foster care before learning that her biological grandmother was alive and living in Thunder Creek. Ada Scott had never even known she had a granddaughter, and now she had Josy, who lived and worked right here in Thunder Creek most of the year— when she wasn't traveling to New York or Europe on buying trips or for a show, or scheduling a week of meetings at her New York offices. In the past few years, Josy and Ada had become as close as if they'd known each other all their lives, and Josy had fit just as beautifully into the Barclay family as she had in Thunder Creek. She and Ty were so happy, so much in love, that whenever she saw them together, Faith's heart ached with pleasure for them.

She only hoped her brother Adam met someone half as wonderful one day. But Adam was too busy working for the FBI to think much about marriage or even a serious relationship.

Not that she could blame him for concentrating solely on his career. Serious relationships were complicated and they could explode like dynamite in your face.

And she had the powder burns to prove it.

But she wasn't here to think about her failed engagement, she reminded herself as she sank into the easy chair before the fire with a cup of coffee, just as dusk settled over the mountains and the sky turned a vivid indigo that seeped peacefully across the mesa.

She was here to relax. To regroup. And to give herself a break from everything she'd left behind in the city.

Like murder cases, domestic assault trials—and the memory of the devastated expressions on the faces of Jimmy Clement's mother and younger brother when the judge gave her what she asked for—the death sentence.

Guilt squeezed her heart every time she thought about Jimmy Clement. It had been that way ever since she found out, two full years after Jimmy Clement's execution, that he had been innocent of murder after all, just as he and his family had claimed.

That justice had somehow gone terribly wrong.

"You've got to let this go," her mother had told her only a few nights ago. "You can't hold yourself accountable for everything that's gone wrong. You've done the best you could—with all of your cases and with Kevin too. Cut yourself some slack, Faith."

I'll try, Mom, Faith thought, taking a deep breath as her fingers tightened around her coffee cup. *I'm sure as hell going to try.*

If any place on earth could help her find some sense of peace again, that place was Thunder Creek. It had been more than a year since she'd been back, and as she gazed out at the darkening sky, she suddenly realized just how much she'd missed it.

The coming night felt quiet and tranquil. And the cabin was always soothing, simple, and homey. The living room where she sat now was furnished with a deep tan-and-beige upholstered sofa and matching ottoman, gleaming wood coffee table, a huge Navajo rug, and a big stone fireplace that dominated the cozy space.

The kitchen was always stocked with canned goods, coffee, soft drinks, and beer, and Great-Grandma Barclay's hope chest in the corner of the master bedroom always held a supply of clean linen and blankets.

And thanks to Josy, she now had ice cream in the freezer, wine chilling in the fridge, and a tin of fresh-baked chocolate chip cookies on the dining room table.

Life was good.

Well, pretty good, Faith reflected as she sipped her coffee. It would have been a whole lot better if she hadn't received that phone call today.

Somehow she knew—every instinct shouted—that it was Hank Bayman on that phone, breathing hard, not saying a word.

He hadn't given up yet. He probably wouldn't for a long time. The bastard was determined to find out where Susan and the kids had gone—and Faith was equally determined that he never would.

Based on everything she'd learned about domestic violence in her years at the DA's office, she knew that if Bayman ever caught up with Susan and the kids, he might well make good on his threats to kill them, all of them.

That wasn't going to happen, certainly not if Faith had any say in the matter. The courts had already let Susan down once. Faith had found it necessary to go one step further to ensure that Bayman wouldn't have a chance to hurt Susan or the children again.

And since only Faith, and not even the administrator of the Sisters in Need shelter, knew where Susan had gone, there was no way Bayman—ex-cop or no—would find out.

All the tracks had been covered. Bayman would try to sniff them out, maybe even harass her for a while, but eventually he'd have no choice but to give up.

In the meantime, she could handle a few annoying phone calls. All it showed was that even now, six weeks after Susan and the kids had moved in secret out of state, he still hadn't given up.

She took another sip of coffee and made a mental note to call Liz in the morning and ask her to contact Bayman's probation officer, make sure he was complying with his sentence, that he was still going regularly to his job and keeping his monthly probation appointments. It wouldn't hurt to see if he was in any way violating his parole . . .

Suddenly her cell phone rang. She jumped, nearly spilling her coffee. *Speak of the devil?*

But after glancing at the caller ID, she smiled as she lifted the phone to her ear.

"Hey, Patti."

"Don't *hey Patti* me. You've been here in Thunder Creek for approximately seven hours and you haven't called me yet? I'm furious with you."

"I can tell." Faith's shoulders relaxed and she leaned back in the chair. She and Patti Maxwell had grown closer over the years than they'd been even as teenagers. Despite the differences in geography and lifestyle, they were still connected and kept in frequent touch. But they hadn't seen each other since Patti had come to Philadelphia six months ago for Faith's engagement party.

Faith had asked her that night to be a bridesmaid at her wedding—when she'd thought there was still going to *be* a wedding.

"Looks like I can't get away with anything these days." Faith grinned. "How do you know how long I've been here? No, don't tell me—Roy."

"Of course Roy. Have you forgotten how quickly news spreads in a town this size?"

"I guess I have."

"Well, let it be a lesson to you." Patti laughed and the familiar warm sound of that laughter took Faith back to countless pajama parties, afternoons stuffing themselves with french fries and Cokes and pie at Bessie's Diner, to summer horseback rides where they just happened to trot by the ranches of boys they had crushes on.

"So when can we get together?" Patti asked. "I haven't

seen you in ages. And now that you're here, there's something I need to ask you."

"Not legal advice, I hope." Patti had married Bob Maxwell three years ago and was blissfully happy—at least she had been the last time they'd spoken. *You've got divorce and splitsville on the brain,* Faith told herself, relieved when Patti answered with characteristic good humor.

"Nope, no legal advice, I'm keeping this big teddy bear guy of mine around for a while. Hold on, hon, I'll be right there," Patti called into the distance; then returned to the conversation. "But I do need your help with something, Faith. How about meeting me at Bessie's Diner tomorrow for breakfast? Is ten okay?"

"Better than okay. I haven't had Bessie's pancakes in forever."

"Then tomorrow's going to be your lucky day. See you then."

Faith set down the phone and leaned back in her chair. It would be good to see Patti. And Bessie, and Ada Scott, who worked the cash register at the diner.

Over the years, coming to Thunder Creek during the summers and occasionally over winter break, she'd become a part of this town, even when she was away. So many of the people here were like family—they'd seen her grow up and she'd known them all as long as she could remember. The Barclay family had ties to Thunder Creek that went back generations, and the current generation was still as closely tied to the town as those that had come before.

She let out a deep peaceful breath. She was beginning to feel a million miles from Philadelphia, from the courthouse, the politics, the pressures.

And she wouldn't have to face any of it again for a whole month.

As soon as I confirm that Bayman is still in Philly and hasn't gotten a whiff of Susan's whereabouts, I'll really be able to kick back, she thought.

And then she made another decision. While Liz was checking up on Bayman, she'd call Susan herself. Just to reassure herself that everything was fine.

Susan's safe, she told herself as she poured more coffee. Stirring in a spoonful of sugar, she listened to the vast comforting silence of the August night, and for the first time in a long while, a semblance of calm stole through her.

Maybe the world will get lucky, she thought. Her fingers curled around the mug and she lifted it to her lips.

Maybe Hank Bayman will manage to get himself flattened by a truck.

The headlights of the U-Haul truck blinded him as he froze in the middle of the street. Where the fuck had that thing come from?

Hank Bayman heard the roar, the screech of brakes. He blinked once, and dove. He smacked into the pavement in front of Smiley's Bar a split second before the front wheels of the massive sucker squashed him.

Hank sucked in a good whiff of cool night air. That and the shock of the truck bearing down on him had sobered him up some.

He swore, staggered to his feet. His knees hurt like hell. His fucking hand was bleeding. He'd nearly been killed!

I need another beer—or three, he thought, and peered around him. Which one to pick? A bar was like a pretty woman, inviting, seductive, and always calling his name.

He turned away from Smiley's and headed instead toward the Peephole. Their waitresses wore skimpier outfits. And their pool tables were in better shape.

He was a big man, but nimble. He'd played football in high school and had been damned good at it. He'd gotten a scholarship to college, but his father had needed him to help out at the gas station. No college for Hank. No, sirree. Just work at that damned gas station, six days a week, nights, weekends.

Working alongside Pop hadn't exactly been pleasant either. Pop was never in a good mood, not since ol' Mom had run off and disappeared. Poof, one night she was tucking him into bed, telling him if the teacher complained one more time about his bullying the other kids at recess she'd have Pop whomp him good, and the next morning—zip. She was gone. She and her Camels and frayed blue robe and bright red lipstick. She'd taken fifty bucks from Pop's wallet while he slept, and ten from Hank's piggy bank.

And left a sinkful of dirty dishes from the night before. And who'd had to clean them up? Not just then, but every day, every night from that moment on, who'd had to do the dishes and listen to Pop grouse, and be the one he smacked around when he got good and mad that nope, there was still no letter from Carolee Bayman, not today. Not ever.

Hank pushed his way through the crowd in Peephole's, unzipped his khaki jacket, and found himself an empty stool at the crowded bar.

"Budweiser," he snapped as the bartender glanced his way. "No, make that a Scotch. Double."

Through the haze of cigarette smoke, he peered at the cute redheaded waitress joking with a bunch of obnoxious fraternity boys.

She was pretty and had a nice ass. But she was a slut. Look at her, look at the way those geeks were looking at her.

She's cheap, she's nothing, he told himself. *Not like Susan. Susan's beautiful and classy and she's your wife. You can't cheat on her. Even if she did get out of line, go a little crazy. You're still married. It don't matter what that stupid piece of paper says about divorce. You took vows, and so did she.*

Till death do us part.

He gulped down the Scotch.

That's the way it's going to be, baby. I told you once, I told you a dozen times. You can't run away from me. You and me, we're forever.

Forever, baby.

"Refill here?"

The bartender waited, watching him, the Cutty Sark bottle in his hand.

"Get that shit away from me." Hank scowled. "What do I owe you?"

He didn't want another drink. He wasn't going to let that runaway bitch turn him into a goddamned alcoholic. He wanted his wife back. He wanted the woman whose snot-nosed kids he'd taken in out of the goodness of his heart. He wanted her and her brats back where they belonged.

But that wasn't going to happen if he didn't get on the stick. He had to do something more than make those stupid phone calls to the assistant DA bitch.

It was time to get serious, he thought, slapping some bills on the bar and pushing himself off the stool. Time to show that tight-ass prosecutor how much she'd under-estimated him.

He was smarter than her. Tougher too. Big-time. Hadn't

he played football and kicked ass for four years of high school—not to mention going through basic training in the army, then acing marksmanship before shipping out to Bosnia? And hadn't he been a damned good cop before getting canned for no good reason?

He knew how to find anyone, how to watch and wait.

And then go in loaded for bear.

Shouldering his way through the packed bar, Bayman stumbled back out to the street. He'd find Susan, all right. He'd give her the surprise of her life. But first he had to sober up. Go on the offensive. The army had taught him that.

You take the fight to the enemy, right on the front lines.

And the enemy was Faith Barclay.

Because whatever Susan thought, whatever she said, all this running away was just a ploy. A stupid female ploy to make him come after her, to prove to her he wanted her back.

And when he caught up to her, he'd show her just how much he did.

Chapter 3

"FAITH BARCLAY! COME ON IN HERE, GIRL— heavens to Betsy, we haven't seen you in here since Ty's wedding!"

Beaming, Bessie Templeton, owner of Bessie's Diner, thunked down the pot of hot coffee she'd just lifted up and bustled toward the front of the diner even as the little bell that announced a customer rang prettily over the door.

She threw her arms around Faith and squeezed. Beneath Bessie's short waves of iron-gray hair, the sharp gray gaze that missed nothing studied the slim young woman with the lavender shadows under her eyes.

"So how are you doing, honey? Not that I need to ask. You look gorgeous as a ripe peach, first of the season. But tired." Bessie tilted her head to the side, birdlike. "Ty said you were going through a rough patch. That true?"

"Don't listen to Ty, Bessie." Faith hugged her back with a rueful smile. "He exaggerates. So does my entire family. I'm fine, absolutely fine. At least I will be after you bring me a plateful of your pancakes."

"Comin' right up. Sit wherever you please. Soon as I get a little break, we're going to have us a chat."

Patti hadn't arrived yet, so Faith chose a booth near the

door. The diner smelled of pancakes and coffee and eggs over easy with toast. She wanted to savor the aroma, the feel of the worn booth cushions, the familiar quiet whir of the ceiling fan, but then, before Bessie could even return to pour her coffee, Patti walked in.

Faith's mouth dropped open. Beneath her long blue T-shirt and khaki capris, Patti's belly was gently swollen.

Her huge brown eyes sparkled like new pennies.

"You're pregnant!" Faith sprang from the booth like a jack-in-the-box. "And you didn't tell me!"

"I wanted it to be a surprise." Patti chuckled as her friend embraced her in a gentle hug. "I'm just starting my fifth month. It's a girl—we did the amnio already. Bob's painting the nursery next week—pink walls, yellow-and-white-striped borders. What do you think?"

"I think it sounds fantastic." Faith grinned at her. Patti, always pretty with her strawberry blond hair and animated features, was positively glowing. "I'm so happy for you," she murmured, and meant it.

"Thanks. That makes two of us. Actually three." They both laughed as Bessie came over and poured decaf for Patti and the real stuff for Faith. She took their orders without bothering to write anything down on a pad and scooted back to the kitchen with the energy of a woman half her age.

"It took me a while to get pregnant," Patti confided. "We tried for eight months before things finally clicked. But it was all worth it."

She added a dollop of milk to her decaf, then leaned toward Faith, her gaze taking in not only Faith's pale yellow T-shirt and jeans and her waterfall of curls, but the slight pallor of her skin, the shadows under her eyes. "Now tell me about you," she demanded. "You look like hell.

What did you do—take an oath of office for the DA that required you to swear off sleep?"

"Ouch. Do I really look that bad?" God love Patti. She was as blunt as always. "Or do you have a camera planted in my apartment?"

"Faith, this is serious." Patti looked worried. "I know things have been rough lately—"

"Oh, no, not you too. What did my family do, put up a sign in the middle of town saying 'Poor pathetic Faith—be nice to her'?" She shook her head in exasperation.

"No, of course not, but . . . look, all I want to say is that I'm sorry about Kevin. That things didn't work out."

"Don't be." Faith swallowed. "The truth is, the marriage would have been a disaster. I'm glad I found out—that we both found out—before we spent a fortune on a wedding and a honeymoon and . . . had kids." She paused for a moment, controlling the painful twinge inside her.

It still shook her to have been so wrong about Kevin, about their entire relationship. She'd thought they'd known each other, that what they had was solid, but it had quivered beneath her feet like quicksand and nearly sucked her under.

Once, she'd believed they were perfect for each other, but maybe that was it—they'd been too perfect. Too alike. Both of them attorneys—driven, competitive, and jockeying for advancement in their respective careers.

"You knew, didn't you?" Faith gazed ruefully at her friend. "At the engagement party, you seemed hesitant, as if you didn't really like him. I could tell."

"It wasn't that I didn't like him. I thought . . . well, you'd just won a conviction on that big rape case and your picture was plastered all over the press and the DA was singing your praises and we were all so proud of you, but Kevin . . ."

Patti broke off, choosing her words carefully. "Kevin

seemed annoyed with it all. He made some kind of a crack like, now there'll be no living with her. It was supposed to be funny, but the tone of his voice—it didn't sound very nice."

Faith felt the familiar knot tightening in her chest. Patti was right. Her career had been taking off, and Kevin had been threatened by that. And she'd been too dumb and too blind to see it. At first.

"It was right around then that things began to change between us," she told Patti quietly. "A week after the engagement party, Kevin was passed over for a promotion at his law firm, and the law, which had always been something the two of us shared, somehow became . . ." She drew a breath. "A minefield," she finished. "He was competing with me—he was jealous, I guess . . ." She shook her head, remembering her confusion and hurt at the time. "I was so wrapped up in work and plans for the wedding that I didn't have a clue that my fiancé was backing off. And those little comments, like the one you heard him make—they hurt me, but I kept trying to laugh them off, to make excuses for him . . ."

She swallowed. "It wasn't until the Clement case blew up in my face that I took a good hard look at where we were."

Patti grimaced. "I heard about that case, Faith. I'm sorry."

Faith nodded and reached for her coffee, her throat suddenly dry. Yes, Patti knew. Of course she knew. Most of the country knew. The story had been picked up on CNN, MSNBC, and AOL. Not to mention all the major newspapers. According to Ty, even the *Thunder Creek Daily* had run a small article about it, because of the Barclays' connection to the town.

She'd successfully prosecuted the final appeal of Jimmy Clement more than two years ago. Clement, who'd been convicted of the rape and murder of a college student named Devon Skye ten years earlier, had spent a decade on death row before his last appeal reached the Supreme Court. At that point, she was assigned by the DA to argue the state's case.

And she'd won. Clement's appeal was denied, the DA's office chalked up a victory, and Jimmy Clement was duly executed.

Justice had been done.

At least that's what everyone had believed—until six months ago, when a middle-aged bus driver named Lamont Elwood was arrested on kidnapping and rape charges. A search of his home turned up evidence from several old crime scenes—including a bracelet that had belonged to Devon Skye. Traces of Devon's blood were found on the bracelet, but that wasn't all. A more intensive search of the shed behind his house turned up photos of Devon before and after her murder, gruesome, sickening photos, along with a lock of her hair, stored in a box with clumps of hair and photos of three other victims of unsolved murders.

Elwood confessed to Devon Skye's murder. And to the murders of the three other women. He had knowledge of all the crime scenes, he boasted of having gotten away with his crimes for years, and he laughed when he related how he'd read every newspaper article about Jimmy Clement's appeal.

When Faith got the phone call about Elwood's confession, when she'd heard and seen the evidence with her own eyes, she'd been devastated.

She'd taken a two-week leave of absence from her job, then gone back to work with a vengeance. And right after that, the nightmares had begun.

"I can only imagine how awful that was for you, Faith. But it wasn't your fault. You had no way of knowing," Patti said firmly.

Faith's stomach clenched. No, she'd had no way of knowing, but that didn't make it any easier. She remembered how she'd been curled up on the sofa in her apartment that first night after receiving the news, sick to her stomach, unable to stop crying. Then Kevin had arrived. She'd been planning to cook dinner for them—lasagna and salad—and he'd picked up wine and tiramisu from Georgio's for dessert.

But he'd found her in tears, her face damp, her eyes red. And no lasagna in sight. The thought of food had only made her more nauseous. A man—the wrong man—had died. And *she'd* prosecuted him. *She'd* asked for the death penalty.

She'd been so sure of his guilt. The evidence had been strong. But it was misleading. And an innocent man had died.

"Kevin tried to console me that night, the night I found out about Clement's innocence," she said softly. "For about five minutes. Then, when I couldn't seem to stop crying, he lashed out. He told me he had a big win in court that day and he was looking forward to celebrating and that I was ruining it for him."

"What?" Patti gasped.

Faith nodded, her neck muscles tight. "He said everything wasn't just about me."

"He actually said that to you?" Anger flared in Patti's eyes. "The guy is even more of an asshole than I thought."

"There was more, but I won't bore you with the details." Faith paused, lifting her coffee cup. "I only wish I hadn't been stupid enough to think I loved a man who was so . . . so . . ."

"Callous and self-centered? Jealous of your successes?"

"That about covers it." She smiled wryly and took a sip of coffee. "Look, Kevin and I are over and done. There's no point in crying over lost fiancés." *Or lost dreams,* she thought bleakly.

Seeing the flicker of pain in her friend's eyes, a flicker that was there one instant and carefully erased the next, Patti quickly lifted her own cup. "You're so right. Let's make a toast never to talk about it again—unless you want to," she added.

"I'll drink to that." Faith clinked cups with her. "Now tell me all about you, aside from being pregnant. What was it you wanted to ask me about?"

Before Patti could reply, a teenage waitress with fuchsia-streaked hair dashed up to their table and nearly dropped plates of pancakes and French toast, jam, syrup, and small dishes of powdered sugar in front of them.

Patti waited until the girl had rushed back to the kitchen before casting Faith an impish look.

"I need your help with something, but I don't want to impose on your vacation. Oh, hell, actually I do—unless you really just want to hang out and veg."

"Vegging gets old fast. I like to be busy, and you know it. Come on, Patti, ask away. I won't be afraid to say no if I don't want to do it."

Patti swallowed a mouthful of golden brown French toast and patted her napkin to her mouth. "We're having a big shindig here in a couple of weeks. The Autumn Auction and Dinner Dance. It's a new event, this is only the second year. It's a charity benefit to raise money for the expanded children's wing of the hospital. I need you to be my co-chair."

"Co-chair?" Faith nearly choked on a bite of pancake. "Me? But I might not even be here—"

"You will be, Faith. The dance is the first week of September, only two weeks away. I heard you have a leave of absence for a month."

"Patti, I'm flattered, but there must be plenty of people who actually live in Thunder Creek who'd love to be involved in this. I'm practically an outsider—"

"Give me a break. Your family's owned land in this county since the late 1800s. Their ties to Thunder Creek go back longer than almost anyone else's. And your brother's the sheriff. Your cousin lives here—you spent every summer of your life here until you went to college—"

"But what about Ada Scott or Bessie, or Tammie Morgan, for that matter? It seems to me this kind of an event would be right up Tammie's—" She broke off. There was a grim look on Patti's face.

And suddenly, light dawned. "Don't tell me. Tammie is involved in this event—she's already working with you, isn't she?"

"She's my co-chair," Patti admitted. "Only because the auction and dance are being held on the Morgan property, at their dude ranch, during the two weeks out of the year when it's closed to guests." Patti set down her fork. "That's why I need you. A third co-chair—to break the tie. Tammie and I disagree about everything. I can't work with her—not unless I have you to mediate and settle all our differences and always side with me," she added with a burst of laughter.

Faith rolled her eyes. "That's all I need. Tammie Morgan."

Tammie and Wood Morgan considered themselves the glamorous, sophisticated power couple of Thunder Creek. They owned several hundred thousand acres of prime grazing land, and had several years ago converted a good portion of their scenic back acres into an upscale dude ranch. Like everything else the Morgans touched, it had turned into a gold mine and a four-star resort. Tammie, who'd had a penchant for self-aggrandizement even in high school, now considered herself the crème de la crème of Thunder Creek society.

Faith had still been an eighth-grade tomboy when Tammie and Wood Morgan began dating in high school, but even then she'd never much cared for her. And that was before Tammie married into the powerful Wood family.

During the last few years, according to everything Faith had heard, Tammie had become more insufferable than ever.

"You're on your own," she told Patti. "I'm trying to get away from politics and power struggles." She paused as she saw the disappointment in Patti's face. "Unless you really need me," she heard herself saying.

A voice inside of her called her all kinds of names, not the least of which was *sucker.* "You really don't think you can handle Tammie all by yourself?"

"Only if I absolutely have to. Look," Patti rushed on, suddenly hopeful. "School's going to start again in a few weeks and I have to start preparing my classroom. I've had morning sickness every single day of the past three months, and I get totally exhausted by the middle of the afternoon."

Seeing Faith's sympathetic expression, Patti grinned. She was almost home free. "To top it off, Tammie and I have fought about everything, and we have so much to do my head is spinning. We still need lots more donations for the auction, we can't agree on the dinner menu, and so far our committee has only sold seventy tickets for the dinner dance, out of a possible two hundred. And you know it's for a good cause," she added, but from the resigned expression on Faith's face, Patti knew she didn't have to say another word. She'd already won.

"Tammie Morgan." Faith groaned. "Damn. But I guess I can't have you working yourself into a funk with a baby on the way, can I? Okay, I'll run interference for you with Tammie. And we have to sell all two hundred of those tickets," she stated, a determined glint entering her eyes.

Patti laughed. "You're still the greatest, Faith. I knew I could count on you. Come by the house tonight for dinner and I'll bring you up to speed on everything."

"It's a deal. But . . . fill me in on something first." Faith had been trying to resist the temptation to ask about Zach McCallum, but now that she and Patti had fallen so quickly back into their old routine of telling each other just about everything, she couldn't pass up the opportunity.

She kept her tone offhand. "What is Zach McCallum doing back in Thunder Creek? And please tell me he isn't staying long."

"You already know about Zach? How?"

"I ran into him. Almost literally." She told Patti about the near collision with Zach and Candy. "I know he inherited the Last Trail ranch after both Ardelle and Stan Harvey died. So is he here to sell it, or what?"

"No. Zach's here—for good, I guess. I don't know all the details of what happened, but after his father died, he apparently cut almost all of his ties in Texas. Oh, he has a manager running his family's ranch there—he hasn't sold it or anything yet—but he's installed himself at the Last Trail. He's also building a major branch office for TexCorp Oil—right on the outskirts of town. I guess he wants to be on-site to make sure it's done right."

"It sounds like a big operation," Faith murmured, her heart sinking.

"You bet it is. This is the biggest business deal to hit Thunder Creek since the Morgans opened the Crystal Horseshoe Dude Ranch. Everyone's been talking about it for months."

"Hmmm." Faith schooled her face into the noncommittal expression that served her well in the courtroom. But she was puzzled. Years ago, Zach had told her about his troubled relationship with his father. But he'd also told her how much he loved Texas. Despite his conflicts with Caleb McCallum, he'd always been loyal to the family ranch and land that were his roots.

"I'm just surprised that he'd leave Buffalo Springs," she said, as Patti shot her a questioning look.

"You don't . . . still have feelings for him . . . after all this time, do you?"

Patti knew better than anyone how Zach had hurt her ten years ago. She was studying Faith, looking worried.

"Please." Faith forced herself to laugh and hoped it sounded natural. "I'm far from being that dumb, love-struck nineteen-year-old, Patti. You got over your first crush, didn't you? Or are you still writing every night in your diary about Joe Dan Foster?"

"Hardly." Patti giggled. "Joe Dan happens to be one of Bob's and my best friends. He's married, prematurely bald, and the father of twins. As a matter of fact, his wife, Margo, is on the committee for the benefit. I'll introduce you at our next meeting."

Bessie appeared at the table, wiping her hands on a striped dish towel. "Is this a private party, girls, or can anyone join in?"

As Faith and Patti urged her to sit down, she slid into the booth opposite Faith and beamed at her.

"Ada's coming over in a bit, but she said to tell you first off that Ty's horses are stabled in her barn and you're to come over and ride 'em anytime you get the urge. Not that you need any encouragement to ride," she added with a snort. "I still remember how you stole your dad's stallion and snuck out in the middle of the night."

"Ending up stranded on Cougar Mountain with a broken ankle," Patti put in, grinning. "Your parents had to send out a search party."

"Won't I ever live that down?" Faith asked in mock dismay. Patti and Bessie laughed.

"Nope," Bessie answered. "Not in a million years. Not in this town."

It was more than an hour later that Faith finally left the diner. Patti had given her Tammie Morgan's cell phone number before heading home for a nap, and as Faith headed to her car, she started punching in the numbers.

But suddenly she heard the rush of feet behind her and the cell phone was knocked from her hand. It clattered onto the pavement as a small boy brushed past, shouting, "Batman! Batman, come. Come!"

At the end of the street she saw a mutt that looked like a cross between a golden retriever and a Lab. It was bounding across the intersection, narrowly avoiding traffic. As Faith knelt to retrieve her phone, she saw the boy dart across the street in pursuit, still calling the dog's name.

But with his eye on the dog, he hadn't looked both ways as he leaped almost directly into the path of a pickup. She gasped, her heart stopping cold as the boy froze before the oncoming vehicle. The brakes shrieked as the driver attempted both to stop and to swerve sideways. With inches to spare, the pickup veered left and came to a halt, narrowly missing the child.

An instant later a huge potbellied man with a bull neck and a gray crew cut jumped from the truck. The boy spun toward the spot where his dog had disappeared, but before he could take off, the man grabbed him by the arm.

"You goddamned little troublemaker. I ought to thrash you from here to kingdom come. Didn't your no-good father ever teach you to look both ways?"

"Sorry—I shoulda looked, but . . . let me go. I have to catch my dog!"

The man jerked the boy closer. "I asked you a question. Answer me right now."

"Let him go, Mr. Harrison." Faith had reached them by then. The boy, who looked to be about ten, was trying futilely to pull free of the rancher's grip, and Faith spotted the red mark on his thin freckled arm.

"Take your hands off him *now*," she ordered.

Fred Harrison squinted at her in the afternoon sunlight, as cars wove their way around the three people in the middle of the street.

It took only a moment before he recognized the woman in the jeans and yellow T-shirt. *Faith Barclay*, he thought darkly. *The little Barclay firecracker. The sheriff's kid sister, all grown up*. And she looked nearly as fierce as her brother when he was breaking up a fight. An ornery bitch for all her prettiness.

Scowling, he released the boy's arm.

"You stay out of this, little girl," he warned her, aware that Sheriff Barclay wasn't even in town. "This is between me and this kid. He nearly got me and himself killed."

"I didn't mean to, mister, but I have to catch my dog!" A note of frantic despair filled the boy's voice. "I'm sorry, I really am." He glanced swiftly between Faith and the big man. "I should have looked, but Batman can only see out of one eye and I didn't want him to get lost or hit by—"

A car door slammed behind them.

"What's going on here?"

"Dad!"

Zach McCallum strode toward them, but he wasn't looking at Fred Harrison or at Faith. He was looking at the boy who ran to him eagerly and threw himself into his arms.

Dad. This is Zach's son. Faith froze as shock ripped through her.

"Dillon," Zach demanded, "are you all right?"

"Yeah, but Batman saw a cat and he ran after it. We have

to find him!" The boy grabbed his father's arm, trying to pull him along.

"We'll find him. Don't worry."

Zach glanced first at Faith, who had gone still as a statue, then at Fred Harrison.

"Your boy nearly got the both of us killed," Harrison barked. "He's a wild one, ain't he, just like you," he added with contempt.

"How did that red mark get on my son's arm?" Zach asked quietly. "Did you put it there?"

Faith saw the muscle throbbing in his jaw, but that was the only visible sign of anger coming from Zach. The rangy teenage boy she remembered from years ago had been volatile as dynamite, and quick to fight—this man was outwardly calm, totally controlled, and radiated quiet authority. Only that one little muscle in his jaw and the iron flatness of his voice betrayed what he was feeling and exactly how much self-control he was exerting right now.

"What if I did put it there?" Harrison sneered. "The boy's arm ain't broken—he got off easy. He practically dove under my truck and begged me to mow him down!"

"It won't happen again. And you'd better never lay a finger on him again," Zach said evenly.

"Now that's real interesting considering what you did to my boy, McCallum," Harrison snapped.

Zach looked him square in the eye. "Pete and I settled that between us, a long time ago. Maybe it's time you got past it too."

"You'd like that, wouldn't you? Does your son know what you did? Did you ever tell him what you did to *my* boy?"

Faith held her breath. The Zach she remembered would have slugged the older man right about now. That Zach would be shouting, striking out. This cool-eyed, dark-haired

man with the impassive features and tight-lipped stare
merely touched a hand to the little boy's shoulder.

"Dillon, apologize to Mr. Harrison."

"But he—"

"Dillon."

The boy looked glumly up at the potbellied rancher
whose face was as fiercely red as his shirt.

"Sorry," he muttered. For the first time Faith heard sul-
lenness in his tone.

"You oughta be, boy." Harrison glared at him, then his
hard gaze shifted to Zach again. "And you—I heard what
you're up to in this town. You're not going to get away with
it either. You watch and see."

Then he stalked past Faith to his truck.

Dillon glanced uncertainly at his father. "What does he
mean, Dad?"

"We'll talk about it later." Zach's expression was grim.
"Right now let's concentrate on Batman."

"Okay, then, come *on*." Dillon tugged on his arm.

"Hold on one more minute, son." Zach looked at Faith.
"What did you have to do with this?"

"Not a thing." She shrugged indifferently, turned on her
heel, and started walking away, her throat tight. Behind her
she heard the boy's quick voice.

"That lady made him let go of my arm, Dad. He
wouldn't listen to *me*. But she yelled at him. Now come on,
we have to hurry—Batman could get run over!"

Faith saw something out of the corner of her eye. Turning her head, she spotted the dog. He must have circled
back around Main Street because he was streaking across
the front of Merck's Hardware, toward the gas station
down the street.

Without thinking, she stuck two fingers in her mouth

the way Adam had taught her when she was eight. She whistled, a high piercing whistle that rang up and down the street.

The dog's head swiveled and he came to a stop. She whistled again, saw him turn around, his ears alert.

"Batman—come!" she yelled, and whistled once more.

He came. Trotting like an obedient pony, he approached her with his tail wagging and his golden fur gleaming in the sun. Behind her she heard Dillon whooping with joy, then the boy raced past her to throw his arms around the dog's neck. The animal sat obediently down in front of Faith as if there was no place else on earth he'd rather be.

"How'd you do that?" Dillon asked, flashing her the biggest, most admiring smile she'd ever seen.

"My brother taught me to whistle when I was even younger than you." She watched the dog lick his cheek and neck. "It works on horses too."

"And you still remember how to do it? That's awesome!"

"Dillon, when you get older you'll learn that there's some things you never forget. And some people too," Zach said beside her.

Faith turned to stare at him. "And some you wish you *could* forget," she retorted quickly.

A smile touched the corners of his lips. "Dillon, this is Faith Barclay. We used to be friends a long time ago."

We were a helluva lot more than that, Faith thought furiously, but she kept her mouth clamped tight and nodded at Dillon.

"Thanks for getting Batman back," Dillon told her, snuggling his face against the dog's furry neck.

"I'm glad I could help. Keep an eye on him, okay?"

"You bet I will!"

She spared only a nod for Zach before heading toward her car, but Dillon's voice carried as she walked briskly away.

"Dad, I wish I had a brother to teach me cool stuff like hers did. Did you hear how loud she whistled? I want to learn how to do that too—in case Batman ever runs away again."

She never heard Zach's response. But as she pulled the SUV onto the street, her mind was racing. Zach McCallum had a son. A son he clearly adored. Well, she knew he'd gotten married, didn't she? This shouldn't be a surprise. And it shouldn't be shaking her up this much, not after all these years.

But it did. It stabbed through her with a jagged pain.

The sight of him with his son brought back waves of sorrow. Her hands shook on the steering wheel.

Was Zach still married to Alicia Andrews, the old girlfriend from home he'd left her for? Was she here too?

Why hadn't she thought to ask Patti about that . . .

Because I don't want to know. Don't care, she told herself sharply, her temples throbbing as she left the town behind and turned toward Blue Moon Mesa.

What difference does any of it make? Nothing about Zach's life has anything whatsover to do with mine.

She needed to stop looking back. What in the world would it accomplish? What did she think she'd find? Some justification for being a totally naive idiot that summer, falling for a boy who was rebellious and dangerous, devastatingly handsome, and unpredictable as lightning? A boy who'd betrayed her, lied to her, let her down?

And made a fool out of her in front of the entire town.

She gritted her teeth. Not to mention running away like some kind of coward from what he'd done to Pete Harrison . . .

Driving into the foothills, she switched on the radio,

desperate to think of something other than the ugly scene she'd just witnessed between Zach, his son, and Fred Harrison. Refusing to wonder what new beef Harrison seemed to have with Zach now . . .

It doesn't matter. None of it. The past is dead. History.

As she climbed up the twisting road into the foothills, the tall pines and gray rocks flew past. And suddenly, the Eagles' "Desperado" wafted from the radio.

She listened to a few bars, her stomach roiling. Then she switched off the song, snapped the radio into silence. That song had always reminded her of Zach. Of the wild, reckless boy with the lonely soul who'd made love to her on Snowflake Mountain.

Des . . . perado . . .

Gripping the steering wheel tighter, she switched the channel in her mind.

Think about dinner tonight at Patti's. The auction. Tammie Morgan.

And a nice long bath before driving out to Patti and Bob's. Whether you want to wear blue jeans or black jeans, the white cotton sweater or the blue silk tank . . .

But when she reached the cabin she found a chirpy message from Patti on the answering machine, one that gave her something else to think about entirely.

"Hi, Faith, it's me, your friendly neighborhood social planner. Dinner's at six. Don't be mad, but you're in for a surprise. Be sure to wear something pretty."

Oh, no. Faith groaned. *I'm going to have to kill her.* She closed her eyes for a moment and then went to run her bath.

Chapter 4

"IT JUST HAPPENED," PATTI WHISPERED IN THE kitchen as she handed Faith the oversized salad bowl brimming with cut-up lettuce, carrots, tomatoes, and radishes. "Bob invited Owen to dinner, I didn't."

"But you invited Rusty Gallagher, didn't you?"

"Well, yes, but actually, it wasn't my idea."

Faith's brows lifted. "Whose idea was it?"

"Roy's." As Faith stared at her, Patti sighed. "I ran into him at the gas station on my way home and mentioned you were coming to dinner tonight. And then Rusty pulled in while we were talking and I saw this big lightbulb go off in Roy's head, and before I knew it, he was saying I should introduce the two of you."

"Patti—"

"And then Rusty came over to say hello, and well, it just sort of happened. I had *no* idea that Bob had invited Owen. Now, how many women would complain about having dinner with two good-looking eligible men? . . ."

"I know you and Bob—and Roy—mean well, but I'm not ready to start dating anyone again."

"Well, why not?" Patti grinned. "It's been months now since you called off your engagement." Piling char-grilled steaks onto an oval platter, Patti continued talking in a reasonable tone.

"Don't you think it's time to get your feet wet again—before you forget how to swim?"

"How to swim? Patti, I'm just trying not to drown right now," Faith shot back, exasperated. "All I want is a good foothold on solid ground."

"Well," Patti murmured in a low tone as they headed toward the dining room, "I can understand that, but it wouldn't hurt you to stick one little toe in the water, would it? I'm not asking you to dive in, and Roy isn't either, but . . ."

Faith had no time to answer because they reached the dining room where Patti's husband, Bob—who had broken all her crayons one summer when she was six because she'd beaten him in a footrace through town—sat at one end of the rectangular oak table, smearing butter on sourdough bread, while Rusty Gallagher's and Owen Carey's gazes swerved simultaneously toward her as she came forward with the salad.

"Damn, that looks good." Owen smiled, but he wasn't looking at either the salad or the steak Patti set down in the center of the table. He was smiling at Faith, appreciation in his crinkly brown eyes as he surveyed the simple V-necked cotton sweater she wore with black jeans.

She'd known Owen forever—his father had been the foreman at Fred Harrison's Flying Devil ranch and he'd been good friends with Fred's son, Pete, both before and after his injury—as well as with both Ty and Roy. He was burly and good-looking in that uniquely attractive outdoorsy way, with dark sandy hair and a ready smile. Patti had told her he was divorced, liked to play the field, but could never seem to find the "right" girl.

"Patti prepared everything—I'm just a guest," she said

quickly, setting down the salad bowl and hurrying back to the kitchen.

Patti was already sailing out with the mashed potatoes and a second basket of warm bread, so Faith had no choice but to take the dish of creamed peas, the last of the side dishes, and return to the dining room.

"Bob mentioned you might be here for most of September," Owen remarked as Faith slipped into her seat opposite him and Rusty.

"If I'm lucky." She smiled. "I've missed Thunder Creek."

"So life must be pretty hectic in the big city?" Owen helped himself to salad as the bowl was passed around the table. "You been keeping busy putting all the bad guys away?"

"Giving it my all." Faith forced a smile.

"Ty is damned proud of you. He loves to talk about how you kick butt in the courtroom. Of course, anyone who knew you way back when would expect no less." Owen winked at her as he lifted a forkful of salad to his mouth.

"Any plans for your stay while you're here, Faith?" Rusty Gallagher's voice was a deep, gravelly Western drawl, which Faith was sure many women found sexy as hell. He was a lean, muscular six-footer, probably in his late thirties, with a handsome square jaw and deep-set, intelligent brown eyes. His hair was the color of wheat, barely touching the collar of his crisp blue shirt. He had the rugged and easy look of a cowboy, but when he'd introduced him, Bob had mentioned Rusty was an attorney employed by Wood Morgan's corporation.

"No plans really, nothing too exciting," she told him with a smile. "I hope to get some riding in and visit with some old friends. Speaking of which—one in particular is determined to keep me busy. She recruited me to help with the auction for the hospital wing."

"Anyone I know?" Bob chuckled and glanced at his wife, who returned his grin. "She's had her hands full with that whole deal. No surprise that she'd rope you in too, Faith."

"My boss's wife, Mrs. Morgan, is very involved in that auction as well." Rusty glanced around the table. "The Morgans are paying half the cost of however many tickets their employees buy—from the ranch hands and guest handlers and cleaning staff of the dude ranch, to all the attorneys and accountants and techies in the company," he explained. "I think Tammie's sold nearly fifty tickets herself just in the past few days."

"Well, good job, Tammie!" But Patti shot Faith a look that clearly said *now there'll be no living with her.*

"So are you planning to go to the dance, Faith?" Rusty asked.

"Yes. I'm going to support the event every way I can."

"The Barclays never pass up a good cause," Owen told the lawyer. "I don't even know if you're aware of this, Faith, but last year, Ty paid the highest price of the night for a saddle that belonged to Wild Bill Hickok. It's hanging on the wall of his study in that big house he built for him and Josy."

Rusty ignored this comment. He was still watching Faith, his intent gaze traveling from the high cheekbones of her lovely serious face to those pretty toffee-colored curls, then to the intriguing V neck of her sweater, which revealed an enticing hint of beautifully rounded breasts.

"I hope you'll save me a dance." His deep-set brown eyes held hers as if there was no one else in the room.

Aware of the silence that dropped over the dinner table

like a heavy linen cloth, Faith fought the impulse to shrink back in her chair. In the courtroom she loved being center stage. In her personal life, right here and now, not so much.

Especially when that personal life had so recently imploded.

She'd never liked being set up on a date with anyone, and now, between Owen and Rusty, she had the impression that she was the main course of this dinner, not Patti's steak and mashed potatoes.

"I'll try," she told Rusty, summoning up a smile. "But I have the feeling Patti's going to have me running around like a headless hen making sure everything goes smoothly all night. I can't make any promises."

"Well if you manage to save one for him, you have to save two for me," Owen countered quickly. "One for now, and one for old times' sake. We go way back, and don't you forget it." He waggled his fork at her, his eyes lit with teasing amusement.

"That's right." Bob leaned forward, nodding at Faith. "Remember that time Owen stood in for Zach, when Sheriff Harvey grounded him before the rodeo? Owen drove you to Casper at the last minute so you could see Ty and Adam in the steer-roping—and then you ditched him for Zach when Zach snuck out of the Last Trail and showed up."

He laughed, then yelped as Patti kicked him under the table.

Faith nearly choked on a mouthful of peas. Couldn't she escape Zach even at Patti's house? Owen, to his credit, looked almost as uncomfortable as she felt at the mention of Zach's name. *And for good reason,* she thought with a pang. Owen had not only been Pete Harrison's friend, he was the one who'd witnessed Zach running away that last night, leaving him lying on the ground, unconscious after decking him in a fight.

She didn't know how, but Owen managed to keep his tone unemotional. "That was a long time ago, Bob." He took a drink of his beer.

"Yeah, I guess so . . . sorry." Bob had it now. He looked embarrassed, and knowing Patti, Faith figured he'd have a black-and-blue ankle by morning. "It just popped into my head all of a sudden . . . I didn't mean to . . . well, you know." He cleared his throat. "Uh, Rusty, how about passing me those peas?"

"Are you talking about Zach McCallum?" the lawyer asked as he handed over the dish. When Bob nodded, Rusty leaned back in his chair. "So you all know him from way back? I thought he hailed from Texas."

"He visited Thunder Creek one summer—a long time ago," Patti explained. "His aunt was Ardelle Harvey and she owned the Last Trail ranch. Zach spent the summer with her and her husband, Sheriff Harvey. Many of us became friends with him then," she added, consciously avoiding glancing over at Faith.

"He was here just that one summer?" Rusty asked.

"Just one," Owen said tautly.

"There was some trouble near the end," Bob explained, speaking more quickly than usual. "Anyway, Zach didn't come back after that."

"Until now." Rusty helped himself to another steak. "Seems like there's going to be some trouble this time too, I'm sorry to say."

"What do you mean? What kind of trouble?" Patti asked the question before anyone else had the chance.

Rusty glanced around the table and saw that he had everyone's full attention, including Faith's.

"Well, first off, let me say he's tried hard to make himself welcome by opening a branch of TexCorp here. That was a smart move—it's good for jobs and good for business, of course. It's great for Thunder Creek's entire economy, and no one can have any argument with that. But he's also got some other project up his sleeve. It's pretty controversial. And folks are going to be hearing a lot more about that venture pretty soon."

"So why don't you tell us now," Faith met his gaze directly. She didn't care for insinuation or instigation, and she was getting the impression that Rusty Gallagher was one of those lawyers who practiced both.

Owen nodded and spoke in a low tone. "You're fairly new to Thunder Creek, Rusty—but you'll find folks here are pretty up-front. Don't feel you have to beat around the bush."

"All right then." Rusty shrugged. "Word is that Zach McCallum has plans for several thousand of the Last Trail ranch's back acres. He's leased it to a nonprofit outfit that wants to build a camp."

"A camp?" Patti looked intrigued. "What sort of camp?"

"A charity camp. You know, along the lines of Paul Newman's Hole in the Wall camp. The idea is to bring in underprivileged kids, mostly urban, some foster kids, maybe even some who've had trouble with the law, and give them a few weeks at this here camp in the mountains, riding, fishing, whatever. I guess the folks organizing it hope that exposure to the great outdoors will get them turned around, or at least headed in the right direction—though I for one fail to see how two weeks at a Western camp can turn a bad kid around, or make much of a difference against poverty."

Rusty took a forkful of potatoes. "And I can tell you

right now, my boss is opposed to the idea. A lot of other folks are opposed too. There've been some private meetings about it, but you'll hear soon enough, there's going to be a fight."

"What kind of fight? Legal?" Bob frowned.

"Possibly. Maybe a petition, a town meeting. Hal Miller's going to be writing about it in the *Thunder Creek Daily,* so everyone will be apprised and welcome to speak out. That's if private negotiations with the Morgans and others don't work out," he added with a slight smile. "Actually, it would be in McCallum's best interests to listen to public opinion and ditch this plan before it goes too far."

"The last I heard, Wood and Tammie Morgan didn't represent public opinion in Thunder Creek," Faith said evenly. "Most of the people here like to think for themselves."

"Just what are the Morgans worried about?" Bob asked. "I seriously doubt a camp in the mountains is going to interfere with the profitability of the Crystal Horseshoe Dude Ranch."

"Well, now, you'd be surprised. That's something that can't be determined yet. Who knows what kind of rowdy kids will be hanging around town? There could be disturbances . . . problems. Thunder Creek is a perfect dude ranch town right now. Small, pleasant, quiet, except when a little hell gets raised at the Tumbleweed Bar and Grill." Rusty smiled genially. "Tourists like the quiet, the quaintness, the clean-cut small-town atmosphere here. And the guests at the Crystal Horseshoe are good for the economy—they shop in town, eat at Bessie's Diner, shop on Main Street for antiques and handmade quilts. This camp could ruin the atmosphere here, the very things that make Thunder Creek special, if there's a bunch of noisy kids hanging around, running wild, possibly getting into trouble—"

"Rusty, this better not be about race," Patti said in a low tone. Her piquant gaze bored into the lawyer's face.

He shook his head. "Absolutely not. It's about a bunch of kids who have no clue about living in Wyoming, getting bused into Thunder Creek—and we're talking lots of kids over the summer—four two-week sessions of camp, over a hundred kids a summer. We just don't know what kind of effect all these high-spirited young people out on their own will have on the town's population, its businesses, and its tourist attractions."

"Our ancestors handled gunslingers, bank robbers, and crooked sheriffs—I expect we can handle some high-spirited kids," Faith said.

"You bet. They'll have the time of their lives." Owen drained his beer.

Before Rusty could argue, Bob spoke warningly. "You might want to remind Wood that anyone who wants to tangle with Zach McCallum should think twice. He's always been a hell of a brawler—and not the type to back down from a fight."

You can say that again, Faith thought, taking a sip of lemonade. She'd never forget seeing him take on three of Thunder Creek's high school football players outside the movie theater when they'd been bullying a younger kid. No one fought as cleanly, as ferociously, and with such angry focus as Zach. Not even her own very formidable brothers.

And yet, Zach had shown remarkable restraint today when he'd been taunted by Fred Harrison. Either he'd really learned self-control over the years or he'd just been more focused on his son than on taking a swing at a man twenty-five years his senior.

At any rate, she reminded herself as she helped Patti

clear the table, none of it had anything to do with her. Zach might well be in for a fight about leasing his land for a summer camp, but that wasn't her problem.

And from what she'd seen in the past few days, he seemed perfectly capable of handling his grown-up life and whatever troubles came his way all by himself.

She left Patti and Bob's shortly after dessert. She was tired and restless, and not in the mood for Rusty Gallagher's not-so-subtle attentions, or even for Owen's good-natured bantering.

"Sorry, next time it'll just be the three of us," Patti whispered as she walked Faith out to her car.

"Dinner was wonderful, don't be sorry."

"Rusty could barely take his eyes off you and I could see you weren't interested. But Owen's fun, isn't he?"

"Very."

Patti said nothing as Faith swung open the SUV's door. "All that talk about Zach—you're okay with it, right?" she asked hesitantly as Faith slid behind the wheel.

"I'm fine." Faith dismissed the question with a smile and a wave of her hand. "Zach McCallum doesn't have the power to throw me for a loop anymore, Patti. You don't have to worry about that. Look." She changed the subject in the next breath. "I never did reach Tammie today. How about if I call her in the morning and let her know I'm on the committee and that we need a meeting within the next few days? Can you make it Wednesday? Bessie's Diner, around three? Coffee's on me."

"I'll be there."

Letting herself into the cabin a short time later, Faith switched on the light and slung her purse over the back of a chair, then kicked off her kitten-heeled sandals.

She checked her answering machine. The message light

wasn't flashing. And there hadn't been any calls on her cell either.

"Damn." She'd been hoping to hear back from Liz about Hank Bayman's work attendance and if there'd been any change in his routine. Or any indication that he might have discovered where Susan and the kids had gone.

But Liz hadn't returned her call yet.

There was one way to find out right now if Susan was all right. She sank down on the sofa, picked up her cell phone, and found Susan's number. As the line rang several times, Faith chewed on her lip, then felt a wave of relief when Susan answered the phone. A television blared in the background—it sounded like the kids were watching cartoons.

"Everything is great, Faith. Couldn't be better." Susan sounded happier, stronger than Faith had ever heard her. She could picture the woman's short black hair, her dark, haunted eyes. She no longer sounded defeated, as she had after Hank's trial.

"Everyone's been so nice. Your friend at the law firm in Phoenix found me a job as an administrative assistant. And the kids love their new school."

"That's great." Faith closed her eyes, smiling at the picture in her mind and the note of confidence in Susan's voice.

"And you use the security system every day?" she asked.

"Yes. Always. But . . ." There was a pause. "The only thing is . . . if Hank ever did find me, I know he'd have a way to get around the system. Any system."

"He's not going to find you," Faith assured her, swinging her feet onto the sofa and leaning her head back against a throw pillow. "Even Julia Kimball at the shelter doesn't know where you are, remember? I'm the only one who knows, and I'd cut out my tongue before I'd tell him."

"I know you would, Faith. You've been wonderful throughout all of this. I . . . I don't know how to thank you." Susan's voice wobbled for a moment. "I . . . I never thought I'd get away. I didn't think it was possible. If it wasn't for you, I'm sure Hank would have killed me by now—and the kids."

"He should have been the one forced to leave," Faith said grimly. "If we hadn't gotten a chauvinistic pig of a judge who let him cop a plea, and then let him off with probation, Hank would be locked up right now. I'm just sorry I couldn't do better for you."

"That judge was never going to give Hank jail time. I could tell by the way he looked at me during the trial. Like this was all *my* fault. But it sure wasn't yours, Faith!"

It was, Faith thought, *at least in part. I failed, and the system failed. I should have been able to get through to that judge. And Hank Bayman should have been kept behind bars.*

But the system wasn't perfect, no system ever was, and despite her best efforts, a battered, desperate woman had been left vulnerable to attack—perhaps even to murder— by a man who routinely put a knife to her throat and punched her until she hemorrhaged.

Up until the Bayman case, Faith had accepted and worked through a lot of crap in the maze of the legal system, and had been able to live with it. But she hadn't been able to just throw in the towel and leave Susan Bayman to the mercy of her husband.

"Call me if you have any concerns," she told Susan as she heard one of the boys calling her. "I'll check back with you in a few weeks."

Reassured that Susan and the kids were all right, Faith turned her attention to the auction. She spent the next couple of hours jotting down ideas for the benefit—thoughts on how to pull in more donations and pump up the totals. Around midnight she fell asleep on the sofa with a legal pad on her lap and a pen in her hands, but she slept no more than a few hours before the nightmare woke her once again.

It was the same nightmare as always. A graveyard surrounded by barbed wire, in a cemetery full of snow and ice and blood. A figure floated straight up out of a sealed coffin, its gaunt face locked in a silent, frantic scream. He was floating toward her, fingers twitching, eyes wide. She recognized him as he bore down on her. It was Jimmy Clement. She tried to beg his forgiveness, but her mouth was frozen. No words could form. Closer he came, blood oozing from his nostrils. Closer and closer and . . .

She jerked awake, shaking. In the lamplight, the cabin was warm, still, and very quiet. *No one's here, it was just another dream,* she told herself, taking deep breaths. But panic filled her chest. Along with a wave of guilt that swept through her, cold and bitter as a January wind.

Faith sat up and raked a trembling hand through her hair. Beads of sweat clung to her skin and her heart was racing. Sleep was not coming back, not tonight. That she knew from experience.

So at four in the morning she prowled the cabin and sipped green tea, trying to forget the nightmare. It came less often now . . . but still it came.

She was wide awake, pacing, when her cell rang.

"Hello?"

As usual, nothing showed on her caller ID. He was either calling from a pay phone or he'd used a calling card.

And as usual, he said nothing.

"Bayman, I know it's you. I'm going to get a restraining order if you keep this up." Faith spoke quickly, her voice awake and alert, clear as a whistle. "It's harassment. And it's only going to get you in deeper trouble. You hear me?"

She heard something then. Something that in the dim solitude of the isolated cabin chilled her blood.

Laughter. Soft, faint laughter.

Then a click.

Faith threw down the phone. He'd hung up.

Chapter 5

HANK BAYMAN WHISTLED AS HE GOT OUT OF his car and slammed the door a block from the Krispy Kreme doughnut shop.

It was impossible not to be in a good mood, now that he had a plan. A damned good plan, for that matter. One that was going to get him exactly what he wanted. Calling Faith Barclay's cell phone had been satisfying for a while, but now it was no longer enough.

Time to take the next step.

The day felt cool, more like autumn than late summer, and he ducked his head against the wind as he reached the doughnut shop.

"Large coffee and a Bavarian cream," he told the washed-out-looking blonde behind the counter. A quick check of the crowded shop showed that Marco wasn't there yet.

Just as well. Better let the place clear out a little first. Too many people around and someone might overhear.

Twenty minutes later, Marco burst in, his cop uniform drawing some smiles and nods, some wary glances.

"Hey, there." The blonde flashed a welcoming smile that deepened the lines feathering her pink-lipsticked mouth. "You want the usual, Officer Washington?"

"That'll do me, Connie. Thanks."

"For here or to go?"

"Here." Marco gazed leisurely around the shop as the woman filled a tall Styrofoam cup with black coffee, then reached into a doughnut rack with a square of wax paper to seize a doughnut.

His eyes met Bayman's, but only a slight nod of his head betrayed any sign of recognition. After he had his coffee and doughnut in hand, he ambled over to the table where Bayman was sipping his coffee and casually took a seat.

"Better make this quick. My partner's on the phone with his wife—she might be in labor—and I've got to get back. What do you want?"

"I want the assistant DA, what else? That Barclay bitch."

"The one who nearly nailed your butt?" Marco stared at him from beneath unkempt black brows. "Haven't you had enough trouble? If you're smart you'll stay away from that one."

"If *you're* smart," Bayman said in a low tone, "you'll shut up and do exactly what I tell you."

"Depends what it is." Marco took a sip of his coffee, wincing as it burned the roof of his mouth.

Bayman leaned forward. "The dingbat who answers the phone at the DA's office said she's on a leave of absence. I want to know where she is."

"Look, I already got you her cell phone number. If you want to keep stalking the ADA, you're on your own."

"I don't think so, Marco."

"Jesus, Hank, you looking to do time? Forget about her. You got off—with probation, for cripes sake. You might not be so lucky next time."

"My goddamned wife is gone, Marco." Bayman's voice

was a soft snarl, ferocious as a wolf. He hadn't touched his doughnut. A fly, emboldened, made a swoop at it, then buzzed away. Bayman's eyes shone like copper nuggets in his heavy-jowled face. "The Barclay bitch has Susan hidden away somewhere. That's fucking not acceptable."

"What are you, stupid? You gotta leave Susan alone. Let her go, Hank. Start over. Maybe take some of them anger management classes they always talk about. If Susan's gone, she doesn't want you anymore."

"Listen, asshole." Bayman's face was flushed, his eyes had narrowed to dangerous slits. In the tiny doughnut shop, his voice whipped across the Formica table, quick, precise. "You're not here to give me advice. You're here for one reason only. I want to know where Faith Barclay is. *Specifics*. How long she's gone, when she's coming back. Her home address, if she's there. Her hotel in Miami, if she's on vacation. I want every last detail, you got it? And I want it by tonight."

Marco stared at him as if he'd just asked to be FedExed to Mars. "You need to chill, Hank. You're going to get yourself in deep—"

"Shut up." Bayman snapped the words so loudly several people in the shop glanced his way. The blonde turned her head, alarm flickering in her eyes.

Bayman didn't care. He was done here anyway. "By tonight, Marco." He forced his lips into a smile and waited until the gapers lost interest before he spoke again. "Or else your sergeant's going to know all about that time you skimmed cash off the Fornelli bust."

The cop's face blanched gray as ash. "Jesus, Hank. You going to hold that over my head all my life? I never done anything like that again. We had a baby on the way and—"

Marco broke off, glancing around. He was sweating now. He looked both angry and scared.

Bingo, Bayman thought with satisfaction. *Marco is so predictable. This shit works every time.*

"Yeah, I am going to hold it over your head, pal. Whatcha going to do about it, old buddy?" With a hoarse guffaw, Bayman shoved back his chair. He left his uneaten doughnut and half-filled cup on the table, clapped Marco on the shoulder, and leaned down.

"By tonight, or I give Sergeant Rodriquez an earful," he warned in a tone that only Marco Washington could hear.

He whistled again as he headed to his car. His mood had lightened again the moment he'd left that doughnut shop. Because if there was one thing he knew better than his own name, it was that Marco, his good ol' pal from the days when they were both rookies on the force, would do anything to keep from getting nailed.

Marco had a wife, kids, a mortgage, and was up for promotion. The last place he wanted to end up was the pokey.

Officer Washington—family man, decorated cop, friend to doughnut shop slackers everywhere—would find a way to get the 411 on Faith Barclay. No question about it.

Chapter 6

"HOW ON EARTH DID I LET YOU TALK ME INTO this?" Faith asked Patti in mock dismay as she gazed around the loud, noisy bedlam of the Tumbleweed Bar and Grill.

It was Saturday night and they were seated at a table under the window. Cool fresh air fluttered the paper napkins and ruffled Faith's hair—Patti had only half jokingly called this the nonsmoking section, or as close as you'd get to one in any drinking establishment in Thunder Creek.

The place was packed. Across from the bar, both pool tables were surrounded by players—men in cowboy hats and women in skintight jeans—but the steady click of pool cues was nearly lost in the din of laughter and talk that swirled through the bar, not to mention the Johnny Cash tune rumbling from the jukebox.

"That's easy—you *wanted* to come here because you've done nothing but work on the auction, ride, and hike around by yourself for the past week. You're lonely as hell. Admit it." Patti pushed a bowl of beer nuts across the table toward her as Faith sipped a beer.

"I'm not lonely, I'm relaxed," she countered. It was true. For the past week, since she'd had dinner at Patti and

Bob's, she'd actually started to unwind. Despite that creepy phone call from Bayman in the middle of the night, she'd wrapped herself up in the calm of the cabin and the serenity of Blue Moon Mesa and had finally felt some of the tension that had wracked her for months beginning to ease.

She'd even slept five straight hours the past few nights. *Progress*.

"What else can I get you all to drink?" A red-haired waitress in a hot-pink blouse and black jeans paused beside Bob's chair and peered around the table.

"More lemonade for me, sweetie." Patti patted her belly with a grin.

Bob ordered another beer and Faith asked for the same.

"We can't stay too much longer actually—too much secondhand smoke won't be good for the baby," Patti said. "But everyone stops in the Tumbleweed at least for a little while on Saturday night. And I knew you wouldn't want to miss out on the action."

"What action? You mean if Big John Templeton or Randy Otis wins the darts competition?" Faith shot back, then grinned. She wasn't really annoyed. The Tumbleweed, along with Bessie's Diner, was a central part of Thunder Creek social life and it had felt good to slip into old jeans and a red sweater, to plop herself into the midst of a crowd of happy people who all knew each other and wanted to have a good time. She spotted Roy and Corinne coming in the door and waved. They headed straight for the table.

"Don't forget, you promised to come to dinner next week," Corinne told her with a smile.

"How are things going at the cabin?" Roy wanted to know. "If you start to feel lonely out there, we've got a spare bedroom. It'll be turned into a nursery in a few months, but it's yours now anytime you need it."

"Thanks, Roy, but everything is great. I love it at the cabin."

"Hello, beautiful lady. How about a dance?"

She looked up into the deep-set brown eyes of Rusty Gallagher. He looked coolly handsome in pressed jeans and a white polo shirt as he held out a hand.

"I figure we should practice up before the dinner dance," he said, easily filling the moment that she hesitated.

"Oh. Yes. Absolutely." Faith had no choice but to take that outstretched hand and walk with him to the dance floor. She was very conscious of the eyes boring into her back as Roy, Corinne, Patti, and Bob all watched Rusty slip an arm around her waist as Garth Brooks came on the jukebox.

"That guy doesn't waste any time," Roy remarked, grinning. "So they must have hit it off at dinner last week."

"Not exactly. Will you just look at your cousin?" Patti popped a beer nut into her mouth. "Does she look *swoony* to you? I've seen more enthusiasm from a third-grader getting put into time out in the corner."

Corinne sighed. "Oh, no, don't tell me you're matchmaking again, Roy. Just because you pushed Ty and Josy together and they ended up falling madly in love doesn't mean your middle name is Cupid."

"You watch," Roy told her. "I'm going to be two for two." He tipped back his beer.

But Bob was looking toward the bar. "Don't count Owen out."

The others followed his gaze. Owen Carey was hunched

on a barstool, sipping a beer as he watched Faith and Rusty on the dance floor.

"I haven't seen Owen scowl like that since Nancy Pruitt broke up with him and skidoodled out of town," Bob said.

"All right, then, maybe we've got a horse race. Let the best man win." Roy put an arm around his wife. "Just so long as Faith is happy."

"Maybe Faith is the best judge of what makes Faith happy," Patti murmured.

Corinne nodded. "Now there's a voice of reason. You should listen to her." She poked Roy's arm. "How about dancing with your wife, cowboy? Or are you going to let the single people have all the fun?"

On the dance floor, Rusty wasted no time in clasping Faith's hand in his, while his other arm tightened around her waist.

Garth crooned from the jukebox, and all around them in the smoky dimness, couples melted together, swaying and shuffling across the floor.

"How are the plans for the auction coming along?" Rusty asked as he guided her smoothly away from the thick of the crowd.

"Terrific. We have over one hundred items donated now—and nearly three quarters of the tickets for the dinner dance have been sold."

"I'm sure you were a big part of accomplishing all that," Rusty said.

Faith tried to ignore the pressure of his arm at her back. "It was very much a team effort."

"Modest as well as beautiful." He grinned. "I like that in a woman. You don't find it too often. Take my boss's wife, for example. Please."

He chuckled at his own joke, but Faith's attention had

shifted to his appearance. His skin was flushed. His eyes shone almost golden in the dim light. And there was alcohol on his breath.

He's drunk, she realized, even as she felt Rusty's hand slide from her waist to cup her bottom.

She reached behind her and pushed his hand away. "You're out of order, Counselor. You lose points for that."

"I'm sorry, Your Honor." He chuckled. "I didn't mean anything by it. How can I get them back?" He leaned in closer to her—a little too close. Faith's spine stiffened.

"You'll have to figure that out for yourself."

"Fair enough." With a wink, he added, "I like a woman who plays hard to get."

And I like a man who waits for an invitation to grope my butt, she thought, but instead said with a cool little smile, "I'm not playing, Rusty. I am hard to get."

He studied her face, the cool gorgeous eyes, that perfect mouth. Slowly he nodded as the song came to an end. "Then I'll have to woo you proper."

Faith barely heard. Zach McCallum had just pushed through the doors of the Tumbleweed, and he wasn't alone.

Candy Merck had her arm linked with his as they paused for a moment to survey the crowded bar.

Faith's heart did a crazy little leap. Then Zach's gaze locked with hers across the room.

For a moment he did nothing but stare at her, then his glance shifted to Rusty, whose arm was still tightly encircling Faith's waist.

She saw a frown darken his face. Then Candy whispered something to him and tugged on his arm. Through the haze of smoke, Faith saw Zach drag his gaze back to the blonde in the slinky red tank top and white leather miniskirt. They turned toward the pool tables.

"Join me at the bar for a drink?" Rusty asked, not moving from the dance floor as other couples drifted back to their tables.

"I'm with friends. I'd better get back." She started to walk away from him, but he yanked her toward him once more, the wide handsome grin spreading across his face.

"Hey, I'm a friend too, aren't I?"

Faith realized his grip on her arm was tight enough that she couldn't break free without a struggle. Which would mean a scene. Already she could see Roy watching them. To her dismay, he looked like he was almost halfway out of his chair.

Enough was enough. "I think you've had plenty to drink for one night, Rusty," she said quickly. "You're stepping over the line."

"I'm bein' friendly. Whass wrong with that?" His grip was hurting her arm.

"Let me go, or my cousin's going to shove your teeth down your throat," she said coldly. "Unless I do it first. Or would you like to be kicked in the balls?"

"Literally or figuratively?" He laughed, his eyes both bright and bleary, and she realized that he was mistaking her anger for some kind of weird flirtation. And he probably had no idea her brothers had taught her a dozen different ways to protect herself from drunken idiots—or worse.

"You're hurting my arm, Rusty. Let go of me—now." She managed to jerk free, only to have him step forward and grab her hand in his.

"One little drink at the bar," he insisted. "Just one—"

Again Faith pulled her hand free, her mouth tight with anger. Alarm ripped through her as she saw Roy launching himself out of his chair, with Bob right behind him. *Damn.*

Then she saw Owen hurrying toward them from the bar, a rare frown on his good-natured face.

"Rusty," she said quickly, "you'd better get out of—"

But she was too late. He was suddenly shoved ruthlessly away from her, and went skidding into a table. At the last instant he managed to grab the edge of it to keep himself from falling onto the floor.

And Zach McCallum stood in front of her, his eyes steely.

"Are you all right?"

Faith was too stunned to speak. She just stared at Zach in amazement. His face was taut with anger, making him look like some handsome avenging devil, and those intense dangerous silver eyes lasered in on hers with the force of a torpedo. A thousand emotions splintered through her, astonishment foremost among them. And in that instant she finally found her voice.

"Of course I'm all right. Who the hell asked you to mess in my life?"

Zach's gaze hardened. And then she saw Rusty lunging straight at him in a flying tackle.

"Look out!" she shrieked.

Zach wheeled around just in time and both men hit the floor in a flurry of fists, grunts, and denim.

"Best step out of the way, cuz." Roy's hands clamped down on her shoulders and drew her back ten feet from the fray.

"You'd better stop them, Roy, or I will!" she demanded, shaking off his protective grip.

"Gallagher has it coming. He was all over you," Roy countered, but to Faith's relief, Owen and Bob were already hauling the two men apart. But not before Zach got in one final punch to the attorney's midsection.

Rusty had quite obviously received the worst of it. He was doubled over, the wind knocked out of him, and a dribble of blood ran from the corner of his mouth. Zach's dark hair was barely mussed.

"That's enough, folks. Settle down." Elam the bartender strode over, holding his hands over his head. "That's all the excitement for tonight." He pointed at Rusty, looking dazed and angry as a gored bull.

"You." The bartender jerked his thumb toward the door. "Out."

Touching a hand to his bruised mouth, the attorney scowled at Zach. "You just made a big mistake, McCallum. Who the hell do you think you are?"

Zach picked up his hat from the floor, dusted it off against his jeans, and set it on his head. "Someone who'll wipe the floor with you if you don't stay out of my way," he said coolly.

He was turning away when Candy dashed up, her heels clattering against the floor.

"For God's sake, Zach, are you okay? Come on, let's get out of here. I'll fix you a drink at my place."

"No." He looked into her wide, worried eyes. "We came here to shoot pool. Let's shoot some."

"Well, if you're sure, honey. Whatever you say." Candy slanted him a smile that would have singed a cat's tail. "But what do I get if I win?"

He never even glanced toward Faith as he guided Candy back to the pool table.

They made a great-looking couple, Faith thought, her gaze following them. Zach, impossibly handsome, tall and dark, and Candy, petite and curvy, with her baby-fine hair and pert little nose. She accepted a cue stick from him with a seductive smile that could have graced the pages of *Cosmopolitan*.

Slowly, the crowd in the Tumbleweed drifted back to their drinks and their conversations. Couples were dancing again.

Faith was silent as she slipped back into her chair.

"Well, now, *that* was interesting." Patti leaned over and whispered in her ear. "Are you all right? Or are you accustomed to men fighting over you whenever you go to the bars in Philadelphia?"

"Oh, sure. Happens every night." Faith reached for her beer and took a long drink.

"He was drunk, wasn't he?" Patti said aloud. "I thought so when he came to the table."

"Zach sure lost no time in decking him," Roy put in with satisfaction as he and Bob took their seats. He threw Faith a thoughtful look. "What was up with that? Are you two . . . friends again?"

"Hardly." Faith shrugged. Despite the fact that she was trying to appear casual, her heart was racing.

Zach McCallum had just jumped into her business, into her life, with both feet—and both fists.

Why?

There was also the little matter that he appeared to be here on a date with Candy Merck. So obviously he no longer had a wife . . . not that *that* mattered, certainly not to her . . .

"I'm sorry I got you mixed up with Gallagher." For once, Roy looked serious. And repentant. "I didn't know he was an asshole."

"How could you have? I'm sure he's only boorish when he's had too much to drink. Besides, I was handling him, Roy. I just couldn't do it fast enough." She stood up, went around the table, and wrapped her arms around her cousin's neck.

"You're the best. And I'll tell Ty and Adam that you took good care of me." She managed a short laugh. "But I think I've had enough fun for one night. Time to get some beauty sleep."

Patti and Corinne promised to call her in the morning, and Roy got up to walk her out to her car. But he stopped as he saw Owen headed over.

"Faith, you're leaving? Can I drive you home?"

"I've got my car, Owen. But thanks."

"I'll walk you out then. You never know what kind of scum might be hanging around."

"In Thunder Creek?" She smiled at him.

"Yeah, in Thunder Creek. One piece of crud just got kicked out of here, and who knows if he's barfing in the parking lot or waiting to hassle some other woman."

He had a point. She fell into step with him as they wove their way across the packed bar. Owen seemed pretty loaded himself, Faith noted as he stumbled once and swore under his breath. She could smell the beer on him.

"I hope you don't think I couldn't have handled Rusty on my own," she felt compelled to tell him. "But nobody gave me a chance to try."

"You shouldn't have had to try. I saw him manhandling you. That guy was way out of line."

At her car, Owen held open the door and waited until she'd slid behind the wheel. But instead of slamming it closed, he held it open a moment, looking down at her with too-bright eyes and an uncertain expression.

"I've been . . . kinda wondering something, Faith. Do you think you and I . . . could . . . talk . . . one of these days?"

Something in his tone made her glance searchingly at him. "Sure. What's on your mind, Owen?"

"I need to ask your opinion about something."

"Care to give me a hint?" She tilted her head to one side, studying him as the cool night air wafted into the SUV.

"Not now." Owen glanced around as a Jeep full of young cowboys pulled into the parking lot, the radio blasting.

"I'll call you, Faith," he said quickly. He ducked his head and turned away. "Soon."

She was curious about what was on his mind, but as she started the drive home in starlit darkness, she was even more curious about what had happened this evening between Zach McCallum and Rusty Gallagher.

On her way out of the Tumbleweed, she'd been unable to resist glancing over toward Zach and Candy shooting pool, but neither of them had even glanced at her. They'd been joking, drinking, concentrating on the game and on each other.

A silly little pain twisted inside her. She unknotted it brutally. *When are you going to learn you can't understand anything about Zach McCallum?* she asked herself angrily as the SUV rattled over the darkened road.

And more important, a little voice responded deep in the recesses of her mind, *why in the world do you still want to try?*

Chapter 7

CANDY MERCK WAS IN HEAVEN.

Even though she'd lost two out of three games of pool to Zach McCallum, she didn't mind a bit. Because now she was dancing in Zach's arms while Patsy Cline sang her heart out. In the midst of a crowded dance floor of romantically swaying couples, Zach was holding her so close she could breathe in the subtle tobacco and leather scent of his cologne, and she could certainly feel the muscular strength of his body against her own, even through their clothes. Her skin warmed where their hands touched and a fevered heat began to beat in her blood.

He had excited her when she was seventeen, and he excited her today. Some men just had that special heartthrob factor that there was no denying. And Zach had it in spades.

Of course he'd never paid attention to her back then when she was in high school. She was younger than Faith and Patti and the other girls Zach had hung out with. She'd been pudgy, self-conscious, and shy back then—until she lost twenty pounds, dyed her hair a lighter, sheerer shade of blond, and learned to loosen up thanks to the judicious help of Mr. Budweiser.

Now every guy in town wanted to date her, dance with her. But so far, not one of them had wanted to marry her.

Maybe it was just meant to be that Zach would come back into her life and be *the one*. Candy smiled dreamily and shifted closer to Zach's rock-solid abs. Maybe his coming back now, seeking her out to handle that land lease, was fate's way of saying *Candy, here's your guy— the one you always dreamed of.*

That one summer he'd spent in Thunder Creek ten years ago had begun with Zach running around with his friends, drinking beer in the back of someone's pickup truck every night, swimming in the creek, or drag-racing on the dirt road that ran for two miles behind the highway. But all that had changed the day he met Faith Barclay.

They'd starting spending more and more time together. By the end of the summer, they'd been inseparable.

And Candy had felt invisible.

But now Zach had returned, all grown up, better looking than ever, rich as all getout, and he'd come looking for *her*. She'd handled all the paperwork he needed to lease his back acres to the Buffalo Kids Camp organizers. They'd been at enough meetings together for her to learn that he was divorced from his son's mother, that he planned to settle indefinitely in Thunder Creek, and that he still had that slow crooked grin that had always had the power to send her into a tailspin.

Candy had worn her sexiest suit today when she drove out to the Last Trail for one last signature. She'd seen Zach notice her snugly cut violet blazer—worn with a sexy silk camisole and a tight black skirt that hugged her bottom. When she'd suggested that they hang out tonight at the Tumbleweed, to celebrate finalizing the deal, he'd only hesitated a tiny second before accepting.

Candy was sure he was just thinking about who would watch his son while he went on a date. But that wouldn't be a problem, since Zach had a live-in housekeeper who was paid to help take care of the boy.

And she was equally sure that Zach wouldn't be turning down anything else tonight either—including what she planned to offer him when they left the Tumbleweed and went back to her place.

"How about one more dance?" she murmured, gazing up into his eyes as the music ended and George Strait came on the jukebox, crooning out another ballad. "This is my favorite song."

"It's getting late, Candy. How about a rain check?"

For the first time, she noticed the distant look in his eyes. What was he thinking about? Or maybe she should ask herself *who*?

It wouldn't take three guesses.

"You wouldn't turn Faith down for another dance, would you?" she blurted before she could bite back the words.

Finally he seemed to focus in on her. Was it her imagination, or did his features suddenly harden, as if her words had made him retreat deep and fast into himself, far away from her, from this dance floor?

"What are you talking about?"

Candy sensed she'd made a misstep, but there was nothing to do now but bluster through it.

"Well, you did jump in there kinda fast when she was dancing with Rusty Gallagher." Try as she might, she couldn't keep the peevishness from her tone. "And it's not as if she even asked you for help. She looked fine to me. They were just talking—"

"Faith Barclay has nothing to do with this conversation, or with you and me."

You and me? Hope surged through her. *So maybe there is a you and me,* she thought, her heart beating faster.

"I'm glad to hear that, Zach. More glad than I can say."

She tossed him a smile she'd perfected by the time she turned eighteen, a sideways, come-hither smile that never failed to get a man's attention. "How about one more drink at my place? I have a bottle of champagne I've been saving for a special occasion. We should have a toast to finalizing your deal with the camp."

Which is how Zach found himself twenty minutes later sitting on a sleek red leather sofa in a small ranch house two miles outside of town. Candy's house was furnished like a Manhattan loft with lots of leather and glass, bold contemporary art, and dramatic geometric rugs on the hardwood floors.

It looked amusingly out of place in the comfortable, down-home coziness of Thunder Creek, but Candy confided her secret goal—that if she ever built up her bank account enough, she'd be headed for the Big Apple. She had her sights set on going east, on selling luxury condos and penthouses in Manhattan and summer homes in the Hamptons. She'd lived her whole life in Thunder Creek and that was enough. She was going for the big time—where a single real estate deal would net her more commission than she earned in Thunder Creek in a year.

"There's only one thing that would stop me," she told Zach, handing him a glass of champagne. She sat close to him on the sofa and took a sip from her own glass. "And that's if I met the right man and he begged me to stay."

"You'd give up your dreams for a man?"

"If it was the right man—maybe." She shot him an assessing smile. "Or maybe I'd just convince him to come along with me. Then I could have it all."

Zach felt a spurt of pity for her. Did she really believe she could have it all?

Well, good luck to her, but based on his own experience, anyone who thought that way was in for a rude awakening.

He'd long ago given up on wanting to have it all—much less believing he ever could.

His wants were much more conservative now. They all revolved around his business—and his son. A good life for Dillon. Keeping his company strong. Those were his goals. His focus. His lifeline.

For himself, personally, he'd long ago given up what he'd wanted, and if there was anything he'd learned over the years it was that there was no going back.

You live with your mistakes, give up your dreams, and move on, making the best of it, he thought, taking another swig of Candy's champagne. It was a philosophy he'd honed in his battles with his father and in his dealings with his wife.

Candy was giggling into her glass. She'd already consumed three beers at the Tumbleweed, and as he'd driven her home, she'd sung pleasantly off-key along with the radio.

"I should be going." He finished off his drink and set it down on her glass cocktail table. "I promised to take my son fishing in the morning. That means a five A.M. wake-up."

"But we just got here." She touched his arm. "Stay. Please. Pretty please."

And before he could stand up, she scooted onto his lap, wound her arms around his neck, and kissed him.

Her lips were moist and puffy, scented with champagne. She was a cuddly handful, and her blond hair tickled his chin. But Zach felt nothing as he kissed her. Nothing but frustration.

She wasn't the woman he wanted to be kissing right now. She wasn't Faith.

He ended the kiss, pulling back. Though she still clung to him, he held her at arm's length.

"I have to be going, Candy."

She blinked twice, looking as if he'd just thrown cold water in her eyes. "C'mon, you can stay a *little* longer, can't you? We're just getting started—"

"Sorry. I have to go." As he saw anger and hurt flash in her eyes, he took a deep breath. "I'm sorry. You've had a lot to drink and I don't want to take advantage of our friendship."

Shifting her off his lap, he stood. "You and I are friends, Candy." His tone was firm. "Good friends. And that's it. I hope we can keep it that way."

Driving home a few moments later, he raked a hand through his hair. He wished he'd never accepted her suggestion about going out to the Tumbleweed together. Then he never would've gotten himself into that damned awkward situation at her house.

Damn, Candy will probably be embarrassed as hell in the morning, if she even remembers anything. He hoped to God she didn't.

But there was something else that never would have happened if he hadn't been at the Tumbleweed tonight. He wouldn't have run into Faith, wouldn't have felt his blood boil when Rusty Gallagher had his hands all over her. He wouldn't have acted like a geeky teen in love when he'd seen Faith trying to push Gallagher away.

She had plenty of protectors: Roy, Bob, Owen. She sure

as hell didn't need him. But he'd acted reflexively, without thinking.

He hadn't done that sort of thing in a long time. Over the years, he'd trained himself to exercise self-control, to think through every action before initiating it.

Tonight, the mere sight of Faith trying to pull away from Gallagher had triggered a grenade in his bloodstream and sent him barreling into battle.

Despite the single beer he'd drunk at the bar and the glass of champagne at Candy's place, he was wound up. A fierce restlessness gripped him as he drove. The night was bedazzled with stars, reigned over by a glittering half-moon of pure silver, and the air was tinged with an early autumn chill that swept straight down from the mountains.

He knew he should go home, get to bed, set his alarm for five. Dillon would be raring to go by five-thirty. But he found himself passing the turnoff to Bear Paw Road, which led to the Last Trail ranch house, and instead heading west, toward Blue Moon Mesa.

Zach stared straight ahead as he turned onto the lonely gravel track leading to the cabin, which was backed by woods and set within tall pines.

The cabin was bathed in moonlight as he halted in the small clearing before the porch and shut off the lights and the engine.

The windows were all dark. Faith must be asleep.

Even if she wasn't . . . what the hell was he doing here?

Yet he sat, studying the cabin, the smoke curling from the chimney into the brilliant night sky. The peace of it enveloped him even in his truck.

He thought back to the night ten summers ago, when the two of them had hiked from here all the way to Shadow Point. Faith had worn cutoff khaki shorts and a white

T-shirt that made her tanned arms and legs look even richer. Her mass of curls had been tamed and twisted into a braid down her back.

She'd smelled of baby powder and Dove soap as they'd kissed over there . . . right beside that juniper tree twenty feet from the cabin. The sun had been shining that day, and her mouth had felt as soft as flower petals.

He'd blurted that he'd loved her—just like that, in the middle of a summer afternoon, with birds singing in the trees all around them and not another human being around for miles.

And she'd said she loved him too . . .

Someone was over there. By the tree where they'd kissed.

In the car, Zach stared through the darkness, alarm surging like ice through his blood. He saw movement, a man's shape, the sheen of eyes, barely discernible through the starlit night . . . and then in an instant the man slipped toward the woods and disappeared into the dark.

What the hell?

Zach was out of the car in a flash. "Hey," he yelled, sprinting forward, scanning the blackness. "Who's there? Stop!"

There was no answer, no sound. Zach kept running, straight toward the spot where the man lurking outside of Faith's cabin had melted like a ghost into the dark.

Chapter 8

A NOISE OUTSIDE YANKED FAITH FROM A REST-less sleep. She shot straight up in bed, her heart racing.

A motor hummed. Tires crunched gravel. Someone was driving up the track to the cabin.

Rusty Gallagher was her first thought. Maybe he was drunk, wanted to "dance" with her some more. Or bawl her out for getting him kicked out of the Tumbleweed.

Scrambling out of bed, she grabbed her gun from the bottom dresser drawer where she'd tucked it atop her sweatpants and zip-up jackets. Then, clad only in her pink tank top and white drawstring pants, she crossed to the window, peered through one of the slats of the plantation shutters, and saw the car outlined in the moonlight.

The lights had been killed. And the engine. She strained to make out the vehicle or someone inside, but all she could see was that it was a pickup and there was a man behind the wheel.

Suddenly, the driver's door was flung open and a tall male leaped out of the car, shouting.

"Hey!"

Zach. She stared in astonishment as he took off at a dead run toward the south end of the cabin. What the hell?

Her breath quickening, she shoved her feet into her flip-flops and snatched a flashlight from the nightstand.

Gripping the gun in one hand and the flashlight in the other, she ran out onto the porch, peering in the direction Zach had gone.

"Zach? What's going on?" she yelled, shining the beam into the brush.

She heard running footsteps and braced herself, until she saw it was Zach emerging from the shadow of the woods.

"Give me the flashlight."

"Like hell I will. What are you doing here?"

"You had a prowler." He strode toward her. He noticed the gun in her hand but ignored it. "Come on, Faith, I want to look around, see if there's any footprints or if he dropped something."

"I can do that myself. What are you doing at my cabin in the middle of the night?"

"Damned if I know." In a movement that took her by surprise, he swiped the flashlight from her grasp and turned back toward the woods. "Go inside. I'll let you know what I find."

"No way. Give that back to me." She leaped after him, grabbed the flashlight back. He gritted his teeth as she marched ahead of him.

"Where did you see him?" she demanded.

"There. By our . . . by the tree."

A stone skimmed across the surface of her heart, making ripples. Did he think of it as "our tree" too? She bit her lip and swung the flashlight toward the tree, making a slow circle of the ground around it.

She didn't see anything except gnarled roots, dirt, and grass.

"He ran past the cabin, into the woods. That way." Zach pointed and she aimed the beam toward the spot, slowly walking forward, shining the light on the star-kissed wheat grass.

There were no clear footprints: some parts looked like they'd been flattened, but that could have been done anytime, by anyone. Even by her. She'd been taking nightly walks all around the cabin, in every direction. And more than once she'd started those walks from the tree.

"Are you sure you saw someone?" she asked at length. Zach had accompanied her as she plunged into the shade of the trees, where the night was even blacker. Glancing at him, she saw grim concern on his face.

"I'm sure."

"Maybe it was a fox or a bobcat."

"Give me a break, Faith. I know what I saw. I think you should call the sheriff."

"The *acting* sheriff." She spoke with disdain. "No."

She was just as stubborn and headstrong as ever. That knowledge made his gut ache, like hot salt rubbed into an unhealed wound.

Faith might be a high-powered assistant DA, she might be a lithe, stunningly elegant woman with a brain sharper than a laser—but she still had the spunk and the spirit of the fiery teenage girl who'd once gazed at him as if he were the sun and the moon. That girl was still inside her, an intrinsic part of the slender, formidable woman beside him, the one with a gun in her hand and a sexy tank top outlining her beautiful breasts. Knowing that made him happy, and it made him hurt.

But Zach knew how to hide what he was feeling. A good portion of his life had been spent learning how to best hide everything that made him appear vulnerable and weak.

He was a pro at concealing his emotions, his thoughts. He'd found that a valuable weapon in the battle of life.

As Faith stalked back to the cabin, he fell into step beside her, his face shuttered in the moonlight. Neither of them spoke.

There was all around them only the sound of their footsteps crunching over the grass, the chirp of crickets, and the whispered rustle of wild creatures scurrying in the night.

He was the first to break the silence when they reached the porch.

"I'm going to take a look inside." He bounded past her up the steps before she could protest. "You left the door open— he could have circled back while we were searching."

"Don't bother. I'll check myself—"

But her words fell on deaf ears—or rather, on *no* ears, because he'd already strode inside and switched on the lights.

Of all the things that might have happened tonight, Zach McCallum walking through her front door sometime after midnight was not one she would have ever imagined.

She followed him inside and closed the door, then set the gun and the flashlight down on the coffee table. For some reason she felt close to naked in her tank top and drawstring pants, her feet in slim flip-flops, and she wondered why she'd feel better, more protected if she was wearing a bulky sweater, jeans, and boots. *Protected from what?* she wondered, her heart skipping a beat. From Zach? Or from herself?

Her own weak, foolish, stupid self?

She couldn't help noticing that when Zach left the

smaller bedroom and headed for hers, his tall, rangy body looked as tense and alert as a special forces operative checking for land mines. She tried not to stare at the way his shoulders filled out his light-blue shirt, or at the corded muscles of his arms. Or at the casual, sexy way his dark hair tumbled over his brow. It was bad enough that his jaw was set in a way she remembered all too well, a way that gave her a pang deep in her heart.

When she looked at Zach, it was as if no time had passed between them. His expressions, gestures, the way he moved, were indelibly engraved into her memory. So familiar, so sexy. So . . . hurtful.

"Are you satisfied now?" she asked when he appeared at her bedroom door.

"You're still as messy as ever, I see." He didn't mention that the sight of a black wispy bra slung over the back of a chair, unlaced Pumas beside the bed, and magazines and folders stacked on her night table along with a handful of earrings and a jar of tangerine-scented body scrub had made his muscles clench, not with irritation but with a heat that came from memories so sweet they scalded.

"No one's under your bed or behind the bathroom door. I'm going to check the last bedroom. Wait here."

He's making too much of this. It was dark out there, he can't be sure he actually saw someone. We didn't find any signs, she told herself as she heard him moving through the third bedroom.

Yet she glanced uneasily at the window and shivered, half expecting to see a face staring back at her.

But there was only moonlit darkness beyond. She drew the curtains and hurried to the front door to lock it.

He found her sitting at the kitchen table, sipping tea from a blue-flowered cup.

"So did you find a bogeyman hiding under the bed?"

He leaned against the countertop, regarding her through narrowed eyes. "There was someone out there, Faith. I'd bet my company on it."

"Well, whoever it was—if there was someone—he's gone now."

Zach couldn't help noticing the tension in her neck and shoulders. She wasn't quite as cool about this as she'd have him believe.

"Any idea who might want to sneak up on you in the middle of the night?"

"None at all." But she wondered if it had been Rusty Gallagher. If he'd been drunk, angry, horny, whatever.

Or . . . She didn't like the other possibility that presented itself, so she pushed the thought away.

"I suppose I should offer you some tea." How stiff her voice sounded, even to herself. As if she were talking to a stranger. *Well, you are,* she told herself, setting her cup down with a tiny clink. *You don't know Zach anymore. He's different—and so are you.*

"Don't trouble yourself. I'm a coffee kind of guy myself. And this isn't—wasn't—intended as a social call."

"Oh?" Faith pushed back her chair, stood up. She shoved a lock of hair from her eyes. "What was it intended as?"

For a moment Zach gazed at her, at a loss how to reply. He himself didn't understand what had brought him here in the middle of the night—how could he possibly explain it to her?

It didn't help that she looked so sexily mussed from sleep, and beautiful as a sunrise. Not only did the pink tank top deliciously sculpt the outline of her breasts, but those drawstring pants hovered sensuously around hips he longed to touch. Her hair . . . hell, he'd always loved to tangle his hands in her hair. It looked like a silken cloud, curl upon untamed curl. It took a conscious effort not to reach out and stroke those thick curls between his fingers, watching her eyes darken with pleasure as they had when she was nineteen.

But they probably wouldn't do that anymore, even if she liked it, Zach thought. Faith seemed to have learned how to guard her expressions. Her face used to reflect everything she was feeling, and he had been fascinated by that. Now what she felt was locked inside her, her outward countenance as lovely, neutral, and cool as a distant waterfall.

She stood before him, spine straight, sexy as hell, her perfect mouth tightly clenched. The urge to banish that damned distant expression from her face, to touch and soften those set lips was nearly overwhelming.

But he had learned discipline and self-control in the past ten years as well. He exercised both now.

"I didn't come here to see you, if that's what you think. Call it subconscious insanity. It just happened."

"Insanity? That I can believe. You're the last person I'd expect on Blue Moon Mesa in the middle of the night."

"Yeah, well, that makes two of us."

"In that case don't let me keep you."

She moved toward the front door and he had no choice but to follow. The sway of her rounded bottom beneath those drawstring pants kick-started his blood.

As he stepped out onto the porch and she still held the door open, he turned back. Faint moonlight illuminated the soft lines of her face, gilded her full mouth.

"Did he hurt you tonight? Gallagher?"

"Of course not. I told you, I could have handled him."

"Yeah. I'm sure you could have—if you'd put a tin can on his head and gotten hold of a rock."

Now, why did he say that? If he'd been looking for a smile, he didn't get one. She was tough, this grown-up Faith. She'd told him years ago, proudly, about how her brothers had taught her to hit a tin can target with a rock nine times out of ten. He'd challenged her to a contest, and she'd won, then teased him about it for days.

But tonight she gave no sign of remembering it, or anything else about that summer. She looked as closed to him as a solid steel wall.

Zach suddenly had the nearly irresistible urge to melt that steel.

Go. Just go. With all her might, Faith willed him to leave. Her heart couldn't return to its normal rhythm, not while he was here. She told herself it was only from the shock of finding him—anyone—on the premises in the middle of the night. And from the hurried search in the woods. But deep inside, she knew that was a lie.

It was Zach. Purely Zach. He looked so frustratingly handsome—so tough and virile and *male*. His thick straight black hair and tanned skin contrasted intriguingly with eyes as gray as a moody sea.

His mouth was thin and hard. At thirty, he was, if possible, even sexier—hotter—than he'd been ten years ago as a rebellious teenage boy.

But now he was very much a man. A man who would dazzle any woman. And the effect he had on her was indescribable.

Memories flooded back. She remembered the first time they'd made love, on the hottest day of July, on Snowflake Mountain. She remembered the sun baking their bare skin, the sweet smell of the grass cushioning her back, and the way his hips had moved against hers.

She trembled inwardly, fighting to stop the flow of

memories, but she couldn't stop wondering if she would burn inside again if they kissed, if he cupped her breast, trailed his hand across her thigh . . .

No, no, she'd never find out. It would never happen. Never again. She glared at him, proving her own strength.

He tipped his hat to her on the porch. Pain sliced her heart.

"I wish I could say it's been fun," she said. "Good night, Zach."

She was stepping back, starting to close the door, when she saw his eyes darken. Something changed in his face, something that flashed through him like a bolt of hot gold lightning, and she sensed the danger like a clap of silent thunder.

Before she could move, he reached her. He held the screen door open with his body and seized her face between his calloused palms before she could do more than gasp.

His gray eyes glinted into hers. His gaze was hard and piercing, and she knew horribly in that one instant that he saw *everything* . . . her fear and shock—and her desire.

His head tipped lower, closing in. Then his mouth slanted ruthlessly against hers and Faith's senses went haywire. The kiss was deep, hard, hot. Like a man sampling, swallowing whole, a delectable treat he'd long been denied.

The coolness of the almost-autumn night vanished. It was suddenly summer again. Warm, sensuous summer, the air thick with the scent of pine, the world a blur of sunlight and heat, of gold and green, she and Zach on Snowflake Mountain, frantic, breathless, dizzy in love . . .

His arms went around her as she nearly slid to the

ground. He held her up, held her close, the kiss changing, gentling, setting off torpedoes of fire through her blood.

Then it hardened again, became almost angry, punishing. She moaned, threw her arms around his neck, begged for more. She drank him in, her own mouth frantic with need, but suddenly he put his hands on her shoulders and stopped.

He just stopped. Just like that. Broke the kiss as quickly as he'd begun it. And stepped back.

When Faith looked into his eyes, feeling helplessly stunned and naked, she saw that his gaze was dark now. Dark and cool and totally unreadable.

"Now," he said quietly as she stared at him, dazed. "*Now* it's a good night."

He turned and walked away, leaving her standing there without so much as a backward glance.

Chapter 9

High up on Snowflake Mountain, Hank Bayman opened another can of beer and drank deeply. The air was cold as a witch's tit at that height, but his campfire and khaki jacket kept him warm. So did the beer.

Tonight had been a close call. Almost too close. How could he have guessed that the Barclay bitch would have company in the middle of the night? Just went to show, no matter how smart and high and mighty she might think she was, she was still a slut.

Which meant she was going to deserve everything she got.

Bayman was more than satisfied with the way things had gone ever since he'd landed at the Natrona County airport in Casper a few days earlier. He'd rented a Dodge truck easy as pie and hit the road, never once even spotting a cop car on his way into Thunder Creek.

Not that he had anything to fear from the cops, he mused, savoring another gulp of beer. Chances were that his dumb-fuck probation officer didn't even have a clue yet that he'd skipped town.

Everything was under control, and he was ready to make his move. With his background, scoping out this speck on the map and finding the cabin where Faith Barclay was holed up had been a cinch. So now came the fun part.

He'd bought enough food and supplies to camp out up here on the mountain until he was finished with her. And that wouldn't be too long. Once he got her alone in that little cabin of hers, it would be quite easy and very pleasurable to get every bit of information he needed to know.

There was a sound from the brush nearby, and Bayman's hand shot to his hip holster, closing on his gun. But it wasn't a mountain lion or a bear. Only a fox slithering through the brush. He set the gun beside him, took another swig of beer, and stared into the fire.

He'd just been checking things out tonight. Getting the lay of the land around that cabin, hoping to catch a glimpse of the whore inside.

Tomorrow he'd wait and watch until she left, then go in, look around. He doubted Faith Barclay would have Susan's new address or phone number lying around, but it was worth checking out. And he might just leave her a little present. Maybe a skinned rabbit or squirrel. Something to rattle her. Something to think about in the dead of night when she couldn't sleep.

I'm coming for you, bitch, he thought, as the flames danced and swayed in the gusty wind. *I'll be there when you least expect me. First you, then Susan. Then those damned sniveling kids she coddles so much.*

His eyes narrowed, thinking about those brats whose father had run out on Susan five months before he met her. He'd been damned good to those boys, taking 'em to the circus, to baseball games, and all that crap. But did they appreciate it? No, they acted like they couldn't stand the sight of him. He knew why too. Susan had made wienies out of them. Neither one of them could hit a baseball worth a damn, and they were too puny to ever go out for football. They hated the fact that he was strong and an athlete and that he didn't hesitate to swat them if they stepped out of line.

Hell, Curt, the older one, bawled whenever someone looked cross-eyed at him. And he was nearly nine. Jesus. And that little one was nothing but trouble. Him and his stupid nightmares. How many times had Brian burst in during the middle of the night when he and Susan were doing the deed?

God, he hated those kids.

But it was Susan's fault they were the way they were. It was Susan's fault that everything had gotten screwed up.

A woman's supposed to stick by her man, right? But not Susan. She had to cut and run.

No one leaves me and gets away with it, baby, he thought savagely, picturing her pale face and the dark hair that had been so long and beautiful when he first met her. *No one goes until I say.*

Bayman chugged the last of the beer. He got up and pissed into a pile of leaves, then zipped up his jeans, stalked back to the fire, and stared down into the hypnotic gold flames.

He remembered how he'd had to hide tonight, when that slut and the jerk who'd shown up had searched the woods for him. They'd thought they could find him, proving that they were even more stupid than he'd imagined. He'd been on the police force, for chrissakes, he had training and smarts and experience.

They'd see. She'd see. The world would see.

He stamped out the last of the fire, ducked inside his tent, and settled down in his sleeping bag for the night.

Tomorrow would be a busy day. This operation was about to kick into high gear.

And as far as he was concerned, the sun couldn't rise soon enough.

Chapter 10

A CHILL WIND RACED THROUGH THUNDER Creek two days later, hinting at the long Wyoming winter to come.

In Bessie's Diner, everyone was ordering coffee or hot chocolate and thinking early about Thanksgiving and Christmas even though it was only the end of August.

"Old man winter's right around the corner," Bessie sighed, pausing beside the table where Faith perused sample menus for the dinner dance.

"Just so long as we don't get snow the night of the auction," Faith replied, glancing up with a distracted smile.

"Don't you worry. Folks in Thunder Creek aren't like those in the big cities. We're all accustomed to bad weather blowing in when it's least needed, and no one hereabouts lets a dozen inches of snow keep 'em away from a good party."

Faith knew there wouldn't be a dozen inches of snow in early September, but for some reason, the past few days she hadn't been able to shake a feeling that something bad was coming. Something she wasn't prepared for and didn't know how to deal with.

And it had nothing to do with the supposed prowler

Zach thought he'd seen at the cabin. If Rusty Gallagher had really come by to hassle her—or perhaps to apologize—she knew she could handle him. It would take more than Wood Morgan's drunken lawyer to tie her insides up in knots.

No, the source of it all went straight to Zach. Why on earth had he kissed her—and worse, why in hell had she kissed him back?

She took a sip of hot coffee, letting the sounds and smells of Bessie's Diner float around her. Bessie and Ada were joking with Katy Brent, Bessie's granddaughter, at the cash register, their laughter warm and comforting. The teenage waitress was serving platters of meat loaf and mashed potatoes to some hands from the Davis ranch.

She could smell blueberry pie. The ceiling fan circled lazily, and outside the diner the wind whipped the awnings of storefronts and blew tumbleweed down Main Street.

You let him do it to you again. Make a fool out of you. Maybe nobody else in town knows, but he *does. And so do you,* she thought bitterly.

You'd think a twenty-nine-year-old woman would know better than to make the same mistake she made when she was nineteen.

Bessie's Diner, with all its cozy warmth and bustle, wasn't helping to calm her thoughts. They circled endlessly, and the knot in her stomach wouldn't go away.

That does it. This goes no further, Faith told herself as she set down her coffee cup with a clatter and drew in a long hard breath.

What you need to do is keep a good half mile between you and Zach McCallum at all times. That shouldn't be too difficult, should it?

"A penny for your thoughts."

She glanced up, startled to see Tammie Morgan standing beside her. Tammie's head was tilted to one side, and there was a broad smile on her coral-glossed mouth. "You don't mind if I join you, Faith? Do you?"

Without waiting for a response, she slipped into the booth across from Faith as if she owned it. Her long amber cat eyes gleamed as she leaned companionably forward.

"Now tell me." She held up one slim tanned hand so that her perfect coral nails and three-carat, emerald-cut diamond ring dazzled in the sunlight. "You must have just loved having all those handsome single men fighting over you the other night. I swear I thought Zach McCallum would *kill* poor Rusty. I'm sure you were quite impressed."

"Actually, Tammie, it takes a lot more than caveman tactics to impress me."

"Really?" Tammie tossed her long black hair. "So does that mean you're not ready to pick up with Zach where the two of you left off?"

Faith stared at her. Could the woman *be* any more obnoxious if she tried? *Yeah,* she thought, *she probably could.*

"What can I do for you, Tammie? I'm sure you didn't come over here to talk about my personal affairs. I assume you want to discuss the dinner dance or perhaps the auction?"

"Well, no. Everything is under control with our little event at the moment," she said, waving a dismissive hand in the air. Her whiskey-soaked voice dropped another notch lower and she glanced around the diner to make sure no one was paying attention to the conversation.

"Actually I do want to discuss your personal affairs—as they relate to Zach McCallum."

"Then we have nothing to talk about, because they don't."

"Oh, but that's not what I saw the other night. And Wood agreed with me. We talked it over this morning at breakfast and we both feel that you could do us a huge favor, one that would also be very important for Thunder Creek. I know how important Thunder Creek is to you, and to Ty, and to all of the Barclays. Your family has had ties here even longer than Wood's and mine."

Faith kept her expression set in courtroom-neutral. "What is it you think I can do for you?"

Tammie nodded. "You like to cut right to the chase, I see. A typical lawyer. That's good, you know—because you understand logic and reason and right and wrong. That's what this is all about."

"Just spit it out, Tammie."

The other woman stared at her reproachfully. "You must have gotten up on the wrong side of the bed today," she said with a shrug. "But I'll make allowances since I'm sure you have a lot on your mind. No doubt you're still getting over your fiancé breaking off your engagement." She smiled slightly as Faith visibly stiffened. "Oh, you know how word gets around in a small town—if there's even one person who knows something, then they tell just one other person and you know what happens next. I'm not saying who it was who let something slip, but there's no reason for you to be embarrassed or anything. You're not the first woman to lose a man before getting him to the altar—"

"Tammie, what is this favor you want to ask me?" Faith asked between clenched teeth. "I don't have all day."

"Well, neither do I, of course. But you and I need to have a good old-fashioned talk. For the good of Thunder

Creek. It has to do with Zach McCallum. He's turning into a problem for those of us who love this town."

"What does Zach have to do with me?" Faith interrupted curtly.

"From what I saw at the Tumbleweed, Zach still has feelings for you." Tammie slanted a look at her from those canny amber eyes. "Very intense feelings. So Wood and I were wondering if you would help us."

That'll be the day, Faith thought, but aloud she said, "Help you what?"

"We need to convince Zach that some of his plans for Thunder Creek are . . . well . . . unacceptable."

"You're talking about the camp."

"You bet your buns I am. It's a damned stupid, irresponsible idea. Busing in kids from all over the country—city kids—who don't know how to ride a horse or sweep a barn or even set up a pup tent. They'll whine every time they get a mosquito bite. They have no business here."

"Zach apparently doesn't agree with you," Faith said. "And neither do I."

"Oh, now, you don't mean that." Tammie's cat eyes widened. "Think about it, Faith. All these kids from sad, underprivileged backgrounds, with no manners, no self-control, no discipline, running wild right here in town. When they flood into Bessie's Diner, it's going to be a mess. Do you want that? Do you want them roaming all over our beautiful, peaceful Main Street, running in and out of our shops, possibly shoplifting, *breaking* things, getting into who knows what kind of trouble?"

"You're making a lot of assumptions about these kids, Tammie. And you have no basis for any of them. Have you sat down and talked about this with Zach? Maybe he can put your mind at rest—"

"Nothing he can say can change the fact that this is bad for Thunder Creek," Tammie stated flatly.

Faith controlled her temper. "Well, it's his property, isn't it? If he wants to lease it out to a camp, that's his right."

"But we've offered to *buy* it from him," Tammie argued. "Wood has made a *very* generous offer. Half again what the land is worth."

Now lightbulbs flashed in Faith's head. At last they were getting to the crux of the matter. "Why did Wood do that? Just to keep a children's camp from operating in the area?"

"Yes, of course." Tammie leaned forward. "If Zach sells us the land, you can be sure that we'll make good use of it. I mean, there's no sense having all that wonderful open land sitting empty."

"Let me guess." Faith studied her coolly. "You want to build on it."

There was a tiny pause.

"Well, yes," Tammie admitted after a moment. "We've had our eye on that parcel for quite a while. It borders the Crystal Horseshoe, you know. And we made a bid on it when Zach first moved back to town. But he turned us down. Can you imagine that? For a camp!" She shook her head in exasperation. "Wood and I want to do something *good* for Thunder Creek."

"Such as?"

"We want to build luxury private condominiums right there in the foothills. The Crystal Horseshoe Ranch condominiums. And . . ." Her amber eyes sparkled. "And we'll build a world-class luxury spa halfway up Thunder Mountain. Now *that* will be fantastic for this town. We'll draw even more tourists in—tourists from all over the world. Every single business in this community will profit from it."

Faith slid out of the booth. "No."

"No?" Tammie eyed her warily. "What do you mean, no?"

"No, I won't try to convince Zach to sell to you, or to give up on the camp. Not that I'd have any influence on him—"

"How do you know if you don't try?" Tammie countered, also sliding from the booth and facing her in the diner. "All I want you to do is think about it. Do you want our town brimming with famous wealthy people who will buy antiques and handmade quilts from our local businesses, who will fill up Bessie's Diner every day, who will spend their money here—or do you want a bunch of unruly kids running wild, scaring away the tourists Wood and I are already attracting with our dude ranch?"

"Frankly, I think we have quite enough tourists already. My answer is no, Tammie. And if it comes to a fight, don't think I'll come down on your side. I won't. And neither will Ty, I can guarantee you."

"You might want to think twice about that." Tammie spoke quickly. "Ty is running for reelection next year, and I've heard he won't be unopposed. Deputy Rick Keene, who's our acting sheriff right now while Ty's away with Josy, has every intention of running against him." Tammie's smile was sweet, but edged in triumph. "Wood and I would really love to throw our support behind Ty, of course. All we ask is some understanding and some cooperation."

"Sounds like a bribe to me." Faith looked her dead in the eye. But Tammie didn't even blink.

"A bribe? Heavens, no." Her laugh was every bit as rich and shallow as she was. "Where do you get these ideas? All I'd like is for you to think about which side you want to be on. Because there will be a fight, and we'll all be choosing sides. I promise you that."

"Count me out," Faith told her in an icy tone.

"Me too." Bessie had come up behind Faith. She

frowned at Tammie. "I'd like to give some city kids a taste of good old-fashioned Wyoming hospitality. What about you, Ada?"

Ada left the cash register and hurried over to stand beside Bessie. "I think it's a grand idea. My own granddaughter, Josy, grew up in foster care, and Zach mentioned to her before she went on her trip that foster kids will be part of the mix. I know she's in favor of it. And Ty too," she added with a dark glance at Tammie. "And besides that, I happen to believe Zach McCallum can do whatever he pleases with his own land. It's nobody else's business."

Angry color filled Tammie's lean, hollow cheeks. She drew herself up straight and said in an icy tone, "Well, Wood and I don't see eye to eye with you on that—with any of you. I guess you just don't care what happens to this town—but plenty of us do. You wait and see."

She flounced toward the door. As the little bell above it rang and Tammie stomped out, Faith glanced ruefully at Bessie and Ada.

"Thanks for the backup. Did you two hear all that?"

"Heard enough to know I don't like it," Bessie muttered.

Ada looked worried. "What Zach's doing is a good thing. I have a special place in my heart for foster kids, after hearing what Josy went through all those years when I never knew her mama and daddy had died."

"I'm sure Zach can handle it," Faith told them. "It'll take more than Tammie and Wood Morgan to make him back down."

But when Bessie and Ada had returned to work, she reached for her handbag, more troubled than she wanted to admit.

Zach and possibly Ty were in for a rough time. She'd

seen and heard enough about the Morgans over the years to know that they'd pull out all the stops to get what they wanted.

And that meant that the ugly incident with Pete Harrison would be brought up all over again in Thunder Creek.

Fred Harrison had already referred to it the other day. He'd talk loudest of all. And many of the shopkeepers and business owners might be swayed by the argument that the condominiums would better benefit the town than a camp. True, it was Zach's property and he could do with it as he wished, but if the community turned against him in a town this size, they could make life pretty miserable for Zach—and for his son.

It's not my problem, Faith reminded herself, but she couldn't shake her anger at the Morgans. Not only were they pressuring her by using Ty and his upcoming reelection campaign, they also seemed to think she could actually change Zach's mind.

As if she ever could.

She was about to leave when she remembered she hadn't yet paid her bill. But as she turned toward the cash register, the bell over the door tinkled, and Zach walked in.

Speak of the devil, she thought, her heart beating a bit faster.

Just seeing him, all dark, tall, and heartachingly handsome, with those quicksilver eyes zeroing in on her like radar, it was impossible not to remember the way he'd kissed her two nights ago—and the humiliating way she'd nearly melted all over him like ice cream on a griddle.

He wasn't alone, either.

Dillon bounced in at his side, his blond mop a striking contrast with his father's dark hair, and yet the resemblance between them was unmistakable. The child had a boyish ruggedness so much like Zach, and the same strong jawline and a dimple in his chin. There was no doubt he'd be a heartbreaker too when he was older, she thought unwillingly. But unlike Zach's darkly unreadable expression, Dillon was grinning, his eyes wide and shining with an earnestness she'd never seen in his father.

"Hi, guess what?" He raced over to her. "I've been practicing how to whistle like you did. Want to hear?"

"Not inside, Dillon," Zach said, walking up beside him.

Faith forced a smile as the boy stuck two fingers in his mouth and showed her how he would blow, without making a sound. "That's great. Does Batman come running every time?"

"Yeah. But he stayed home today," Dillon explained. "I'm not taking any more chances."

"Good thinking." Sensing Zach's gaze on her, Faith struggled to keep the smile on her face. It was a relief when Dillon suddenly spotted a friend sitting with his mother at another table.

"I have to talk to Brett, Dad, about bringing walkie-talkies on our trip. I'll be right back," he exclaimed, and darted off. Only then did Faith allow her facial muscles to relax.

But her heart was beating much too fast and her chest hurt. It would be the final insult if she let Zach McCallum give her a heart attack.

"He's going to the Grand Canyon for a week with the Graysons," Zach said, breaking the silence that had fallen when Dillon left. "It should be quite a trip."

Faith started toward the cash register. "If you'll excuse me, I'm on my way to a meeting," she said frostily, but he immediately snagged her arm.

"Faith. Wait. We need to talk."

"No, we don't." But he continued to hold on to her, and she glared at him. "I'm late."

"You're running away."

"From you? Get over yourself." She managed a light laugh. It cost her, hurting her throat, but she managed it. From the corner of her eye she saw Dillon and his friend eating french fries coated with ketchup while the boy's mother spoke to Bessie.

She had to get out of here.

"You and I have nothing to talk about," she said with finality.

"That's not true. Don't tell me you've forgotten about the other night." His tone held a note of determination she remembered. As his gaze bored into hers, Faith realized he wasn't going to let this go.

"Do you want to talk about the fact that you kissed me right now, right here in front of Bessie and Ada or—"

"I didn't kiss you!" Faith whispered furiously. "It was the other way around and you know it!"

"If it makes you feel better to tell yourself that, go right ahead," Zach said. To her fury, amusement gleamed in his eyes.

She wanted to hit him. Or kick him where it would really get his attention. Instead she drew in a deep, civilized breath.

"What do you want from me? I won't have this conversation here."

"Good thinking. We'll do it on neutral ground. I'll pick you up at six. We'll talk over dinner."

Dinner? Her heart stopped. "Why would I *possibly* want to have dinner with you?"

"We can discuss that over a couple of steaks."

She yanked her arm free. "I'm late."

"See you at six."

His gaze followed her as she nearly ran to the cash register. She obviously couldn't get out of the diner fast enough, he thought, taking a seat in the nearest booth. But she hadn't said no. Still, frustration overwhelmed him. *What the hell was he doing—aside from screwing things up?*

Kissing Faith the other night after all these years apart was the last thing he ought to have done. It wasn't fair to her—and it was driving him crazy. There was nothing between them anymore and he'd had no right to behave as if there was—as if no time had passed and they still belonged to each other.

They'd been kids back then, that summer they'd lived and breathed for each other. Stupid, young, anything-is-possible-when-you're-in-love kids.

Now they both knew better. He sure as hell did.

Why on earth had he gone to Blue Moon Mesa anyway?

And worse, why couldn't he forget what it had felt like to kiss Faith again? To hold her. Different from the last time. This time had felt more dangerous, more heady. Like spiked liquor, 200 proof. Delicious but sure to burn his gut in the end.

And it did.

He'd stayed up half the night, trying to forget the softness of her lips against his and how right her slender curves had felt in his arms. Just as right as she had felt all those years ago.

His mouth on hers, he'd wanted to taste her, every part of her, slowly and completely. He'd longed to slide his hands under her tank top, cup her breasts, watch the heat simmer across her face.

Though it almost killed him, at least he'd stopped at just a kiss.

Just a kiss? Who was he kidding? Kissing Faith could never be just a kiss.

But she was so different now from the carefree girl he remembered. That laughing, daring girl. She was withdrawn, complicated, cool as lake frost. At least to him.

But she was sexier than ever. And just as fascinating.

What the hell had happened to her in the intervening years? Was it all his fault, the way he'd left her, let her down? Or had someone else hurt her? Maybe life itself had wounded her. He knew what that was like.

Let her go, man, just let her go, Zach thought as the waitress with the pierced eyebrow set place settings and water glasses on the table.

He'd said the same thing to himself the other night, until five in the morning.

There was only one problem. He wasn't sure anymore that he really wanted to let her go. He'd done that once, and he had the scars to prove it. But maybe, just maybe, there was a reason why he was back here now in Thunder Creek, and she was too.

Maybe fate was trying to tell him something.

The idea of it, the flick of hope, teased him that night like the perfumed caress of a mermaid, a dreamy figure splashing away as the sun came up.

Faith. If he could try . . . if he could get through to her . . . tell her . . . ask her . . .

But with sunrise had come reality. He'd pushed the hope away. And yet, sitting here in Bessie's Diner, watching her hand over some bills to Ada, chatting with that warm affability she reserved for everyone but him, he realized something.

He wasn't quite ready to let the dream go—a dream he'd thought he'd relinquished ten years ago.

"Dad. Dad! Can I go to Brett's after lunch? His mom said it's okay. His boxer just had puppies—five of 'em!"

He dragged himself out of his thoughts and focused on his son. "You can look at them, but don't bring home another pet or Neely's going to up and quit."

"Nah, she won't. She likes us too much." His son grinned at him, his eyes dancing, and Zach ruffled the boy's hair.

It was worth it, everything was worth it, for this. For Dillon's smile. His stability, sanity. He leaned down suddenly and hugged his boy close.

"Dad!" Dillon squirmed away, embarrassed, afraid his friend would see. "Let's order fast, okay? I want to go see those pups!"

They sat facing each other and as usual Dillon ordered a hamburger with fries and a Coke.

"You're going to turn into a hamburger one day," Zach warned him dryly, but his son, who'd heard the comment too many times to count, paid no attention.

He was watching Faith walk past them to the door. When she gave the boy a faint smile, he waved at her.

"How do you know her again?" he asked after she'd left.

"I met her here in Thunder Creek that summer I visited."

"The summer when that boy . . . your friend . . . got hurt," Dillon said in a low tone, glancing around.

Zach had told him everything following the encounter with Fred Harrison. Needless to say, Dillon didn't really understand it all. All these years later, Zach wasn't sure he did either.

"She's nice," Dillon declared as the teenage waitress set his Coke in front of him. He stuck the straw in it. "She made that mean man let go of me."

He took a slurp of his Coke. "And she's pretty. *Real* pretty," he added.

Zach's brows rose. "You have a crush on her?" *Like father, like son.*

"Eeewww, no." Dillon made a disgusted face, the same one he made whenever he talked about any girl at school. "Girls are gross," he said. "But . . . you like them. Maybe *you* have a crush on her." He grinned suddenly. "Do you?"

Zach's eyebrows quirked. "What's this all about? Why all this talk about Ms. Barclay and how pretty she is?"

Dillon shrugged. "It's just because . . . sometimes I wish I had a mom who lived with me. Like Brett and Ethan do." He hesitated a moment, then went on slowly. "I try to picture what she would look like, you know, tucking me in at night and stuff, but I can't ever see her face."

Zach was stunned. He stared at his son, feeling unaccountably guilty. "I didn't know you felt that way." He cleared his throat. "You miss your mom a lot, I know, but—"

"It's okay, Dad. I don't miss her as much as I used to. I like living with you and Neely and Gabe. Besides, Mom wouldn't let me have any pets, not even a goldfish," he said, adding quickly, "That doesn't mean I don't like seeing her or anything. I do. Sometimes I . . . I wish I could live with both of you."

He took another slurp of his Coke. "But don't worry, I'm gladder than anything that I live with you—and with Batman and Jelly and Zena and Tigger."

"That's good to know." Zach paused as their food arrived, hoping he was handling this right. He didn't have much of a role model when it came to parenting. His own mother had been too distracted with her clubs and her charities and her social life to pay much attention to either Zach or Jock, and his father had single-mindedly worshipped one son and despaired of the other.

He intended to do a lot better than either one of them when it came to raising Dillon.

So Zach had read some books, but mostly he was going by instinct. Suddenly, though, as Dillon took a huge bite out of his burger, Zach had a startling thought.

"Are you trying to tell me that you were thinking about Faith Barclay for a . . . a mom?" he asked in astonishment.

Dillon blushed. "Maybe. I don't really know her that well. I like Brett's mom too, but she's already married. But Ms. Merck . . ." Dillon shook his head as he chewed. "She's pretty and all, but . . . she wears all that icky perfume. Last time she came over, the house smelled so bad I wanted to throw up."

"Really." Zach still hadn't touched his own burger. "Do I get a choice in who your new mom should be?"

"Sure. I mean, if she's going to be your wife, you should at least like her a lot," Dillon said carelessly, but his eyes twinkled. "So . . . does this mean you're looking for a new wife?" he asked, sounding hopeful.

"At the moment, no." But the crestfallen expression on his son's face made him add, "I have a lot of business dealings to get settled over the next few months, and we're still getting settled in at the ranch. But, eventually, if you want . . . maybe I'll see what I can do."

"Maybe?" Dillon said challengingly.

Zach crumpled up a napkin and tossed it at the boy, who caught it, giggling delightedly.

"Give me a break. I'll think about it."

"Thanks, Dad." Dillon popped a french fry into his mouth. "And you should keep Ms. Barclay in mind," he added.

"It probably won't be her," Zach warned. "She doesn't like me much these days."

"Why not?" Dillon stared at him. "Were you mean to her?"

"As a matter of fact . . . I was." Zach grimaced. "I didn't mean to be, but I was. I left for home at the end of that summer I was here without saying good-bye."

"Is that all? Sheesh, why don't you tell her you're sorry? That's what you always tell me to do when I hurt someone's feelings."

Out of the mouths of babes. Zach drew a breath. "I could try that, Dillon," he said. "But sometimes—with grown-ups—things are complicated."

It would be better if he didn't even tell Dillon that he and Faith were having dinner together tonight. It wasn't exactly a date, and it wasn't as if something was going to come of it. In fact, it could be the last time they ever spoke.

He didn't want the kid getting his hopes up.

Like you are? he asked himself as Dillon ordered chocolate cream pie for dessert.

He had the uneasy feeling that edging his way back into Faith Barclay's life might be a disaster for both of them.

Did he really want to risk that?

It's only dinner, he told himself.

And the other night was just a kiss, a voice inside of him jeered.

Zach told the voice to shut up.

Chapter 11

FAITH WAS PULLING ON HER BOOTS AT FIVE fifty-five when her cell phone rang. She shoved her feet into sleek black leather and scooped up the phone from her bed.

For a moment there was a split second of silence and she thought it was Bayman again, but then a familiar voice spoke crisply in her ear.

"Faith, it's Liz. Sorry it took so long, but I've got that information you wanted on Hank Bayman. It isn't good news."

Her stomach dropping, Faith gripped the phone. "Hit me with it," she said.

"His probation officer ran a check and found he hasn't reported for work in nearly a week."

"Damn it. That's the last thing I wanted to hear." She sat down on the bed, biting her lip. "Has he been seen around his apartment?"

"I asked Will to check it out when he was off duty, and you're not going to like this either," her assistant said. Will was Liz's brother—a detective who had worked with Faith on several racketeering cases.

"No one's seen him go in or out of the building the past six days."

"Where the hell is that bastard?" Faith muttered. She raked a hand through her hair, trying to ignore the sinking feeling in her stomach.

"I wish I could tell you." Liz sighed. "The probation officer's issuing a bench warrant. I'll have Will keep his eyes open. Anything else you want me to do?"

"No—thanks, Liz. I'll . . . I'll take care of it. But let me know as soon as you hear anything or if he turns up."

"Will do. How's Lightning Creek?" Liz asked.

"Thunder Creek. It's just fine and dandy."

Faith asked about the status of two upcoming cases, then snapped the phone closed. She swore under her breath as she began to pace around her bedroom.

She had to call Susan, warn her. Even though there was no way Bayman could have found out where she'd gone, she had to let Susan know that he'd dropped out of sight. It would scare her to death, but at least she'd be on alert—just in case . . .

Faith groaned, a sound of frustration and muted rage. Merely by disappearing, Hank Bayman had the ability to terrify Susan and her children again. She couldn't bear thinking about it.

Flipping open the phone, she punched in the number.

She nearly winced when Susan answered cheerfully on the second ring, hating that she had to spoil whatever serenity she'd found.

"Susan, it's Faith Barclay. I don't want you to panic but—"

"Oh, God," Susan gasped. "He's coming, isn't he? He found out where we are and—"

"*No.* Listen to me, Susan. He doesn't know where you are. I'm ninety-nine percent sure of that. He hasn't been to work in almost a week and he's dropped out of sight, but he can't possibly know where to find you."

"He'll find a way." Susan sounded on the verge of tears. "He always finds a way."

"Not this time, he won't." Faith took a deep breath. "There's something else, Susan. I think he's called me a few times on my cell phone. I don't know how he got the number, but I think it's him. He doesn't say a word, but I know he used to do that to you, right?"

"Yes. All the time. And then he'd just be there. I'd come out of the shower and he'd be standing beside my bed. Or I'd wake up in the night, open my eyes, and he'd be leaning over me—" Her voice quavered.

"I have to get out of here, Faith. I have to get my kids someplace else . . . someplace safe."

Faith heard the sound of a car coming down the lane. Damn. Zach was early. She moved into the living room, her attention still focused on the woman on the phone. "Hold on a minute, Susan, someone's here. Don't hang up until I tell you my theory."

She saw Zach striding toward the porch and opened the door as he reached it. She motioned him inside, trying not to be distracted by the way his tall, lean cowboy frame filled out a navy shirt and gray slacks, or by the way his gaze lit as he took in her appearance—which was stark and serious, in her opinion. She was wearing jeans, boots, and a black sweater—and no jewelry except silver hoop earrings.

Bright little sex bomb Candy Merck she wasn't.

"I'll be right with you," she muttered, and he nodded, stepping inside. As he closed the door behind him, Faith paced toward the opposite windows, near the dining room, then back, her boots clicking over the hardwood floor.

"Hank always called you first, before he showed up, didn't he?" she said into the phone.

"Ye . . . es. I think so. Yes. But—"

"Well, he's not calling you, Susan. He's calling me. At least, I have every reason to believe he's the person behind these calls. I don't have any other enemies I can think of— certainly not the kind who would do something asinine like this."

"So . . . you think Hank's trying to frighten *you*? To come after you?"

"I think it's possible. He suspects that I know where you are. Maybe he thinks he can scare the information out of me. If so, he's in for a surprise. I'll slap stalking and harassment charges against him so fast his eyes will spin."

"Be careful, Faith," Susan warned. "He's dangerous. He likes to sneak up on you, not let you see him coming. Once he has you cornered—" Susan took a deep breath and changed the subject.

"So maybe you're right," she said softly. "Maybe he doesn't know where I am yet. Do you think I should move, though, just in case?"

"No. Stay put. You're settling in now, Susan, don't let him push you around anymore, even from a distance. As far as we know, he hasn't a clue where you are." Faith stopped pacing and put all the reassurance she could muster into her words. "I only called to warn you. It's good to be alert, but there's no reason to panic."

"Yes . . . you're right. I know you're right."

Faith could picture Susan, chewing on her thumbnail as she'd done every time Faith had met with her or seen her in court.

"I don't want to scare the kids," Susan said in a calmer tone. "But I'll sure keep my eyes open. You need to do that too, Faith. Hank is resourceful. And he just loves his sneak attacks."

Faith promised to call again when she heard anything further. After ending the call, she turned to find Zach studying her with a frown.

"That sounds like some bad kind of trouble."

"Nothing I can't handle."

Her tone was brusque, shutting him out. He was getting used to that, but it didn't make him like it any better.

"Where are we going for dinner?" she asked, grabbing her purse, slinging it over her shoulder. "Or would you rather just forget the whole thing?"

"We did that once," Zach said evenly. "I'm not going to make the same mistake twice."

Her gaze flew to his face, but he was already opening the door. "Come on. We have a long drive ahead of us."

"Where are we going—Texas?" she shot back.

"Not quite that long. Casper."

She froze, staring at him, as he held the door for her—a dark, rugged cowboy with the face of a fallen angel. And eyes that gleamed with grim amusement.

"Excuse me, but what's wrong with Bessie's Diner? Or that pizza they serve now at the Tumbleweed—"

"I'm taking you away from the eyes and ears of Thunder Creek, Faith. Someplace where we can talk."

"Talk? What do we have to talk about? There's nothing I have to say to you—not anymore." A lie. A terrible lie. There was nothing she was *willing* to say to him. A big difference.

"Then we'll be quiet together. Remember those days? We were really good at being quiet together, Faith."

"That was another century—another lifetime ago, Zach." She stalked past him. Her eyes were cold. She refused to meet his gaze, to acknowledge all the memories—of long afternoons lying in the grass in each other's arms, or evenings in the hammock behind the Last Trail ranch, or up on Snowflake Mountain, kissing in the moonlight beneath a canopy of stars.

She vaulted up onto the seat of the black pickup before he could help her, and stared straight ahead as he circled it around the drive and headed back toward the road.

The night was chilly. As lavender-tinted shadows descended over the Laramies and crept across treetops and canyons, the breath of oncoming winter seemed to sweep away the vestiges of late summer, even the hint of a bright, crisp autumn. It was too soon, Faith knew. Golden autumn must come before the freeze, which would lock Wyoming in the throes of deep white winter, but tonight she almost tasted winter on her tongue and felt it brush like the first snowflake against her skin.

Why was she here with Zach? She could have refused. She could have opened her door, told him she changed her mind, and closed it again.

But she hadn't. And the reason disturbed her more than she could say. She hadn't wanted to.

Now she had to pay the price. Hours of driving alone with him, to Casper and back.

And nothing to say.

He apparently had nothing to say to her either. He drove with ease and surety, slowing around the curves, swerving to avoid a fox that slunk across the road.

Not like the young daredevil who had often made her scream and gasp as he sped on narrow roads, took hairpin turns at speeds that bordered on mania.

And, she reminded herself, she was nothing like the idiotically foolish girl who had opened her heart to that wild, lost boy. She was wiser, smarter, harder.

So why was she letting him call the shots?

"I really don't understand why we're doing this." A half hour had passed. A half hour in which there was nothing but silence between them, except for the rumble of the pickup's tires over the road.

"In case you haven't noticed, Zach, we're over. We've been over for a long time. And that was your choice. So . . . what's the point?"

"We have unfinished business."

"We've had that for ten years." She stared straight ahead out the windshield at the deepening dusk. "Why the hell do you want to dredge it all up now?"

"Because you're back here in Thunder Creek and so am I. At the same time. Maybe someone's trying to tell us something."

"Like one of us should leave?"

He shot her a frown, then turned onto the highway. "I'm not going anywhere. In case you haven't heard, I'm building a major branch office of my company right here. Settling down."

Those were two words no one who'd known Zach ten years earlier would ever have expected to hear. "Because of your son, I'm sure," she said slowly.

"Yes. My son." His eyes were fixed on the road, but his profile was somber. His five o'clock shadow stubbled his jaw, accentuating the tough handsomeness of that completely masculine face. She ignored the flutter in her stomach and concentrated on keeping the conversation in neutral territory.

"Dillon seems like a very nice boy."

"He thinks highly of you too."

She raised her brows, glancing at him. "Oh? Because I whistled and Batman came back?"

"I'm sure that has something to do with it." He glanced over at her. "His latest idea, aside from wanting to be a vet and work for Doc Brent in his clinic, is that I should get married. Possibly to you."

She stared at him, astonishment sweeping through her. "Is that . . . why you asked me on this date?" she demanded incredulously.

"Sure. Whatever my kid wants, he gets." Zach grinned at her. "I'm kidding, Faith. *Kidding.* I'm starting to believe you've been locked up in the DA's office so long you've lost your sense of humor. In case you've forgotten, I married someone I didn't love once. For your information, it didn't work out too well, and I'm damned if I'm going to do it again."

Her throat went dry. Silence whispered between them for a full minute.

"Alicia?" She licked her lips. "You . . . didn't love Alicia?"

"I told you I didn't—the summer we were together."

"That was before you left me high and dry to go back to her."

Her voice had returned, thank God. And her wits. The words came out clipped and brisk as if she was saying *Your Honor, the people request that bail be denied.*

"Now you're going to tell me that you weren't ever happy?" She practically sneered.

"That's an understatement." Beneath the calm of his tone, she heard bitterness . . . and something else, something that sounded like pain.

"I always thought . . ."

"What?"

"That you adored her." She forced the words out. "There

were photographs in the newspapers right after your wedding . . . in *USA Today,* even in *Newsweek* once . . ."

"Yeah, the oil scion and the Dallas debutante. Don't believe everything you see."

But you left me, without ever saying good-bye, she thought. *You went back to her. Without a note, without a word* . . .

She'd always wondered if Alicia had been pregnant. Always secretly hoped it was that—and not that Zach loved her more. Over and over after that summer, she'd pictured different scenarios, different reasons . . .

And Dillon was about the right age . . .

But none of that mattered now. She wasn't about to lay her heart on the line for Zach ever again, or even to ask him about that night. She refused to open up the pain. Better to switch to safer territory.

"Do the two of you share custody? Is Dillon only with you for the summer?"

"No. He's mine, full custody." His tone was firm. "Alicia hasn't even seen him in about eighteen months."

"Why not?"

Zach's mouth twisted. "She's been pretty busy bouncing in and out of detox."

Faith stared at him. "Drugs?"

"Yeah. Among other things." Zach passed another car on the highway and in the gleam of light she saw grimness in his eyes. "Alicia and her second husband aren't much into kids and pets and horses and baseball," he said. "They prefer bourbon and Scotch and the occasional line of coke. Easy to get when they spend their lives partying in London and jetting between South Beach and L.A."

"I'm sorry—for Dillon," Faith said in a low tone.

"Yeah, me too. They don't seem to mind showing him

off to their friends when he's around, but on a scale of one to ten, Alicia's mothering instincts register around negative five."

His voice was hard now. And angry. It wasn't because of whatever pain his wife had caused *him,* Faith realized with a sharp intake of breath. It was because of how she'd treated Dillon.

Her heart cracked, an opening that was narrow as a crevice. During those first few years apart, she'd always pictured Zach contentedly married to the daughter of his father's oldest friend. She'd imagined them on the McCallum ranch in Texas, like king and queen of the prairie, raising children, entertaining friends and business associates, living the good life of those who traded in power and money. She'd even imagined that marrying Alicia had somehow softened his father's antipathy toward him.

Maybe she'd been wrong. About his marriage, at least. But not about any of the rest of it, she thought. Not about the fact that he'd left her without a word—and never looked back. Never called her, or wrote. Never hesitated in cutting himself off from everything that had happened between them—and marrying a daughter of Texas royalty without regard to the promises they'd made to each other on Snowflake Mountain during all those sweet, pine-scented Wyoming nights.

"Well." She tried to sound casual, indifferent. "Dillon seems to have survived her pretty well. I assume he owes that to you."

"He's not going to grow up like I did."

She couldn't help it—his determination stirred a twinge of compassion. Zach had shared more than French kisses and hot caresses with her that summer. He'd poured out his heart in a way she'd suspected he'd never done before.

He'd told her how his father had always compared him unfavorably to his brother, Jock. How Jock had excelled in school, had been the valedictorian of his class, and returned home with an MBA to help run TexCorp Oil, while Zach was still slacking off in high school, getting expelled for telling his physics teacher to go to hell, and running around with girls from the wrong side of the tracks.

Caleb McCallum hadn't minded some high-spirited high jinks in his offspring, but he considered Zach much too rebellious and restless for his own good.

Two months before Zach was shipped off to Thunder Creek for the summer, Jock had been killed when the TexCorp company jet had crashed on landing at the Denver airport. With his death, Caleb's dreams and visions for the future had crumbled like a mountain of dust. Pain had turned to anger and anger to rage—all of it directed at Zach, who had let him down in all the ways Jock had pleased him. Zach could do no right. He wasn't Jock, he never would be, and in the two months following Jock's death, Caleb never missed an opportunity to remind his younger son of his shortcomings.

In response, Zach had grown wilder and ever more defiant. On the day when father and son had nearly come to blows, the decision was made to send Zach away. Zach was only too happy to go—he knew that the very sight of him sliced his father like a knife, and more than ever, they had become like oil and water.

So Zach was sent packing to his aunt and uncle in Thunder Creek. If anyone could control the boy, Caleb had decided, it would be Ardelle's husband, Sheriff Stan Harvey.

But even Sheriff Harvey had been unable to bend or break Zach. Nevertheless, for his aunt's sake Zach had pretty much toed the line. Until the end . . . until that night . . . the night before the end-of-summer dance—the last night she'd seen him.

Memories of Pete Harrison in his hospital bed flicked through her mind. She didn't know why Zach had fought with Pete—they'd always gotten along. She only knew what everyone else knew—that he'd left Pete lying there, unconscious, and caught a flight back to Texas—before Sheriff Harvey arrived on the scene, before he could be arrested.

People had called him a coward. She had called him that herself, silently, over and over.

He'd not only hurt Pete and run away, he'd abandoned her and everything they'd shared.

Back then, it had seemed unimaginable that the boy she loved would do such things, but now . . . today, it seemed even more impossible. The man Zach had become possessed an aura of solidness, of quiet authority and strength. Everything about him exuded steadiness and calm.

And he was clearly devoted to his son. She had to hand him that, no matter what he'd done in the past.

"I'm sorry about your father," she said at last. "I heard about his passing."

"He never gave an inch even at the end." Zach's gaze was focused straight ahead on the road, but she had a feeling he was looking at something else entirely. "Even in his sickbed, he was as ornery and uncompromising as ever. I told him I loved him. He couldn't bring himself to do more than grunt. Dillon, now . . ."

He shook his head. "I brought Dillon in to say good-bye to him. And the old man told Dillon he was the best, smartest, toughest boy in the world, and to never let anyone beat him in a fight. How do you like that? What kind of thing is that to say to a nine-year-old?"

"He stayed true to form, I'll give him that."

"Ten times over." Suddenly, Zach smiled, his entire face lightening. "He probably thought if he'd tried to say I love you, even to Dillon, the words would stick in his throat and choke him to death. He did love Dillon though," he added quietly. "I'll grant him that."

"He loved you too, I'm sure. He just didn't have a very good way of showing it."

A short laugh burst from his lips. "You don't need to try to make me feel better, Faith. I'm not that wild, hurt kid anymore. And I can handle whatever my father dishes out ten times over, even from the grave. What about you?"

Startled, her eyes flew to his face. "What about me?"

"You're more beautiful even than you were at nineteen." His tone had changed, it was serious, quiet now. "But you're nothing like that girl. Her laughter rang out so easily, like lovely music you never want to stop. But . . . you're different now. Other people might not see it, but I do." He glanced away from the road then, to look into her face, his eyes keen and gray and searching in the darkness.

"What the hell happened to you?"

Chapter 12

CANDY MERCK CLOSED HER EYES AND SWAYED to the music in the Tumbleweed. Clint Black sang of love and loneliness and she hummed along, pretending she was dancing with Zach McCallum, when really it was only Owen . . .

Not that there was anything wrong with Owen—he was cute enough, and sweet as a peck of peaches, even when he was drinking, but Zach was dangerous and sexy and more handsome than Tom Cruise. She'd had a crush on him since the first day he'd ever set foot in Thunder Creek ten years ago.

The music stopped and she forced herself to open her eyes, peering up into Owen's face. It was a little flushed, and as friendly and open as ever. And just as uninteresting.

"How about a game of pool?" he suggested as they walked off the dance floor arm in arm.

All around them, people milled around, drinking, laughing. One of the waitresses, scurrying back to the bar with a tray of empty glasses and bowls of nuts, nearly collided with her, but Owen steered her gently out of the way. He'd always been a real gentleman.

"What I'd really like is another beer." She grinned up at him, batting her eyes just for the hell of it.

"I can sure arrange that. But only if you let me drive you home. You're in no condition to be out on the road, Candy."

"Sweet of you to worry about me," she murmured as he held her chair and she sank down at a small round table near the dart board at the rear of the bar.

Zach wouldn't worry about me. He only worries about Faith Barclay. Even now. He wouldn't care if I drove off the edge of Wolf Canyon, she thought with a sad, sinking feeling in her stomach.

Owen ordered refills for each of them. The noise of the bar pounded in Candy's head as she swigged her beer and listened to Owen talk on and on about his quarter horses. He was trying to impress her, she could tell.

But she wanted to dance again. Only not with Owen. With Zach. *Damn Zach. And damn Faith.*

"Another one," she muttered, pushing her glass toward Owen. "Please."

He looked worried. "How many've you had, honey? It's only seven-thirty and you're loaded." He covered her hand with his. "If you go on much more, you'll be sick as a dog. Why don't you let me take you home now, before you lose it."

Sure, she thought. *You want to take me home. But not because you care about me. You just want to get me into bed. Everyone wants to get me into bed . . . except Zach.*

"I'm going to the little girl's room now," she announced, and stood. But the floor tilted. *Ooops.* Owen grabbed her arm and she got her bearings. She shook off his hand in irritation.

She wanted to get drunk, wanted to pass out. Anything to forget about the humiliating way Zach was treating her. She wasn't some shy, dopey high school girl anymore—she was beautiful. Lots of men had told her so, and she could see it when she looked in the mirror. *Beautiful. Smart. Successful.*

Maybe she'd invite Owen to her place after all. Let him

take her to bed. Maybe having sex with him would help her calm down, get Zach out of her head. Maybe she'd even see a side of Owen she'd never seen before. It might be fun.

Candy pushed open the door of the women's restroom and stared at her reflection in the mirror.

Gawd, she looked like hell. It had been a bad day all around. A client had stood her up, another had backed out of buying the old Trumble place on Beaver Road, and she'd spilled red wine on her favorite powder-blue blazer.

And now she was at the Tumbleweed with no one but Owen Carey for company and Zach was . . . where?

Getting it on with good ol' Faith?

She hiccupped and dug in her purse. A comb, and cherry-colored lipstick. That helped.

But she was thirsty. Wobbling a little, she made her way back to the table.

Another ice-cold beer was sitting there waiting for her. So was Owen.

She ignored him and grabbed the frosted glass.

"Thirsty," she muttered in between gulps.

"Candy, how about it? Let me take you home now."

"You'd like that, wouldn't you, Owen? You want to get me in the sack. Admit it."

His lips tightened. "I'm trying to make sure you get home safe—"

But Candy interrupted him with a loud, ringing laugh that turned heads even in the noisy bar.

"Liar, liar, pants on fire. You want to make sure you get me in bed, don't you? They all do. All of 'em. But—" She stopped herself. She'd almost said it. They all wanted to take her to bed, but they didn't want to marry her. She knew it was true. But she didn't know why. What was wrong with her? Why didn't anyone love her?

Tears filled her eyes. She pushed back her chair, staggered away from the table. "I'm going outside. I need air . . ."

"I'll come with you—"

"Who asked you?" she snarled. At the next table, two cowboys from the Double O ranch turned and stared back and forth between her and Owen.

"I'll be . . . right back," she mumbled, scowling at him. "Here, I'll leave my damned keys. I just need—" To be sick, that's what she needed. She tossed her car keys in Owen's lap and rushed for the door.

Once outside she took deep breaths of the clear night air and tried to keep from barfing. But nausea roiled in her throat.

She rushed toward the scraggly bushes at the end of the parking lot, bent over, and heaved.

When she was all done, she shoved a stick of gum in her mouth and knelt weakly on the pavement. She was disgusted with herself, disgusted with the world. Disgusted with Thunder Creek and everyone in this stupid town. She wanted to go someplace else, someplace far away . . . as far away as she could get.

She heard a car door slam from a distance. Then a man stood over her. Candy squinted up at him, but there was no moon and it was hard to see him through the shadows.

"Who are you? What the hell are you looking at?" she snapped. The dark shadow of the man moved closer.

Candy felt the first hint of fear. She tried to stand, but her legs weren't working properly. She opened her mouth to scream. Help, she needed help.

But the man leaned toward her and the words wouldn't come.

"Help," she finally gasped. But her tongue was thick and the words were soft. Too soft, too weak.

Too late.

Chapter 13

"NOTHING HAPPENED TO ME, ZACH."

Faith's shoulders were so tense her neck ached. "I grew up, that's all. My take on the world isn't the same as when I was a teenager, just as yours isn't. Or are you going to try to tell me you haven't changed as well, when it's clear that you have?"

"I can see why you make a good lawyer, Faith. You're quite adept at dodging the issue."

Her spine stiffened against the back of the seat. She wasn't about to unburden anything about herself to Zach. Not now, not ever.

"My life isn't an open book for your inspection," she retorted. "But if you must know, it's a good life and I'm happy with it. I enjoy my family and my friends, I've been successful at my career—" She broke off, her stomach clenching. "Well, I have been, up until recently," she muttered. Her tone was bitter. "I'm sure you heard about it. Everyone else has."

He glanced over at her. "That death penalty case. The real murderer turning up later." He'd read it in the paper, every word. "That must have been rough."

"You could say that." Unbidden, an image of Jimmy

Clement, white-faced in court, and of his mother and young brother weeping behind him, flashed in her mind. Pain throbbed in her temples. She tried to blink the images away.

"It wasn't your fault, Faith." Zach passed the sign for Casper. "You were doing your job, based on the evidence you had—"

"Do we have to talk about this?" she interrupted him. "I came to Thunder Creek for a vacation. To forget about work for a while."

"Sorry." Obviously he'd touched a nerve. The case meant a lot more to her than she was willing to let on, Zach thought. It must have devastated her more than he'd even imagined.

"Anything else you need to know, Zach?" she asked in a low, angry tone.

"Actually, I was wondering if there's anyone special in your life these days."

"No."

The curtness of her answer had him glancing over at her. Another sore spot. There was someone—or there had been. He'd been tempted to ask Roy or Patti or Bessie, but it hadn't felt right. Anything he needed to know from Faith he had to find out firsthand. He owed her that. And a lot more.

Before he could ask her anything else though, she leaned forward and switched on the radio. Glen Campbell blared into the car between them, singing "Wichita Lineman"—loudly. Too loudly for conversation.

Okay, Faith, he thought, settling back in his seat. *We'll play it your way—for now.*

The restaurant in Casper was a steakhouse, big as an old-fashioned saloon but with a private section that had large and small banquettes tucked away in the dark back room. A few lanterns and some fat votive candles on the white-clothed tables provided the only light.

In this private room, cattlemen and oilmen made million-dollar deals in the quiet dimness over steak, whiskey, and cigars.

But tonight there were only a scattering of couples in the sumptuous red leather booths. Faith sat across from Zach, studying the menu intently.

This was feeling a bit too much like a date. And it seemed absurd to go on a date with Zach. She bit her lip, pretending to read about aged prime rib and filet mignon, about potatoes au gratin and ranchhouse salad. But she was intensely aware of the man sitting across from her, and of the determination she'd noticed in his expression as they drove across the county.

He ordered a bottle of wine. They selected entrées. Faith had never felt more uncomfortable. Not when she was in law school, not when she was in court—even when she was being blasted by Judge Kirkpatrick while trying her first case. This odd formal silence with Zach was driving her crazy.

She took a long sip of her wine, then another. Across the table, he studied her with those intent silver-gray eyes of his, and she suspected he saw much more than she wanted him to see.

"Is it me?" he asked abruptly. "Am I rattling you, or was it that phone call? Maybe it's time you told me who Hank is."

She nearly choked on her wine, then swallowed and set her glass down with a soft thump. The truth was, she'd almost forgotten about Bayman and her phone call with Susan until he'd just mentioned them.

She drew a deep breath. "Hank is Hank Bayman. He's a

jerk, a scumbag." She was almost grateful for the chance to talk about something that wasn't personal between her and Zach. "He almost killed his wife a couple of times and he'd try again if he could. Nothing seems to stop him—not personal protection orders, not getting arrested. The guy's a bully who belongs behind bars."

"And you prosecuted him?"

She nodded. "Unfortunately we got stuck with a judge who has a mind-set from the 1800s. He only gave Bayman thirty days and probation instead of the tough sentence I requested. In other words, he basically let him back out on the street to terrorize his wife and kids again."

She paused until the waiter had set a basket of sourdough bread and a plate of honey butter in the center of the table.

"While he was serving his thirty days, Susan and her children were in a women's shelter, recovering mentally and physically from his latest illegal visit. I helped her get out of town while he was still locked up."

Zach said nothing, but his mouth was set in a grim line.

"She's in hiding now, out of state, with her kids. She has a new name, a job—and I made sure no one knows how to find her. But—"

"He's out now," Zach said. "And he's been nosing around."

"I'd bet on it." She told him how Bayman had gone missing, but Zach wasn't ready to let the subject drop there.

"He's been calling you," he said. "That's what you told Susan."

Faith shrugged, but her eyes slid away from his. "I'm not worried about it. He has no idea where I am."

"Is he calling your cell phone?"

"Yes, but—"

She broke off as the waiter, who'd been about to set down their salads, hesitated a moment. The man had caught the dark expression on Zach's face and looked for a moment like he was going to beat a quick retreat. Then he set the bowls down before them and hurried back to the kitchen.

"How the hell does he have your cell phone number?" Zach growled before she could say anything. "And how does he know you helped Susan leave town?"

"Bayman used to be a cop." She picked up her fork. "Until he got busted for taking bribes, that is. He still has contacts on the force. That's why I was careful to keep things close to the vest, but . . . someone must have found out something and filled him in."

"What does he say when he calls you?"

"Nothing." Faith didn't like talking about Bayman. Especially to Zach. Bayman was her business, her problem. Zach had nothing to do with her life. "He's silent. Except . . ." She suddenly remembered the soft laughter. "Except the last time," she finished.

He was studying her much too intently. "What happened the last time, Faith?" he asked in a deliberate tone.

"It was . . . a little different. He . . . laughed. This weird kind of creepy laugh." She fought off a shudder. "He was probably hoping to scare me out of my wits—which he didn't do," she added firmly. "That worked on Susan, because he knew where she was, and he liked to call her and then just show up in the middle of the night."

Zach listened, his eyes narrowed.

"It didn't matter if Susan had an alarm system, double-bolt locks on the door, whatever—he'd find a way in and she'd wake up and find him standing over her." Faith's tone hardened. "He beat her with a baseball bat one time—ripped up her sheets and pillows with a knife another. He's into fear."

She stabbed a forkful of salad and paused with it in midair, meeting Zach's eyes.

"I'm not," she said coolly. "He doesn't get to me."

Zach saw the stark determination in her eyes, and something plummetted inside his stomach. No, Faith wasn't into fear. But he was afraid for her. He leaned forward.

"And that man I saw the other night sneaking around outside your cabin? Maybe that was Bayman—maybe he's found you. Did you ever think of that?"

"It crossed my mind." She spoke casually, though in truth, the idea had made her skin crawl.

"If he has, you're in danger, Faith."

"You don't know if he has, and neither do I. But if he wants to tangle with me, I'm ready for him. A lot more ready than Susan ever was."

"What does that mean?"

"It means I own that gun you saw the other night—and I know how to use it. My father taught me when I was a kid, plus I've taken classes in both gun safety and marksmanship. Don't worry, Zach, I have no qualms about protecting myself. If Bayman comes after me—"

"You might never get a chance to pick up that gun," he said sharply. "What the hell are you doing staying alone out on Blue Moon Mesa when a psychopath is looking for you?"

A muscle twitched in his jaw. He looked ready to hit someone. Faith felt pretty sure it was Bayman. A tiny shock reverberated through her.

Why did Zach care so much what happened to her? They hadn't had any contact, not one word, since the night he'd walked out on her—not until she returned to Thunder

Creek and found out he was here as well. And all of a sudden, he was sticking his nose into her business—worrying about her?

"I don't know that Bayman is here, or even that he knows where I am," she said. "But if he is here, and if he does happen to cross my path, that's really my problem, isn't it?"

"Somehow I don't think your big brothers Ty and Adam and your cousin Roy would see things that way." His tone was rough. "Maybe I should drop a hint in their ears. Maybe you should move in with Roy and Corinne instead of staying alone at the—"

"Maybe you should mind your own business!" Faith jumped out of the booth, her eyes sparking. But at that moment the waiter appeared again, bearing their meals, and she gritted her teeth under his startled gaze, then slowly sank back into her seat.

"I want you to promise me you won't say anything to Roy," she said the moment the waiter left.

Zach controlled the anger and concern rushing through him. But his mouth tightened as he met her furious gaze.

"I don't make promises anymore that I can't guarantee I'll keep," he said slowly.

Faith froze, staring into his eyes. They were locked on hers and she couldn't look away.

So . . . he remembers. That night. That last night we were together . . . the promises he made me before he left and blew everything to smithereens.

She steeled herself against the pain clenching her heart, against the memories of those long-ago days and nights, against the old broken longing and the almost overwhelming desire to reach for his hand, to reach for him . . .

"What do you say we call a truce, Faith?" His tone had

altered. So had the hard expression in his eyes. He looked at her quietly and she felt emotion well in her throat. "No more arguments for the rest of the night. For the next few hours, why don't we just try to enjoy each other's company?"

You don't ask for much, do you? The old pain was lodged in her throat, making it difficult to speak. She took a deep breath, trying to get a handle on the rush of emotions he still had the power to evoke in her.

She was a grown-up woman now, not a devastated teenager—she wouldn't let him see her wearing her heart on her sleeve.

"I have no problem with that," she lied, and even managed a small indifferent shrug. "What would *you* like to talk about?"

Something neutral that won't make you close up like a clam, he thought, noting the rigid line of her beautiful throat, the mulish tilt of her chin.

It didn't take him long to think of a safe topic. As she cut into her steak he regarded her with a quizzical smile.

"How about money?"

Chapter 14

IT WAS NEARLY MIDNIGHT WHEN ZACH MADE A right turn onto the narrow darkened road that would take them to Blue Moon Mesa.

Beside him, Faith sat with her head tilted slightly away from him, gazing out the passenger side window.

He couldn't begin to imagine what she was thinking.

He'd spent the past few hours over coffee and dessert and the ride home telling her about the million-dollar donation he planned to make to the hospital-wing fund and outlining what he wanted done with it—including instituting a new pediatric and trauma center.

He specified that he wanted his donation kept secret and announced at the dinner dance, with the hopes that others would be inspired that night to give as much as they could.

But his gut tightened when he remembered the way Faith had looked at him after he'd made that statement. At first there'd been delight and pleasure in those beautiful eyes—and, he swore, appreciation. Then her entire body had stiffened.

"What's wrong?" he'd asked. "You're looking at me like I'm one of your clients who just confessed to murder."

"I've just realized why you're doing this."

"Yeah? And why is that?"

She'd tried to sound nonchalant but he'd heard the coolness in her tone. It flayed him like a whip. "It's good PR. You want to gain the support of the community. For Tex-Corp Oil and for that camp you're planning."

He hadn't spoken for a moment. And when he did, his voice had been rough, thick with sarcasm. "You got me," he lied. "You've really got me pegged, Faith. When did you become so cynical? Or should I say, so smart?"

"It's all right," she'd said stiffly. "I'm not judging you. The donation is unbelievably generous and it will go to good use. But . . ."

"But I'm doing it to manipulate people in this town who might not trust me . . . or who might oppose my plans?"

"I didn't say that."

"You didn't have to. It's obvious. Right?"

Without waiting for her answer, he'd called for the check. They'd left the restaurant moments later and there had been little conversation on the ride home.

So what? Zach asked himself as they drove past Shadow Point, Thunder Creek's famed makeout spot, where he and Faith had spent countless evenings kissing and groping each other in the dark.

So she thinks you're a manipulative jerk. The same guy who put Pete in a coma and married Alicia and never gave her another thought. When the hell do you care? Since when do you give a damn about what anyone thinks—except Dillon?

But when it came to Faith, he did care. It was crazy. No one could hurt him anymore, but Faith Barclay could look at him with disappointment or wariness in her eyes and it was like an axe hacking through his heart.

Screw it, he thought. *There's no way to get a second*

chance, no way to make things right. Too much bad history. The girl who believed in Zach McCallum that summer doesn't even exist anymore.

He pulled up before the cabin and braked sharply. She'd left a light on and it glowed cozily golden through the window.

Automatically, he scanned the grounds, assuring himself that the figure he'd seen the other night wasn't lurking in the darkness.

There was no sign of anyone. Still, he got out of the car as she opened the passenger-side door and stalked around to escort her to her door.

"You don't need to—" she began, but stopped at the grim expression on his face. Silently, she walked beside him to the porch, up the steps.

"It was a lovely dinner," Faith began. Then she caught the bitter darkness in his eyes and the words died in her throat.

"I'm sorry, Zach." It was a whisper. For some reason, she wanted to cry. "I was . . . wrong."

He faced her on the porch, his face hard. Closed. "Yeah? About what?"

"You're not manipulating the town with your donation. That was stupid of me. I apologize." She swallowed. "The boy I knew would never do something like that. I did him a disservice."

"I'm not that boy anymore, Faith," he told her curtly. "You don't know a thing about me. About what I've done these past years or about who I am."

"I know enough. You never did suck up to people. You never gave a damn what anyone thought. You don't need the goodwill of Thunder Creek to do whatever you want with your money and your power. I should have remembered that."

His eyes glinted angrily in the moonlight. "Damn straight."

Suddenly, he looked so much like the wild, angry boy she remembered that she smiled, her heart filling with a rushing warmth that took her by surprise. "Come here," she said impulsively.

She didn't know why, but she grabbed his hand and began to run, tugging him along with her. She ran to the tree where they'd kissed that summer and pulled him beneath the branches with her in the darkness.

"Rememember that day we hiked all the way to Shadow Point from here? I thought I knew you better than I knew myself that day. I'd never felt so close to anyone before."

"I remember." His tone was rough. "I thought we'd be together forever."

Her hands gripped both of his. "It was a long time ago, Zach. Too much has happened and we're both so different now. But I should have known that some things don't change. Whatever was between us then is gone, I know that, but you never were a suck-up and I was wrong to imply that—"

"You're wrong about something else, Faith. Whatever was between us—it's not gone." He took a step closer, his fingers closing around hers. "It's never gone away. You're either blind or you're lying to yourself. And the girl I knew didn't lie to anyone."

She gaped at him. *It's not gone. It's never gone away.* She shook her head. "We don't even know each other anymore. We have different lives. Different dreams. Zach, you *left* me—you married someone else." To her dismay, her voice trembled as the unexpected rush of words poured out of her. "You never even told me you were *leaving*—"

"I was dumb and young and an idiot. Maybe it's time we cleared that up," he said.

But she tore her hands from his grip and began backing away. "No. Don't explain. I don't want that. I've moved on, we both have, and you don't owe me any—"

She stumbled on something, and cried out even as she fell backward. She landed on her rump in the soft grass.

Zach started toward her. "Are you all right?"

But he stopped suddenly and stared down through the starlit blackness. He was staring at the darkened grass, at what had tripped her.

Faith stared too. Horror rose in her as she felt warm stickiness on her hands and the moon drifted out from behind a cloud—and she realized what that long dark shape was.

That's when she started to scream.

Chapter 15

IT WAS 3 A.M. BEFORE THE ACTING SHERIFF, Deputy Rick Keene, the coroner, the county medical examiner, and the other deputies investigating the murder scene finished their photographs, notes, questions, and sketches, and left the crime scene on Blue Moon Mesa.

Before heading out of the Barclay cabin, Keene paused and studied Faith, huddled white-faced and exhausted on the sofa.

"I'll be contacting your brother to let him know what's going on."

Despite his sympathetic tone, Faith thought she saw a certain steely appraisal in his eyes—one she recognized well, even at three in the morning.

I'm a suspect in a murder investigation. Talk about the shoe being on the other foot.

"I'll be calling him too," she said wearily. "If there's anything else I can do, you know where to find me."

At that moment Zach stepped through the door of the cabin. Keene's nearly black eyes glanced from one to the other of them, then he touched his fingers to his hat and made one final statement.

"Don't go near that crime scene. I'll need both of you to

stop in tomorrow and go over your statements once again. It's just routine," he added.

As he left and Zach closed the cabin door at last, a shudder ran through her.

Candy Merck was dead. She'd been bound, gagged, and stabbed to death, less than twenty feet from the Barclay cabin.

"Are you all right?" Zach sat down beside her. Hours ago, he had asked her the very same thing. Seconds before they learned that a woman they'd known for years had been murdered, her body sprawled between them in the shadowy Wyoming night.

"I'll be okay. I need . . . to take a shower."

"And you need some sleep."

So do you, Faith thought. He looked almost as exhausted as she felt. His hair was rumpled, and the fine lines around the corners of his eyes looked deeper, harsher against the drawn contours of his face.

They had been questioned separately, as was standard procedure—Faith inside the cabin, Zach in the sheriff's Crown Victoria. Even now, with Rick Keene's empty coffee cup sitting on the side table, the smell of Deputy Marsden's Brut aftershave wafting through the cabin, and the knowledge of the yellow crime-scene tape circling a bloody section of the mesa, it all seemed unreal. Like a harrowing other-dimension dream, a nightmare from a horror film.

"Who could have done this?" She gazed at Zach through aching eyes.

"Let's start with the guy who was lurking around here the other night."

She sighed. "I'm not sure Keene believed you about that."

"He wrote it down."

"They always write everything down. But he looked skeptical." She dragged a hand through her hair, tension throbbing through her. "I should have called and reported it when it happened. You were right about that."

Guilt rubbed at her. What if it *had* been the murderer prowling around the cabin that night? If she'd notified the police, maybe he would have been caught. Maybe Candy would still be alive . . .

"Hey, we searched for him, remember?" Zach seemed to be reading her thoughts. "We didn't find any trace of him. The police might not have either. By the time they arrived, he probably would have been long gone."

She nodded, but a bleakness filled her heart. "They suspect us, you know. At least for now. That's how it works. Everyone's a suspect until they're ruled out. We found the body . . . we knew the victim . . . "

Her voice trailed off. *The victim.* Candy. With her too-blond hair and overly defined mouth. Her rich laugh and affinity for low-cut purple shirts and skintight black jeans.

Faith had never liked her very much. They'd gotten along fine back in those days when they were teenagers, but they'd never really connected. Now grief and guilt and shock raged within her, and she covered her face with her hands, squeezing her eyes shut, trying to keep the tears inside.

"Faith." Zach drew her into his arms. He held her close, stroking her hair as she fell against his chest and the tears tumbled down her cheeks.

"I know, baby, I know. Let it go."

She felt so fragile, so soft in his arms. Her grief tore a hole through him. He was remembering the last time he'd seen Candy—how he'd left her drinking alone.

Damn it. He'd considered her a friend, nothing more,

and he sure as hell hadn't encouraged her to think there was anything more, but . . . hell.

His gut clenched as he remembered the blood-slicked grass and the stab wounds that had made a horror of her body.

"They'll catch him, Faith," he said quietly. "Whoever did this—he'll pay for what he did to Candy."

It took a while, but her sobs eventually slowed. He felt her shoulders stop shaking and stroked her hair as she lay, spent and quiet, in his arms. When she stirred at last and peered up at him, he felt a pull of tenderness deep in his gut.

He loosened his hold, putting some distance between them.

"How about a drink?" Zach cleared his throat. "I could sure use one."

"There's wine chilling in the fridge." She wiped at her damp eyes. "Glasses in the cabinet. Would you mind getting them?" She shivered. "I need to take a shower. Get out of these clothes . . ."

Her gaze trailed down to the blood on her boots, on her jeans . . . and she felt sick.

Considering all the cases she'd prosecuted, and all the brutal photographs of death she'd seen and presented in excruciating detail to a jury, she should have been hardened to it. But this was different. This victim was someone she knew . . . and she'd fallen over the body. Candy's blood was on her clothes, her skin, perhaps in her hair. She began to shiver again.

"Faith, are you sure you're okay? You're not going to faint in the shower, are you?"

She shook her head. *Pull yourself together,* she thought wearily. *You deal with death for a living.* "I'm not usually a wuss . . . it's just . . ."

"You don't have to explain."

By the time she'd showered, sudsed her hair, and rinsed off the blood and sweat and grime of the night, she was beginning to feel a little more in control. She towel-dried her hair, ran a comb through it, then wrapped herself in a thick white robe and padded barefoot back to the living room.

Zach was talking to someone on his cell phone, two glasses of white zinfandel on the coffee table before him.

"Yeah, Neely knows you're coming. She has the security system on, but I want you to check everything out. Then make yourself comfortable in the spare bedroom. I'll see you in the morning."

He glanced at her as she took a seat beside him on the sofa. "Feel better?"

"Yes. Who was that?"

"Gabe Hawthorn, my foreman. I spoke to my housekeeper while you were showering."

She stared at him. "You woke them at this hour?"

"Dillon gets nightmares sometimes and comes into my room in the middle of the night. I didn't want him to find me gone and be afraid. When I'm going to be away all night, I tell him in advance."

"You're going to be away all night?" She gaped at him. "Where are you going?"

"Nowhere." He handed her a glass of wine. "I'm staying right here."

Surprise left her speechless for a moment. "I don't think so," she said at last.

"Let's not argue about it." He shot her a wry smile. "We've been getting along so well."

"Let's keep it that way. You know, I'm fine, Zach, really I am." She took a gulp of wine. "I was shaken up at first, and in shock, but . . . I'm not afraid. You don't have to babysit me, for God's sake—"

"Save your breath, Barclay." His tone was unexpectedly gentle. "I'm sleeping right here on this sofa until daybreak. And unless you think you can physically evict me, there's no point discussing it."

God, he was infuriating. But . . . strangely comforting to have around. She was startled by how much she appreciated having him here with her right now.

"The killer won't be back. They don't usually return to the scene of the crime the same night," she muttered, giving him one last chance to bow out. "And I do have a gun, as I told you earlier. There's no reason—"

She broke off. Zach was shaking his head.

"We need to talk about something, Faith."

"What?"

"There's something you haven't addressed. You didn't even bother mentioning it to Keene. I'm talking about those phone calls you've been getting from Hank Bayman."

Faith's nerves jangled at the name. She gripped the stem of her wineglass. "It's irrelevant. Bayman would have no reason to murder Candy. It's his wife he's mad at—and me. He's an anger freak, an abuser. A bully and a stalker, definitely, but not a killer—"

"Candy's body was found no more than twenty feet from your front door. Maybe he was trying to tell you something."

She fell silent. The same thought had occurred to her briefly but she'd pretty much dismissed it. It just didn't fit.

"It's too much of a stretch," she told Zach at last. "If Bayman wanted to scare me or hurt me, he'd come after *me*."

"You sure about that?"

"Pretty sure." But a tiny voice inside of her whispered

that she couldn't completely rule Bayman out. The man loved fear. Loved to create it, to draw it out, to watch it in his victim's eyes. Susan had told her that sometimes he would talk to her, tell her exactly what he was going to do with the baseball bat, or the knife, then watch the terror build in her and smile like the devil when she began to cry.

Had Candy's murderer taunted her too? Told her what he was going to do? Was it Bayman, had he gone over the edge? Maybe he was getting off on another woman's fear, trying to send Faith herself a message at the same time, to make her afraid before he even came for her. So afraid that when he showed himself she'd blurt out Susan's where-abouts . . .

As if that would ever happen, she thought, then pushed the entire theory away. It was unlikely—highly unlikely. Candy's murder was about Candy. She'd either been killed by someone with a grudge against her, or she'd seen some-thing she wasn't supposed to see, gotten picked up by the wrong stranger . . .

She drained the last of her wine, aware that Zach was studying her. She felt much too vulnerable to his acutely perceptive gaze. She was simply too exhausted, too shaken right now to keep up her defenses—much less to try to an-alyze the motive behind Candy's killing.

"I need to get some sleep, Zach. Tomorrow I'll have to go into the sheriff's office for more questioning—and so will you. God, I wish Ty was here."

He nodded. She looked paler than he'd ever seen her—and like a spring breeze would knock her over. Tense and fragile and exhausted beyond words. "It's going to be all right, Faith. We didn't do anything wrong and as soon as they get a little deeper into the investigation, they'll realize that."

"I hope you're right." Faith wanted to believe that Rick Keene would follow all the threads, but she'd had experience with too many cops who got a notion in their head and then tended to ignore everything else.

"You've been seen with Candy quite a bit lately," she said in a low tone as she carried her glass over to the sink. "And I had words with her at the Tumbleweed. There were witnesses. And now . . . God, Zach, we found the body—*together*."

"We have ironclad alibis," he reminded her. "The waiter and dozens of other people saw us at the restaurant. We can be placed positively in Casper from eight o'clock until the time it took to drive back here after dinner . . ."

He broke off suddenly at the frown creasing her brow.

"And it doesn't mean anything, does it?" he said. Why hadn't he realized it before? "Our entire alibi depends on the time of death."

Faith nodded. "If the medical examiner finds she was killed earlier, before we even left for Casper . . ."

"We could still be suspects," he finished for her. "Suspects who provided themselves with an alibi before pretending to 'discover' the body."

"Yes." There was no point in denying it. "That could be a problem. But . . ." She took a deep breath. "Since we didn't kill her, there won't be any physical evidence to tie us to the crime."

Saying the words aloud, knowing they were about Candy, struck her anew and she felt her temples throb. "Who would want to hurt Candy?" she whispered. Against her will, her brain was kicking into prosecutor mode. "Is there some psycho roaming around Thunder Creek—or was it personal? A real estate client who thinks he got a bad deal, some man she threw over or cheated on—"

"Hey. Madam Prosecutor. This isn't your case. You don't have to solve it."

"It's what I do," she sighed. "I can't help it. And I can't stop thinking about it."

"Let's wait and see what kind of physical evidence the police come up with."

"As if they'll tell us," Faith murmured. She struggled to suppress a yawn. It wasn't always a good thing to know the way the police and DA worked. Sometimes, despite the best intentions, justice managed to get all screwed up.

Zach went to her and took her arm. "Come on—bedtime. The investigation can wait until morning. You need to get some rest."

She knew he was right. She was too exhausted now to even think straight. A few hours' sleep would put everything in sharper focus.

"If you insist on staying, I need to at least get you a blanket and a pillow. Wait here."

She emerged from her bedroom a moment later with both and dropped them on the sofa, then glanced over and met his eyes.

"You're sure you want to do this? You must have a very comfortable bed in your own home. I doubt this sofa is on a par with it."

"You got a bulldozer? Because you'll need one to get me out of here."

Something trembled inside her. A smile touched her lips. *It's gratitude,* she told herself wearily, *that's all.* Gratitude that she wouldn't be alone here for the rest of the night after finding Candy's body.

"Sleep well, Zach." Her voice was soft. Too soft. She hurried into her bedroom and closed the door.

Leaning against it, Faith tried to block out the memory

of his arms around her, of his comforting strength and warmth and steadiness, of his deep, even voice.

Stop it. You're losing it. You have to stop thinking about him.

But the alternative was thinking about Candy. About what had happened to her, and what kind of monster was loose in Thunder Creek.

Dropping her robe over the back of a chair, she slipped on a gray camisole and matching drawstring pants, then sank like a stone into bed.

That's when she realized she hadn't locked the door. But she knew there was no need.

What separated her and Zach was a lot stronger than any bolt or lock, she told herself in the darkness.

And she couldn't forget that.

Any more than she could forget what had happened to Candy.

Chapter 16

"I HEARD DEPUTY KEENE QUESTIONED OWEN Carey for the third time yesterday." Patti set down her half-empty coffee cup in Bessie's Diner and looked across the booth at Faith with worried eyes. "What do you think that's all about?"

"I wish I knew." Faith shook her head. "It's not as if Owen would ever hurt Candy. Even Keene must know that. It's probably just routine," she added quickly, seeing the concern on Patti's face. "I wouldn't worry about it."

Across from her, seated beside Patti, Bessie Templeton snorted. "Routine? I'm not so sure, Faith, honey. They questioned Owen for nearly four hours. Now, I've known that young man all his life—he's no more a murderer than I am."

It was the afternoon lull in the diner and Bessie had taken a break, sinking her small spry frame into the booth with them to sip tea and nibble at a slice of one of the strawberry rhubarb pies her granddaughter Katy had whisked from the oven this morning.

Candy Merck's funeral had been yesterday—a grim affair attended by nearly the entire town. No one could talk of anything else.

In a town this small and close-knit, every death was like a death in the family. But the murder of a young woman, one of Thunder Creek's own? No one could imagine any of their friends or neighbors committing such a crime. It had to have been a stranger, a madman, a monster. And everyone in town drew protectively closer together at the common threat to their tranquil community.

Poor Ned Merck, Candy's widowed father, who owned Merck's Hardware, was walking around in a grief-stricken fog at the loss of his only child. Silently he endured the sympathy of friends, nodding woodenly, his face the color of dead gray leaves, but he seemed unable to shed a single tear.

"Bob saw Owen at the gas station after he was questioned this last time and he said Owen looked pretty shaken up." Patti stirred sugar into her decaf. "Keene was really curious why Owen had Candy's car keys, and why, if Candy had gone out for air, Owen didn't call the police when she didn't come back. I guess he kept hammering away at that, over and over."

"Well, did Owen tell him what he told me?" Bessie asked, frowning. "He looked all over for her in that parking lot and finally he concluded she'd gotten a ride home with someone else. He was just hanging onto those keys until she wanted them back."

"Well, I don't think Keene was buying it," Patti muttered. "It sounds to me like he has Owen in his sights. And one of the waitresses at the Tumbleweed told me they only questioned Elam once—and nowhere near as long as they questioned Owen."

"Owen was with Candy most of that night, and he's probably one of the last people to see her alive," Faith pointed out quietly. "Keene may not consider him a suspect at all. He might just be hoping Owen will remember something Candy said or did that night that might be significant in finding the killer."

"Hmmm, I guess you could be right," Bessie said, looking hopeful.

Faith took a sip of coffee, grimaced, and set the cup down. It tasted not only cold, but bitter. Even the pie, one of her favorites, didn't look appealing. Not today, when the topic of conversation was Candy's death. Not when she could still remember the brutal shock of tripping over her body . . .

"Faith, honey, I'm sorry." Reaching across the table, Patti touched her hand. "You're going a bit green on us," she murmured. "We'll talk about something else. I can't even imagine what it felt like to find the . . . the . . . um, Candy."

Bessie peered at Faith with ready sympathy. "It's going to take awhile to get over that shock, honey. You just take it easy."

"I'll be okay." Faith mustered a smile. "I work in a prosecutor's office. I'm tough, remember?"

"Tough enough to get the job done." Bessie looked her square in the eye. "But underneath you're only a human being, like everyone else. And I'll bet that with all the cases you've prosecuted and all those corpses you've viewed in the morgue and in photos, it's a whole lot different when you actually discover the body."

That's for sure. Faith took a breath. "I'm all for that change of subject." She looked at Patti. "For example, what time do we need to get to the Crystal Horseshoe on Saturday to set up for the auction?"

It was a relief to discuss the details of the benefit, but it wasn't long before the subject turned to the dance itself.

"Do you . . . have a date?" Patti asked, trying so hard to sound casual that Faith's radar went off.

"No. No date. Unless you want to loan Bob to me," she replied with a grin.

"Sorry, you hussy, he's taken. But I thought by now you'd have snagged an escort."

"If you mean Owen or Rusty—" Faith began, but Bessie interrupted her impatiently.

"No, not them. Out with it, girl. We heard all about your date with Zach McCallum. He took you all the way to Casper. To a steakhouse." Bessie was smiling. "Sounds to me like you two have mended your fences."

Patti was grinning too. Faith stared back and forth between the two of them, her stomach sinking. "Does this entire town remember that Zach and I went out a few times when we were teenagers?" she asked in disbelief.

Patti patted her hand as if she were a foolish child unschooled in the ways of the world. "You've been away too long. You don't remember what small towns are like, do you? Especially Thunder Creek. Of course the entire town knew what happened back then. Everyone knew you two were crazy about each other—and that Zach ran out on you the night he put Pete Harrison in a coma."

"And," Bessie added, "everyone's been wondering what would happen when you met up again. Especially after that run-in between Rusty Gallagher and Zach at the Tumbleweed."

Faith closed her eyes. "Oh, no."

"And now we heard you went on this date—all the way out of town, presumably so no one would see you together, and . . ." Patti waited until Faith opened her eyes before continuing with a mischievous grin.

"Don't you want to tell us what *that* was all about?"

She gaped at them as warm color rushed into her cheeks.

"Can't two people have dinner together without everyone thinking they're . . . they're . . ."

"Involved," Patti supplied helpfully. "And the answer is no."

Faith leaned back against the booth. "It was nothing," she said. "We talked about the benefit. That's it. He wants to make a donation, quite a large one."

"Oh, I know all about that." Patti waved her hand airily. "He called Tammie the other day and made a pledge. It's supposed to be a secret. She's over the moon. But he didn't ask her to go out to dinner with him. He just told her on the phone. Don't tell me you really believed that was the reason for the date."

"It wasn't a date."

Bessie reached out and laid a small, blue-veined hand on Faith's arm. "It's none of our business, Faith, and you have every right to tell us so."

An impish grin curved the corners of Patti's mouth. "But we haven't had a wedding in Thunder Creek for nearly a year—"

"That's it. If you're going to talk about weddings, I'm out of here." Faith stood up, grabbing her purse, but Bessie waved her back into her seat.

"You stay right there," she ordered. "Have another cup of coffee. We won't torment you anymore. I have to get back to work, anyway."

"Actually," Patti sighed, "I have to leave too. I need to get home and start supper."

"Don't let me keep you," Faith grumbled, but couldn't help a chuckle as Patti hugged her good-bye.

When they had both gone, Faith sat alone for a few more moments, trying to concentrate on her to-do list before the benefit Saturday night. She had to pick up nearly a dozen items being donated, tag and catalogue them, meet with Tammie one last time . . .

But her mind kept shifting back to the conversation— actually, the *inquisition*—about Zach.

She didn't care about what other people thought, not really. But she wondered what he was thinking. There was a time when she understood him almost better than she understood herself.

But not anymore. Too much time had passed. Too many turns in their lives, turns that had taken them in opposite directions.

She hadn't even heard from him since the morning after the murder. He'd barely spoken to her after she woke up, and had left as soon as the sun came up. At Candy's funeral he'd made an appearance, extended his sympathies to Ned Merck, and left with barely a nod to anyone else—including her.

But he didn't owe her any explanations, Faith told herself. And she had better things to do than think about Zach kissing her, taking her to dinner, and holding her so close when she'd fallen apart after the murder.

Enough already. Sitting in the diner, thinking about Zach, her stomach was churning. Amazing that before she came back to Thunder Creek, she'd actually toyed with the idea of staying here awhile, perhaps indefinitely. It had been nothing but a stupid fantasy—the idea of extending her vacation, of leaving the pressure and politics of the DA's office behind. Of opening a small law practice in Thunder Creek—spending the winter curled up in the cabin, warm and cozy, the summer outdoors, hiking, riding, maybe even buying a horse of her own . . .

But reality had slapped her in the face. Some vacation

this had turned out to be. A reunion with the guy who broke her heart and a murder.

She should have gone to Hawaii.

When she left the diner and walked outside beneath a breezy cloudy sky, her mind turned to the one piece of information Ty had shared with her when he'd called her from New York after hearing about Candy's murder. According to what Rick Keene had told him, all of the preliminary evidence pointed to Candy being killed right where her body was found. The killer had brought her there, right to the cabin on Blue Moon Mesa, and then killed her.

Which led to a whole new set of questions that had kept her up last night.

Why had the killer picked that particular spot—a spot almost within spitting distance of the cabin, where it would easily be discovered?

Had it been circumstance or a deliberate choice? Faith wanted to believe it was coincidence, but her gut and common sense were whispering something else.

What if Candy's murder really was linked to the man Zach had seen skulking around the cabin? Rick Keene had seemed to pay scant attention to that information, but what if there really was a connection?

And what if that man was Hank Bayman—trying to frighten her or send her a message? What if he'd lost it, gone over the edge . . .

She hadn't heard from him since Candy's murder. He'd either given up after she'd threatened him, or he'd gone underground.

He might actually be here in Thunder Creek.

As this thought sent a tingle of alarm through her, she

rounded the corner at Main and Third and collided with a man coming fast from the other direction.

The impact slammed her backward and she cried out, nearly falling, but strong arms shot out and steadied her.

"Sorry." Rusty Gallagher gazed down at her through those somber, deep-set eyes. "Did I hurt you?"

"No." Faith started to move past him, but Rusty quickly blocked her path, to the surprise of the group of three young men he'd been walking with.

Faith glanced at them—they didn't look like ranch hands, more like kids right out of college, and one of them carried a laptop computer. No doubt employees of the Morgan Group.

"I'll catch up with you at the diner," Rusty told them curtly. "Run that new spreadsheet, Boles. I want to study it before the meeting," he told the young man with the laptop.

"Faith." He turned toward her, his tone changing from authoritative to persuasive. "I need to talk to you. Give me a minute, that's all I ask."

The young men brushed past her, but Faith scarcely noticed them. She was eyeing Rusty with cold dislike.

"You're not drunk today. There's no excuse for blocking my path. I suggest you get out of my way—now."

"Come on, Faith, just hear me out. I know I was way out of line at the Tumbleweed. I'm sorry about that. Give me a chance to make it up to you."

"There's nothing to make up for. Forget it, clean slate."

"Then we can be friends?" He smiled broadly and a glint of relief showed in his eyes. "You'll let me take you to dinner? As my way of apologizing, of course."

"I don't go to dinner with men who grope me in bars, or who stop me in the street even when I ask them to let me by," she said evenly, but there was a spark of fire in her pure blue eyes. "We're not going to be friends, Rusty. And we're not going to date. And we're definitely not going to bed."

The smile faded from his face. "You're quite a little bitch, aren't you?"

"When it's called for." She stepped past him quickly and walked away. She didn't look back as she headed for her car.

But suddenly as she pulled her keys from her purse, a strange quiver brushed down her spine. Like cold death breathing against her bones.

She whirled around. Rusty was gone. The street was nearly empty, and she saw nothing—no one—unusual.

She found herself scanning faces, looking for Hank Bayman. Her heart beat faster as she turned her head quickly, looking back and forth, up and down Main. But he wasn't there. And in a moment, the sensation faded, evaporating like mountain mist into the crisp Wyoming air.

Faith started the car and sat for a moment, letting the beating of her heart slow. *You're imagining things. Getting jumpy, spooked. Cut it out,* she told herself.

And that's when her cell phone rang.

"I'm sorry I haven't called you in a few days."

When she heard Zach's voice, she felt almost dizzy with relief. In the background there were sounds of a bulldozer roaring and some banging and shouts.

He must be at his construction site, she realized.

"I've been dealing with some business problems," Zach shouted as the noise level swelled behind him.

"You don't owe me any explanations."

"That's a lot of bull, Faith. We both know that isn't true.

Come over to the ranch and have dinner with me tonight. We need to talk."

She knew she should refuse. She *wanted* to refuse. She took a breath and started to do just that, but instead found herself saying, "What time?"

"Six-thirty." The crescendo behind him grew deafening. "See you tonight," he shouted into the phone and hung up.

She told herself it was only dinner. His son would probably be there, and even if they did manage to find a moment alone, it didn't matter *what* he had to say. Talking about the past, getting it out in the open, wouldn't fix or change anything.

But as she drove through the winding beauty of the foothills even as the clouds began to darken over the mountains, and the smell of approaching rain circled in the air, she wondered what she was going to wear.

Not that it matters, she told herself, trying not to wonder what the evening might hold. *It doesn't. Not to me. Not at all.*

Owen had watched Faith walk down Main from the checkout line at Lucy's Grocery and Drugs. He'd heard about her and Zach going on that date together to Casper, and every time he thought about it, his stomach turned upside down. Were they getting back together?

Or was the past still standing in their way?

He needed to talk to her—to someone. He needed to tell the truth.

Sweat trickled down his forehead as he stood with his basket of Wonder Bread and frozen pizza, steaks, and beer. Candy's death had triggered a fresh surge of guilt in him, one that was nearly pushing him to the brink.

Why didn't I go outside with her the other night? Why didn't I follow her, make sure she was all right?

If I had, Owen thought in despair, *she'd probably be alive right now.*

It was bad enough, living with everything else he'd done, and knowing the ugly secret he'd been keeping all these years, but now he had Candy's death on his conscience too.

Owen's head was pounding.

Suddenly, all he could think about was Faith. He had to talk to her, tell her . . .

As she reached her brother's SUV and opened the door, he felt a surge of urgency so desperate he thought he was on fire. He glanced around, hoping no one could see the weakness inside him. He'd always been weak. And now even though he was old enough to be strong, to know better, to do what was right, the weakness still held him back.

It always will, a mocking voice inside told him, but he tried not to listen to the voice. He hated that voice. Hated the guilt that ate at him. Now more than ever.

He'd talk to Faith. She'd been his friend long ago. And she still was. He'd confess to her, and she'd help him.

Wouldn't she?

No, the voice mocked. *She serves the law. She deals in justice. She'll hate you.*

But they said confession was good for the soul. He should just do it . . . confess—

"Hurry up there, will you?" he snapped at the teenager at the cash register.

He had to get outside before Faith left.

The teenage boy ringing up groceries flushed the color of overripe tomatoes and threw him a resentful glance.

Owen blew out his breath. He considered leaving his

groceries, running after Faith before she could pull away . . . and then what?

Tell her the truth? Just like that?

There's no need for drastic measures, the little voice whispered in his ear. *Do you really want to tell her? You should just keep your mouth shut.*

He moved up in line as the woman in front of him set several brown paper bags into her basket and shuffled toward the door.

At the same moment, Faith's SUV pulled away from the curb. He caught one glimpse of her lovely, fine-boned profile as she drove away.

Too late, the voice inside him murmured. *Too late, too late, too late.*

Owen didn't look at the checkout kid or anyone else as he paid for his groceries and left the store. He went out into the overcast grayness, drove himself home, put away his purchases. All except the six-pack.

He sat down at the kitchen table and tipped back a beer.

Coward. Weakling. Failure, the voice whispered in his head.

Why didn't you stay with Candy the other night? Why can't you do anything right?

He finished the can and reached for another.

"I'll tell Faith tomorrow," he mumbled to himself. He almost believed it. "I'm going to tell her everything."

He chugged the second Bud, but he could still taste the lie, bitter as a sucked lemon in his throat.

He grabbed a third can and flipped the tab.

By the time he swallowed the last drop in the six-pack, he didn't taste a thing.

Chapter 17

ZACH GLANCED UP FROM HIS DESK AT THE sounds of boyish shouts and laughter wafting through his window. Dropping the contracts he'd been studying, he went around the desk to the window and grinned at what he saw going on near the corrals.

Dillon and Brett Grayson were chasing each other around the yard with squirt guns, their shrieks and howls of laughter ringing above the breeze sweeping down from the Laramies. Then Batman came bounding from the trees, barking up a storm, and the noise level jolted up a good five notches. Even the quarter horses in the corral shook their manes and started to frolic.

This is much better than video games and watching DVDs, Zach thought. His grin deepened. There was nothing better for a kid than some good old-fashioned fun. He and Jock had waged their share of squirt-gun fights, he recalled fondly. Not to mention wrestling matches, and horse races on the back roads behind the ranch. Boys loved to compete, to challenge themselves and each other. And Zach had won a good share of those competitions, despite the fact that Jock was older. But there was one contest he'd never won.

The contest for their father's affection.

He'd come to terms with that a long time ago. It was all in the past. But after Dillon was born and became the light of his life, he'd vowed that if he ever had another child, a son or a daughter, he'd love her or him every bit as much as he loved Dillon. He couldn't imagine raising a child any other way. Not when he knew what it was like to be on the outside looking in.

The mere idea of having another child sent his thoughts spinning toward Faith. He couldn't seem to stop thinking about her.

Especially about her living all alone out at that cabin.

Blue Moon Mesa was a lonely spot. Too damned lonely, out in the middle of nowhere, with a killer on the loose.

She belongs here, he thought, his gut tightening. *She belongs in this house, in my home, Dillon's home. She's still a part of me—and she has been all these years, even when we were apart, even when I wouldn't let myself think about her.*

There were other things that dragged at his mind . . . Candy's murder, the kids he'd promised would have a camp, the trouble brewing from Fred Harrison and Wood Morgan and that slimeball mouthpiece, Rusty Gallagher.

But he could deal with all of that. The one thing he couldn't deal with was the hurt and wariness he still saw in Faith's eyes when he was with her. The way she refused to trust him, to lean on him, to open herself to him.

That carved a deeper slice out of his gut than any other. And he knew that everything that happened that final night in Thunder Creek all those years ago still stood between them, like a stone barricade. His chest was tight with pain because he knew it always would.

As the boys threw down their water guns and raced

toward the barn, he checked his watch. Faith would be here soon. He should shave, change his shirt. And remind Dillon to put on dry clothes.

Then he heard boots clumping hard and fast from the back of the house and he turned toward the study door to find Gabe frowning at him. As the foreman entered the study, Zach noticed the steely center of Gabe's eyes and somehow knew his plans for the evening were about to go up in smoke.

"I just came from the building site, boss. All hell is breaking loose—you need to get over there pronto. We got ourselves some real trouble."

Faith drove slowly up the long paved road lined by rows of juniper and pine that led to the Last Trail ranch house. It loomed before her at last, a great winding two-story house, five thousand square feet of spaciousness and grace that had been in Zach's aunt's family for four generations.

As she parked the car in the front drive, her heart caught at the sight of the horses chasing each other in the corral, of the big dog that came thundering out to greet her, barking authoritatively and wagging his tail to beat the band.

She got out of the car and extended a hand for him to sniff, then stroked his head, surprised that Zach hadn't come out to greet her as well.

Perhaps he's still working, she thought as Batman nudged closer. *He's a busy man, after all. And you're not the center of his world, not anymore—if you ever were. He has a company to run, an office to build, and international obligations to meet. Not to mention a son who owns his heart.*

Maybe he'd forgotten she was even coming.

As Batman began to bound in happy circles around her, she straightened and gazed before her at the grand ranch house that looked every bit as magnificent as it had when she'd come here with Zach several times. The first time, she'd drunk a cup of after-dinner tea with Ardelle Harvey before Zach had pulled her away and shown her around the house. From the first, Faith had been fascinated by its lofty dimensions, bronze chandeliers, and charming antique furniture. From the painted mirror and pier table in the foyer to the fresh flowers gracing the carved oak dining room table, the Last Trail ranch house had been a stunning mix of antiques, Western art, and homey charm on a large scale.

Best of all, it boasted wide generous windows that opened in every direction to soaring vistas of wild Wyoming splendor.

Steeling herself, she started forward, long-buried memories swirling through her. That first evening, with its delicate breeze and the hint of thunder in the air, held some of her most beautiful—and painful—memories. She and Zach, ducking out onto the back porch, alone with the night and the summer lightning, the hum of crickets, and the beating of their own lovestruck hearts . . .

"Hey!" Dillon burst out the front door and across the porch, clutching a grape Popsicle. A red-haired boy with tiny freckles sprinkled all over his face raced after him. His Popsicle was yellow. Batman instantly wheeled and bounded toward them, his tail wagging madly.

"You're having dinner with us tonight," Dillon announced, skidding to a stop right in front of her.

Faith had to laugh as she looked at him, at both boys. They were sopping wet, hair dripping, shirts and pants stained with water marks.

The squirt guns on the ground near the corrals confirmed her guess. "Who won?" she asked, gazing from one to the other.

"I did!" both boys chimed in simultaneously.

She laughed again, strongly reminded of her brothers, Ty and Adam, during all the years they were growing up. Except for one thing. Dillon wasn't a Barclay. He was a McCallum through and through.

She'd never seen a picture of Zach as a young boy, but she knew he must have looked very much like Dillon— only Dillon looked so happy-go-lucky, so carefree, and she doubted Zach had ever felt that way.

Her heart twisted as she gazed at his son. Finally, she forced herself to look at his friend instead.

"And what's your name?"

"This is Brett," Dillon informed her before the other boy could speak.

"Brett Grayson," the red-haired kid piped up.

"He's staying for dinner too." Dillon took another lick of his dripping Popsicle. "Then we're sleeping at his house and leaving in the morning."

"Leaving for where?" Faith asked as she fell into step with them, headed toward the house.

"The Grand Canyon." This time it was Brett who explained, even as Faith remembered Zach mentioning the trip. "My parents are taking us for two whole weeks. My uncle's a ranger there," he said proudly. "We're going to camp out with him on the rim."

"And ride down all the way to the bottom on mules." Dillon took the porch steps two at a time. "How awesome is that?"

"Very awesome. Awesomely awesome." Faith smiled. She peered around the high-ceilinged foyer, almost exactly as she remembered it, half expecting to see Zach coming toward her down the stairs, but no one appeared—except a sleek marmalade cat that pranced down the carved oak staircase and whisked around the corner as if late for an important appointment. The only sound was that of drawers slamming and some ominous banging coming from the back of the house, probably the kitchen.

"Is your dad around?"

"He had to leave—he said there was something he had to take care of at work, but he'll be back for dinner—"

"Dillon McCallum, you're letting that Popsicle drip all over my nice clean floor!" Neely rushed into the hallway, her bushy iron-gray hair sticking out from behind her ears, her scowl as dark as the aged leather boots on her feet.

"You're that Barclay woman," she sniffed. She eyed Faith as if she'd just slithered out from a hole in the hard-packed earth beneath the porch.

"Yes, I'm waiting for—"

"I know who you're waiting for." Neely snorted. "He doesn't tell me until this very morning that you and Brett here are both coming to dinner. How do you like that? You'd think it would kill him to give me advance notice."

Startled, Faith found herself fumbling for words. "Well, I didn't mean to cause any extra work—"

"This is Neely," Dillon interrupted her, grinning. "She always complains. You *do*," he told the woman with a giggle. Brett was laughing too and slurping at his Popsicle to keep it from dripping on the floor.

"And she always has tons of food, even if it's only me and my dad, and sometimes Gabe. I end up having leftovers for lunch for *days* at a time." Dillon rolled his eyes.

"My mom does that too," Brett chimed in.

"Are we having fried chicken, Neely?" Dillon looked

hopefully at the stout housekeeper in her jeans and baggy yellow-and-blue flannel shirt, apparently unfazed by her frown. "That's my favorite and Brett's too."

"Is it now? Hmmph, I had no idea."

The boy only grinned wider.

"You'll have to wait and see." She glared at him. "March upstairs and get out of those wet clothes this instant, both of you. Brett, you put on some of Dillon's clothes until yours are dry. And wash your hands—they look sticky as a couple of cinnamon buns. No, no, first go in the kitchen and throw away those Popsicle sticks. I swear, you and those wild animals of yours will be the death of me."

"Wild animals?" Faith raised a brow at Dillon.

"They're not wild. They're just not tame . . . like people," he explained seriously. "I have one dog . . . that's Batman, you know him—one cat named Jelly, one kitten named Zena, and my rabbit, Tigger—he got loose in the house one time—*only* one time," he added quickly. "Plus my own horse, Rocket Boy. I had a hamster named Sonny, but he died. And I turned my frog loose yesterday, so it could be free."

"I'll tell your father to sell them all if you don't throw out those Popsicle sticks right now and change your clothes," Neely grumbled. "You'll get pneumonia and then he'll fire me for sure."

When the boys were gone, pounding up the stairs at last, and Jelly the cat had nudged open the screen door and slipped outside, Neely shrugged, addressing Faith.

"You can wait in the living room, I guess. Or Zach's study. Whichever you prefer. I have to go back to the kitchen and slave away some more."

"Why don't I help you?" Faith suggested.

"I don't need help." She scrutinized the slim young woman standing before her in cream-colored pants and a chocolate-colored sweater, rich curls tumbling loosely to her shoulders. This Faith Barclay was not only pretty, there was intelligence and warmth in her face. She couldn't have looked more different from that high-strung, flitty blond witch Zach had married.

Suddenly Neely shrugged again. "You want to help? How about peeling potatoes? I have to turn the chicken and season the soup and take out the pie—sometimes I think I need five hands, between Dillon pestering me and cooking all day and night, and all those animals running loose."

"Then by all means, I'd love to peel potatoes."

"You know how?" Neely narrowed her eyes. "Lots of girls these days, they don't know how to boil an egg, much less peel a potato or fry up a mess of chicken."

"I've been peeling potatoes for my mom since I was seven," Faith assured her. "And I've fried up more chickens than Colonel Sanders in his prime."

"Well, then." Neely sniffed, turning toward the kitchen. "What are you waiting for? Come along."

"Mr. McCallum, you seem to be up to your neck in trouble every which way you turn."

Deputy Rick Keene faced the CEO of TexCorp Oil, inspecting him like he was a laboratory rat under a microscope.

"That's one way of looking at it." Zach controlled the flicker of anger that licked through him. "But someone just faked a bomb threat to my company and shut down my construction site for the rest of the day, maybe two days. I expect you to find whoever is responsible."

"That's my job and I'll surely do it." Keene nodded, holding the other man's gaze. "Just like I'm going to find out who killed poor little Candy Merck. Interesting—there's not a whole heckuva lot of crime in Thunder Creek—but *you* happen to be involved in two of the most unusual kinds of crimes in small towns, and they both occurred during the very same week. Do you believe in coincidence, Mr. McCallum?"

"What's your point, Deputy?"

"Just thinking out loud." Keene offered a hard smile. "You got any enemies, Mr. McCallum?"

"Most powerful men have enemies. I don't know of any who would threaten my building and scare my workmen. But maybe someone's trying to disrupt the construction of my office."

"Why would someone do that?"

"Isn't it your job to find that out?" Zach retorted. He turned away, staring out at the construction site where moments ago a group of sheriff's deputies had blown up a black duffel bag found behind a pile of two-by-fours. No bomb had been discovered inside—only a couple of old local telephone books.

There had been a note pinned to the duffel bag. Someone had sliced up newspapers and magazines and used the printed letters to spell out a message.

It said: *Go home, McCallum. You've been warned.*

Now the site was empty of workers. Sheriff's deputies and a bomb-sniffing dog prowled the equipment and debris, searching for clues.

"I need some information from you to get me started." Keene was also looking over the site. He made a clicking sound with his teeth, and his pale green eyes held a glint of speculation. "There's bad blood between you and Fred Harrison, isn't there? Someone mentioned that a while back you assaulted and seriously injured his son."

Zach's jaw tensed. "Mr. Harrison blames me for his son's injuries," he said curtly. "But it was a long time ago. And Pete recovered. He lived another four years before dying in a small plane crash—on a business trip for his father."

"Yeah, I heard that. Can you think of anyone else here in Thunder Creek who might want to harm you or your business?"

"I can. Some people don't like my plans for leasing a back parcel of my land. You'd have to ask them if they'd stoop to bomb threats and intimidation to try to stop me."

"And these people would be?"

"You know damn well who they are," Zach said evenly, his gaze hard as he met the deputy's stare. "You signed the petition they started to pressure me to change my mind. Your name is number thirty-two out of ninety-seven."

Deputy Rick Keene scratched his head. "Are you accusing Mr. or Mrs. Wood Morgan of doing this?" he asked. "That's a pretty big accusation against one of the finest families in this town."

"Even fine families have black sheep, Keene. And they've made it clear they don't want me here any more than they want the camp I'm allowing to be built on my property. Seems they want to build on it themselves."

"Have they said this to you in so many words?"

"Yep. Wood Morgan offered to buy the land from me. He wants to expand his dude ranch—to build luxury condominiums in the foothills. I refused his offer. You take it from there."

"I know how to do my job," Keene said flatly. He spat

on the ground. "Can you think of anyone else? Employees you fired? Old girlfriends who might hold a grudge?"

Zach shook his head.

"You know, that reminds me." Keene looked him directly in the eyes. "Did you date Candy Merck?"

"No. And what does she have to do with this?"

"Not a thing. But right now hers is the other big case I'm working on. So as long as you're here, I just happen to have a few questions." The acting sheriff's smile was both cool and fleeting. "I heard that you were seen with her at the Tumbleweed Bar and Grill. Isn't it a fact that she was your date? And wasn't there an altercation that night involving Faith Barclay?"

"You seem to already know the answer to those questions."

It seemed obvious to Zach that he wasn't going to get much help finding out who was behind this bomb threat until Ty Barclay returned to his sheriffing duties. Rick Keene, no doubt seeking Wood Morgan's endorsement in the upcoming election for sheriff, wasn't about to turn the spotlight on Morgan or anyone connected with him. That would include Rusty Gallagher and Fred Harrison, who'd been first in line to sign Morgan's petition opposing the camp.

Talking to Keene and expecting him to question Wood Morgan himself was a waste of time.

Speaking of time . . .

Zach glanced at his watch. Damn, it was after seven. Faith had probably come and gone from the ranch. She'd no doubt left when he didn't show up by half past six. And his chance at dinner with the boys was blown too. Not to mention the fact that he still had to get Dillon and Brett back to the Grayson house for an early bedtime before their trip.

"Let me know what you find out," he told Keene abruptly, knowing full well he'd never hear that a suspect had been arrested. "When can my crew get back to work?"

"Tomorrow." A distant roar of thunder followed his words. Glancing up at the clouds rolling in, Keene started toward his Crown Victoria. "Or the next day," he said, smiling over his shoulder.

The sun was setting in a molten blaze of mauve and gold as Zach roared to a stop in the long driveway right behind Faith's SUV.

He was about to head into the house when he heard laughter and voices inside the barn. The door was open, and Faith's soft laugh sounded above his son's giggles.

He couldn't believe she was still here.

He stepped inside and saw them kneeling in the corner, playing with the cats. Jelly was chasing a string that Dillon dangled and zigzagged. Faith had the kitten cuddled against her shoulder, while Brett and Batman chased each other in circles.

Zach stood perfectly still, taking in the scene. He hadn't seen that expression of pure relaxed happiness on Faith's face since that long-ago summer. She was smiling warmly at his son, her eyes soft, approving, and his chest tightened.

Things could have been so different. If he hadn't gotten Alicia pregnant, if he hadn't had to fly back to Texas that night, Dillon might have been his and Faith's son. They might have spent the past ten years together, close and loving, a real family . . .

She looked up then and saw him.

Zach saw the laughter fade, saw the wall of mistrust swing back, lock into place.

Even the truth couldn't break down that wall, he thought, despair settling upon his shoulders.

It was too late. Ten years too late.

"Dad, Ms. Barclay taught Zena her name—watch! Zena! Zena, come here!"

As Faith set the kitten down on the floor, it peered over at Dillon inquisitively, made a tiny mewing sound, then took a swipe at the string in Dillon's hand.

"See how smart she is?" Dillon cried in delight.

"Mr. McCallum, can we bring Batman back to my house tonight?" Brett asked before Zach could answer. "I want him to meet China's puppies."

"Not tonight. You boys are leaving early tomorrow morning, remember? I bet your folks have their hands full without having to bring Batman home at the crack of dawn."

"Our foreman, Randy, can do it," Brett pleaded. "He's in charge of China and the puppies while we're gone—he could bring Batman home—"

"Another time, Brett." Zach smiled at the two boys. "Did everyone have dinner?"

"Yeah, fried chicken!" Dillon grinned.

"And french fries," Brett added happily.

"Not to mention corn on the cob—and watermelon." Faith rose. "Neely's an excellent cook."

"Did she bite your head off?" he asked in some amusement. "She takes a while to warm to people—I meant to be here to introduce you—"

"Don't worry, Dad, Neely *likes* Ms. Barclay," Dillon interrupted him, scooping Jelly up with a big smile on his face. "Ms. Barclay made the french fries!"

"Did she now?" Zach raised his brows as Faith actually laughed.

"One of my many talents," she murmured with a wry grin.

"Charming Neely must be one of them," he told her. "She doesn't let just anyone enter her kitchen, you know, much less touch the potato peeler."

"She didn't seem charmed to me." Faith remembered the way the woman had twisted her lips as Faith had first peeled a dozen red potatoes, then sliced them into finger-length wedges. "I've seen hanging judges with friendlier expressions."

"You should see her if she *doesn't* like someone," Zach assured her. "She'd have shoved you out of her kitchen so fast your eyes would cross."

"Neely's a big grouch." Dillon looked earnestly at Faith. "But she really liked you. I could tell."

Zach saw warmth in the smile Faith gave his boy, but also something else . . . a flicker of sadness. What was that all about?

"Okay, you young cowboys," he said aloud, more than ever determined to have some time alone with her, "let's get your gear loaded. We've got to hit the road."

As the boys scooped up the cats and left the barn, Zach watched Faith dust off some hay clinging to her jeans. She looked beautiful—far more alluring than any socialite or Texas debutante he'd ever seen. In her dark brown sweater and cream-colored pants, she looked sensuous and classy all at once and he fought the urge to drag her into an empty stall, kiss her breathless, and make love to her before the boys came back.

"Sorry I missed dinner," he told her instead. "Something came up at work."

"That's what Dillon told me. Trouble?"

She found herself wondering at the tension she saw in his eyes. Zach wasn't one to show emotion, and he'd hidden it while the boys were there, but she knew him well enough to recognize the shadow of worry now that they were alone. With his next words, she understood the cause.

"There was a bomb threat at the construction site of my new offices." As she drew in her breath, his face tightened.

"It was a hoax—this time. Probably someone trying to send me a message."

"What sort of message?"

"Don't build the camp," he said shortly.

She searched his eyes, and wasn't surprised at the grim resolve she saw in them. Zach would never back down from something he believed in.

"There's a petition being circulated in town," she told him, biting her lip.

"I've seen it."

He paced toward the stalls, reaching in to pat the horses that thrust their nuzzles toward him. "I never thought I'd say this, Faith, but I'll be happy when your brother gets back. I might not be Ty's favorite person, but he wouldn't let that interfere with doing his job. Deputy Keene isn't exactly a model of law enforcement professionalism."

"I got that impression." She went to the bench along the wall where saddles hung on hooks. "Does Ty give you a hard time—because of . . . *us*?"

"We ignore each other." Zach grinned, a dark swarthy grin that showed he wasn't the least bit intimidated by Faith's big brother. "I can't blame him for hating me. I treated you badly. If I had a sister and someone treated her the way I treated you . . ."

His voice trailed away as he saw the expression in her eyes. Was that the shimmer of tears? It was hard to tell in the dimness. She blinked quickly, and he thought he must have been mistaken.

"Don't," Faith said. "Don't talk about it. It's over, Zach, we can't go back."

It was the first real glimpse he'd ever had of her pain. It shook him. What he saw was an anguish deeper than he could have ever guessed. For that one flashing instant he saw what lay beneath the cool facade, the artless sarcasm, the careful distance.

"Faith—"

"What's the point, Zach?" Faith lashed out, thankful for the flare of temper. "Our lives have gone in completely different directions, and there's no going back—"

"Who says?" He clamped his hands on her shoulders and her eyes widened on his.

"I say," she bit out. "To . . . to think anything else would be ridiculous—"

"Stop thinking then." Zach's voice was rough. His eyes were hot, glittering shards. "Just tell me what you feel."

"I—"

He pulled her toward him so quickly the next words were forgotten. Then all words were silenced. And all thoughts. The kiss was hard, demanding. His mouth moved over hers, so warm and compelling that rational thought evaporated and all she knew was a heated desire that filled every inch of her.

She wanted to push him away, to run and not look back, but she found herself leaning into him, melting into the kiss as if it were the most natural thing in the world. As his arms tightly encircled her, she murmured sounds of pleasure, her blood racing, making her heart skip beat after beat.

His hands slid upward, tangling themselves in her hair, gliding through the loose curls as his mouth continued its burning assault on hers. He was playing dirty, she thought dimly, woozily. Kissing her in a dark, needy way that stole both her breath and her defenses.

He was too good at this. Much too good at this. And she couldn't think anymore, not at all. Which was exactly what he wanted.

She meant to push him away. She did. But instead she pulled him closer, her arms sliding around his neck, her mouth hot and hungry against his.

Was she insane?

Oh, God, yes.

His hands eased down her body, rubbing, enticing. They stroked over her hips, then dipped lower, past the waistband of her pants, until he cupped her curved bottom tight against him. Faith moaned with pleasure as his strong hands caressed her, aroused her as she hadn't been aroused in years, even when she was with Kevin. The barn and the hay and the horses blurred.

Her hands flew to his shirt, unbuttoning buttons, touching his warm skin, brushing across the crisp dark chest hair even as his mouth tore at hers.

She felt hot, dizzy, exhilarated, and terrified all at the same time. Her eyes were closed, her senses intensified, and raw need whistled through her as their kisses deepened and her body awakened and the tempeature in the barn soared as if the hay were on fire . . .

"Aw right!"

The childish voice split them apart in a flash. As one they both spun toward the door, where Dillon and Brett stood grinning.

"Does this mean you're going to get married?" Dillon asked eagerly, racing forward as his father and Faith Barclay stared at him, looking stunned and embarrassed.

"No." Zach took a deep breath, still feeling shaken from the kiss, and hoping to hell he didn't show it. "It doesn't mean anything of the sort." His voice was hoarse, dammit. He cleared his throat.

"How long have you two been there? Didn't I teach you not to sneak up on people?"

"We weren't sneaking, Mr. McCallum," Brett explained, unable to squelch his grin. "We've got Dillon's duffel and backpack, and we just came to tell you we were ready and—"

"I should let all of you get going," Faith interrupted breathlessly. She smoothed a trembling hand through her hair as sanity surged back. And with it, mortification.

"Come with us for the ride." Zach caught her hand as if sensing her instinct to run. His gaze was warm on hers. She knew she shouldn't . . .

"Yeah, come with us," Dillon repeated. His eyes shone with a hopefulness that split open her heart.

Brett added to the chorus. "Yeah, come on. You can see China's puppies!"

Zach squeezed her hand. Her slim fingers felt engulfed by his gentle encompassing grip. Uncharacteristic indecision held her silent and before she realized what was happening, all four of them piled into the pickup, along with Batman, his tail thumping wildly.

He crouched undetected upon a rise fifty feet away, shadowed by newly fallen darkness. A light thrumming rain began to fall as he watched them drive away.

The night-vision goggles he'd ordered online perfectly illuminated the scene in weird greenish detail. He noted their expressions, the laughter of the little boys, the tension in Faith Barclay's profile. The slight smile on Zach McCallum's face as he turned on the windshield wipers.

What a moment this was. His fingers and arms were tingling with excitement.

And a white-hot anticipation.

To think he'd never known about this before. About what it felt like to slaughter a human being. He'd never done anything like it before, and now he couldn't wait to do it again.

It was like a drug pumping through the blood, filling him with energy, with power. With joy.

Much better, he thought, the goggles following the pickup until it disappeared from sight, *than hunting stupid animals. And, incredibly, even better than sex.*

He'd never felt anything as erotic and sublime as that white-hot surge of dark lovely power that came with extinguishing a human life.

But ever since that night, when he'd driven the knife over and over into the blond whore's soft flesh and shredding bone, he could think of little else except doing it again.

He couldn't wait to take his knife to the assistant district attorney. He couldn't wait to watch the terror in Faith Barclay's eyes before the very first thrust.

But he would make himself wait. He would draw it out. Scare her some more. Keep her awake at night until she was exhausted and weak and dizzy with fear. She mustn't get off easy.

And then, when he'd practiced some more, savored some more, let her move and breathe and sweat in terror just a little longer, he would finish it. He'd stand over her and demand answers.

There were so many questions—they screamed every minute in his head.

But let them. She would tell him everything before she died.

And she'd never see it coming.

Soon, he thought, standing in the darkness so near to where she'd passed only a few moments ago. *Soon I'll show myself to you and you'll see what comes to whores like you.*

No mercy.

She gave none, did she? She was so sure she was right. So sure she'd get away with it. But she was all that stood between him and what he wanted more than anything in this world.

Damn her. Stupid, arrogant, condescending bitch. He would sing with joy as he cut her, cut her, cut her down.

Chapter 18

"HOW LONG WILL DILLON BE GONE?" TENTATIVELY, Faith broke the silence in the pickup as they neared the turnoff leading to the Last Trail ranch house.

Batman had settled down across the backseat on the drive home and was softly snoring. The only other sounds were the cacophony of crickets in the darkness and the occasional howl of a coyote from the hills.

"Two weeks." Zach avoided the raccoon crouched at the side of the road, and turned the pickup onto the tree-lined drive.

"I'm sure you'll miss him. You two seem very close."

"We are. And I will. But I'm glad he's leaving right now." He glanced at her. "I don't like what's going on in Thunder Creek these days. He's better off away from here until things settle down."

"You mean the bomb threat. And the petition against the camp."

"And Candy's murder." Zach's mouth looked hard as cement. "We have pretty good security at the ranch house, but until whoever killed Candy is caught, I'd rather have Dillon safely away."

"That's understandable."

He braked in the driveway and killed the lights as, in the backseat, Batman stirred and clambered to his feet. "It's time to finish that conversation we started earlier. Are you ready?"

"Just so long as the conversation is the only thing we finish," she retorted, stepping out of the car.

"I'll just follow your lead," Zach assured her, but there was a purely male glint in his eyes as he opened the door for Batman, a glint that had her setting her jaw.

She hadn't forgotten what had happened in the barn. And she wasn't about to let anything like that happen again.

"See that you do." She started toward the house, trying to appear confident, but her heart was thumping. "Let's make this fast. I need to give Susan a call and check on her and I have some work to do. Let's just stick to the point and settle whatever it is you think we need to settle with each other."

"Ten years' worth of questions, hurt, and doubt, Faith? Settled in a ten-minute conference, like a meeting in the judge's chambers? I don't think so." Zach brushed past her and held open the screen door, a hard gleam in his eyes. "You don't owe me a thing, Faith, not after the way I treated you—and the promises I broke. But you do owe it to yourself to hear the truth."

The truth. She had devoted her life to the law, to justice . . . and to the truth. There were times—like in Jimmy Clement's case—where the search for the truth had gone tragically awry. But not on purpose. She had sought it the best she could.

And with Zach, she had heard it, analyzed it, digested it. But never understood it.

"Fine. Let's get this over with." She marched ahead of

him as he turned off the beeping alarm, schooling her features to an expression of icy calm, while all the while her heart pounded with the need to stay in control. To keep her cool and her focus—and her mouth shut.

The Last Trail ranch house felt different with Dillon and Brett gone. It felt bigger, quieter, more elegant—and far more subdued.

The marmalade cat scooted along the hallway toward the kitchen, with the kitten following behind. Batman was still outside, and a peaceful silence gripped the high-ceilinged entry hall and all the rooms that branched from it on the main floor.

Neely appeared to be nowhere about.

"Can I get you a drink?" Zach asked as he led her into the living room.

"No. Nothing. Let's just do this."

He studied her as she took a seat on the graceful rose and blue upholstered sofa. A short while ago, with the boys and Batman around, she'd looked relaxed, she'd laughed, there'd been warmth in her eyes. Now she looked stiff and wary. A Tiffany lamp shone golden, burnishing her hair, streaking those lush, loose curls with glints of fire, but also revealing the dark shadows smudged beneath her eyes. It didn't take a genius to figure out she hadn't been sleeping well, not for a while.

"All right. We'll do this your way, Faith. No beating around the bush." He paced to the mantel, gazed a moment at the banked logs, then turned to face her.

"I never should have run off that night and gone back to Texas. I should have talked to you first. Explained."

"You were afraid," she said, her tone wooden. "You

didn't know if Pete Harrison was going to live or die. You . . . panicked."

"No." The forcefulness of his reply startled her. She stared at him, astonished by the anger tightening his face. "I didn't panic. Not about Pete. What I did that night had nothing to do with him. It was about you. And me. And Alicia."

Zach scraped a hand through his hair and took a step closer. "The night of the dance . . . when I was supposed to pick you up—Alicia called me from Texas. She was hysterical. She told me she was pregnant. And that she was going to kill herself."

Faith felt the blood draining from her face. There was so much pain in Zach's eyes she knew without a doubt he was telling her the truth.

"I was in shock," he said in a low tone. "We'd used protection, but it failed us. I'd told you Alicia and I had broken up three weeks before I came to Thunder Creek." His gaze held hers. "She'd known she was pregnant for nearly two months before she called me that night and told me. She'd wanted to end the pregnancy—she'd made two appointments under a false name with a clinic fifty miles from Buffalo Springs, but she couldn't go through with it either time. Thank God," he added, his face almost gray in the lamplight. "When I think of not having Dillon in my life . . ." He drew in a long breath.

Faith sat perfectly still, her blood cold . . . cold as Rocky Mountain snow.

"Alicia was terrified of her father finding out—either that she was pregnant or that she had an abortion. Deke Andrews indulged her, spoiled her, but he cracked the whip plenty." Zach went to the sofa, dropped down beside

Faith, forcing himself to continue, to get it all out, before he studied her reaction.

"He expected Alicia to play Daddy's good little girl in public, before his friends and business associates—an unmarried pregnancy would have sent him through the roof."

Faith felt like the ceiling was dropping down on her piece by piece. She didn't know what to say.

"I . . . heard the rumors." There had been plenty of them after Zach left town. Rumors and whispers and sidelong glances. She'd gone back home and left for college a week later, and the rumors had still been swirling. A few had gotten back to her in the months that followed. Some had said he ran off because he'd knocked up a girl in Texas and his father had forced him into a shotgun marriage. Some said he'd run off to escape assault charges and jail after putting Pete into a coma.

She'd only known that he'd abandoned her without a phone call or a letter or, as far as she was concerned, a thought.

And the past ten years hadn't shown her one damned thing different.

"What do you want me to say? That I understand?" She pushed herself off the sofa and walked away from him to the window, where creamy lace curtains were pulled back with gold satin ties, framing the night.

"I do understand," she said in a low tone. *Stay calm. Stay controlled.* "You did the honorable thing."

But not where Pete was concerned, a voice inside of her whispered, the same voice that prosecuted people who committed a crime and left the scene. The voice couldn't understand how someone could run off and leave a person they'd injured, whether it was deliberately or inadvertently.

"You don't owe me any explanations, Zach. Especially not now."

"That's a load of crap."

She heard heavy footsteps behind her, coming fast, and she turned to face him. His hands clamped down on both shoulders, gripping her tightly.

"I hated myself, Faith. I hated the mess I'd created, I hated my life. I hated everyone that night—my father, my aunt and uncle, Alicia, everyone. Except you."

"You could have fooled me." Unbidden, the words broke from her lips. "Do you call what you did *love*? Do you remember what we said to each other that very afternoon? On Snowflake Mountain? Do you?"

She was trembling beneath the grip of his hands. Her eyes glittered with all the pain and fury she'd kept rigidly in check for ten years.

"I remember every word, Faith." His hands suddenly cupped her face. "I told you I loved you—that I always would. That we would be together, that you were the only girl I'd ever marry—"

"That lasted a long time, didn't it? What was it, four, five hours?" The bitter, sarcastic words exploded from her. She pushed at his chest, knocked his hands aside.

"Don't touch me, Zach. Don't you ever dare touch me again. If you had called me—just once—and told me what happened, about Alicia, about Pete . . . if you'd thought about me for even one second after you got that phone call from Alicia—"

"I did. Damn it, I did. I thought about you, about how I'd dragged you into the mess of my life. I knew my going back to Alicia was going to hurt you. But I figured I deserved for you to hate me, and that it would be better for you if you damn well *did*. It'd make it easier to forget about me and go on with your life."

Bitterness thickened his voice and in his eyes she saw the flash of anger and long-ago desperation.

"I knew, Faith, I knew that night—I was never coming back. I was marrying someone else, a girl who'd never meant more than a beer and a laugh to me, a girl who had told me flat out that she had a bottle of sleeping pills under her pillow, enough pills to kill a horse, and if I didn't get back there, she was going to swallow them all, kill herself and our baby. Did you need *that*? Did you need to be dragged into all that crap I faced when I left Thunder Creek, crap I created and had to drown in, and that had nothing to do with you?"

"Nothing to do with me?" Hard, almost hysterical laughter bubbled up. "How dare you? I loved you, Zach. I wanted to spend my *life* with you. And you swore the same thing. Then you locked me out without a word. You could have explained, you could have said good-bye. Maybe there would have been a way to work it all out, together— a way for us to have a future—"

"That was never going to happen. Deke Andrews would have made sure I married Alicia even if I'd wanted to balk—which I never would have done. And my own father would have shot me if I'd tried. There was no room for you in that situation, Faith. I wanted you to hate me as much as I hated myself. I wanted for you to never look back—"

She slapped him. The loud crack of her hand across his face echoed through the room.

"I've done nothing but look back," she whispered in agony. "It was *never* finished, Zach. I told myself a million times it was a teenage crush, first love, it would never have lasted anyway. But I couldn't stop thinking about you.

Wanting you. I had other boyfriends. I was even engaged." Her voice broke. "But I never felt again the way I felt about you—"

"And now?" He cut her off, his gaze burning into hers. "How do you feel now?" He caught her to him, his arms tight around her. "God, Faith, tell me there's a chance— any kind of chance—"

"Why? So you can marry me to make your son happy?"

For a moment, Zach was stunned. Then his face tightened and he released her so abruptly she nearly stumbled.

"Maybe you're right, Faith. I guess it is too late for us."

"That's what I've been trying to tell you." But her stomach was dropping. Oh, God, that last remark . . . talk about a low blow. It was as bad as when she'd accused him of trying to manipulate the town with his donation. Both of them no doubt more painful than when she'd slapped him. What was wrong with her? She'd turned into a bitch. She wasn't sure whom she hated more . . . herself or Zach.

"It's no use," she whispered, turning away. "This is all . . . pointless. I have to go." The tears fell. She brushed at them with the back of her hand, reached for her purse on the coffee table. Grief wracked her heart and the tears fell faster. Zach intercepted her as she moved toward the door. He stopped her, took her hand, enclosed it gently within his.

"Why are you crying, Faith?"

"Because I . . . hurt you. Because it's . . . too late."

Zach felt like he'd just been spit out of the eye of a hurricane. Hope like a patch of blue sky after darkness filled his vision. "If that's how you feel, maybe it isn't," he said softly. "I have an idea."

"What? You hit me back and then we're even?"

"No. Hit me again. Let it all out," he suggested. There

was a faint smile at the corners of his lips, but his tone was serious.

"Don't be ridiculous." She sniffed and, with her free hand, swiped at the tears on her cheeks. Outside, the silence of the night cracked with a slow roll of thunder.

"I mean it. I have it coming," he said. "Come on." He lifted her hand, touched it to his stubbled jaw. "Right here, Barclay. One big one."

He released her fingers then. And waited, watching her beautiful, expressive face.

"Zach . . . I'm going."

"You're passing up your chance?"

"Fool that I am." A ghost of a smile flickered in her eyes as she started to move around him.

But Zach seized her again and drew her gently into his arms. "I'm not a fool. And I'm not passing up my chance."

He pulled her closer. His hand swept through her hair, touching those wild toffee curls, sliding down to caress the feminine curve of her jaw. He saw her eyes widen, soften, saw the alarm in the center of them, felt the quiver run through her. It wasn't fear or distaste he saw in her face, satisfaction pumping through him. It was yearning. Desire. Her mouth trembled and he felt her body quiver against his.

"Your housekeeper could walk in any second, Zach. Let me go."

"I gave Neely the night off. And the next few days as well. She's leaving at six in the morning to vist her sister in Santa Fe."

Faith's heart beat faster. Realization struck. "You planned this . . . you *lured* me here—"

"You wanted to come. The way you kissed me today—"

"*You* kissed *me*."

"I believe it's time we settled that once and for all."

He didn't wait for permission. Or for protest. His mouth captured hers in a kiss that blew the lid off her calm, her focus, her self-protective instincts.

Faith wanted to push him away, but instead she clung to his shoulders, feeling her insides dissolving, her knees turning to oatmeal. Kevin had never kissed her like this. Like he couldn't get enough of her, like she was air, light, sun.

Zach kissed her like she was life itself, and he tasted like fire and spice, musk and wine.

The past faded away. So did the future. There was only now . . . now as his tongue slid along hers, now as his hands dipped inside the V of her sweater, now as they slipped beneath the lace of her bra. She made a sound of pleasure, a plea for mercy, a murmur for more, even as she raised herself on tiptoe, drew his head down to her and took the kiss deeper, drawing him into her, craving him, all of him, with an intensity that had her tearing at the buttons on his shirt, squirming eagerly beneath his caressing hands.

She grabbed at his unbuttoned shirt, dragged him with her to the sofa, and, ignoring his chuckle, pushed him down beneath her on the cushions.

"That's right, have your way with me," he groaned against her lips as she straddled him, her mouth never leaving his.

"Be careful what you wish for, Zach," Faith half gasped, half laughed as she struggled with his shirt and managed with his help to drag it off his broad shoulders and down those heavily muscled arms.

Her lips caught at his and sank against his warm mouth, unexpectedly soft for such a tough man. Her body sank against his too. She couldn't get enough of him. Kissing him, touching him, was so familiar, so wonderful, and yet it was all new, different from what she remembered. If anything, the pleasure was hotter, sweeter, than before. Though Zach's teenage technique had never lacked for firepower, he was a man now and knew just how to touch her, just how to kiss her to make the pit of her stomach melt like butter on a griddle.

He dragged her sweater over her head and nuzzled at her breasts even as his fingers unlatched her bra. It landed somewhere on the floor, but Faith didn't give a damn where because her breasts were on fire and Zach's mouth was lighting the flames. She moaned, throwing her head back as he licked and sucked at her nipples. They had hardened into rigid aching peaks so sensitive to his touch she had to bite back a scream of pleasure.

Squirming, groping, they twisted together on the sofa, stripping each other of all their clothes, of every barrier between them. Zach flipped her over, bracing himself on either side of her with his forearms, gazing down into her face, sheened with desire.

"Zach," she whispered, and there was no playfulness in her eyes or her tone anymore. Now she was gazing at him with need. Raw, naked need.

He recognized it instantly in those glorious dream-blue eyes, in the restless movements of her hot body beneath him, because he felt it too. Oh, God, did he. He'd never wanted anyone so much.

"Come inside me, Zach." Faith pulled his head down to her, her fingers locking around his neck. "Now. Please."

"Not just yet, baby." He smiled gently, but the sensuous shimmer in her eyes and the feel of her soft, sleek body beneath him was making him wild. Tension pulsed through him and he fought to retain control. Tracing his tongue around the soft edges of her mouth, he slid his hand down-ward, across her belly, and then between her thighs. Her body clenched and her breathing quickened as he began to stroke the silky curls. She was slick, hot, and very ready, and he groaned against her lips.

"I've dreamed about this, Faith. So many times. I've wanted you. Only you." Fire burned in those wolf-gray eyes. He pushed her thighs apart. "Always you."

Her heart cracked into a thousand shimmering pieces. He kissed her eyelids, her cheeks. Her mouth. She pulled him down to her, holding him as if she was afraid he would disappear in a puff of mist, wanting him close, closer as hot sensuous pleasure drowned her and he slowly licked her ear as he pushed himself inside her.

Gasping, she opened herself to him, her nails digging into his back. She bucked beneath him, wild and desperate as the wind tore at the windows and Zach made love to her with his body and his mouth and his eyes, taking her to a place of lightning and thunder and kisses soft as rain.

When the explosion came and rocked them both to their core, Faith felt shudder after shudder. Tears sprang to her eyes at the moment of release, and when their breathing began to slow she kissed his neck, buried her face against his shoulder, and tried to lock him inside her.

"Don't leave me," she heard herself murmur as if from a great distance.

Her arms were still tight around his neck. "Stay."

He did, kissing her throat, stroking her face. After a while he groaned and laughed, shifting just enough so that she lay beside him, cradled in his arms, their bodies touch-ing everywhere, her hair soft as silk beneath his cheek.

They lay like that for a while in the silent house, until at last Zach stirred and pushed himself off the sofa. He stood naked and comfortable and magnificent beside her.

"Come on, Sleeping Beauty."

"Where?" she murmured, her eyes soft as blue clouds in the lamplight. At that moment she was so easy she knew she'd follow him if he leaped off Cougar Mountain.

Zach saw that the wariness was gone, and his desire spiked again.

"Someplace where we can be more comfortable," he promised her.

As she tilted her head questioningly, he gave her the slow grin that had made her fall in love with him and scooped her up in his arms.

"Where do you think, Barclay? I'm taking you to bed."

Sometime after 2 A.M. they both came up for air.

The sheets and blankets on the king-size bed were twisted and scattered across the floor, and the black-and-white geometric down quilt half covered their sweat-sheened bodies.

"I think we've *almost* made up for lost time," Faith muttered exhaustedly against Zach's shoulder. She was limp and breathless, and knew she'd probably be sore tomorrow, but a peaceful kind of euphoria filled her.

"I feel like I'm nineteen again," she confessed, pressing a kiss to his chest.

"I feel like I'm alive again." Zach stroked her back. "Like I've been asleep ever since that day when I left here, running through a black tunnel that led nowhere like some idiot kid."

"Which you were," she reminded him. "A kid, not an idiot. Zach, I should go home."

"No way, baby." He leaned over her, gently pinning her to the bed. "You're staying put. We're having a sleepover, as Dillon would say."

"Um, we're not getting much sleep," she pointed out.

"Yeah, well, who needs sleep?"

Faith smiled as he kissed her, and her hands smoothed his tousled hair. She ran her finger along the dark stubble on his jaw and felt wonder fill her, and joy—and a nagging doubt.

"You didn't seduce me just so I wouldn't go back to the cabin alone, did you?"

"That was just one of my many complex motivations. Got a problem with it?"

"As a matter of fact, I do. On general principles."

He laughed. "Doesn't surprise me, Faith. Go ahead, I know you'll do it anyway. Explain."

"I'm a smart, very capable woman and I can take care of myself. I strongly resent the notion that I need to stay here with you to be safe. I have a gun, a security system, a phone, a car . . ."

"I have all that here too."

"But this is your home and I don't need your protection—or Roy's," she said quickly before he could interject. "Or anyone's—"

"What if Bayman is out there—watching you, planning to come after you? What if he knows by now where you're staying and that you're alone? It's going to be a lot harder for him to get to you here," Zach said. "Once you move in, he won't necessarily know where to look for you—not to mention the fact that there's people around this place all the time—"

"Move *in*?" she interrupted, staring at him as if he'd lost his mind.

"Batman can guard you when I'm not around—"

"And what about your son—Dillon? Remember him?"

"Won't be back for two weeks. Maybe Bayman—or whoever killed Candy—will be caught by then."

"Zach." She leaned forward, touched her mouth to his. "You're . . . moving kind of fast, aren't you?" She pushed herself to a sitting position and sat up. Zach shifted, lounging beside her, unable to keep his gaze from the sexy bounce of her breasts as she sat up or from the sensuous tumble of her hair past her shoulders. Her slim body looked creamy white and delicate in the big, masculine master bedroom with its black plantation shutters, square gray rug over hardwood floors, and the oak furniture that had been in the family for generations. He usually paid little attention to the room, but with Faith here, it seemed brighter, more in focus and more cozy, a handsome comfortable backdrop for her sensuous, effortless femininity.

"I'm not moving fast at all. It's been ten years since we last made love. You don't get much slower than that."

"True." Her lips quirked. "But making love is one thing . . . moving in with you just because Candy Merck was murdered is quite another."

"She was murdered on your property. Within steps of your front door." All of the teasing and amusement was gone from his tone. Zach's eyes were thunderstorm dark now, as serious as she'd ever seen them.

"There's a connection there, Faith. Add it to those phone calls you've been getting, and Bayman's history of violence and instability. You have something he wants. He's disappeared from view. I can't prove that he's here, that he killed Candy for some reason known only to him, but I feel it. And so do you."

She bit her lip. The evidence wasn't in, but it *was* a theory. A solid one. And in her gut . . .

She remembered the creepy feeling in town that someone was watching her, a sense of unseen evil . . .

"All right." She raked a hand through her hair. "You win. I'll stay tonight. Maybe for a few days. Let's see where Keene's investigation goes."

"I knew you had a brain beneath all that beauty."

She laughed and tossed a pillow at him.

He caught it and threw it back.

Before she could escape, he dove at her and pinned her beneath him once more.

"Make love, not war?" Faith gasped, pretending to struggle, but actually wrapping her legs snugly around his.

"Now you're talking, baby."

Faith closed her eyes as he kissed her long and languidly. She drank in the kisses and stroked his muscled back, opening herself to him and taking him deep inside her once again.

Chapter 19

"THERE'S SOMETHING ELSE WE NEED TO TALK about." Zach poured a skillet full of scrambled eggs onto a large blue platter and set it down on the kitchen table beside a basket of toast. "The auction."

"Don't tell me you're making another donation." Faith smiled at him, knowing she was enjoying the morning together far too much, but unable to help herself. She couldn't keep from gazing at him, all six foot two of shirtless, magnificent male, wearing only jeans and boots and shower-damp, mussed-up hair. He looked so *good,* so lean and warm and sexy, that she wanted to leap out of her chair and kiss him—to slide her hands down that sun-browned muscular chest and taste the lips that had teased and tormented her so ruthlessly last night.

But she didn't move. Last night was . . . last night. Now opal sunlight spilled across the enormous ranch house kitchen and the smell of fresh-brewed coffee filled the air.

And things felt different. Zach had been downstairs already when she woke up alone in his bed just after seven o'clock. She'd taken a quick shower and borrowed a toothbrush, then found her scattered clothes from last night draped across the leather recliner in the corner of his bedroom.

When she'd pulled them on quickly and come into the kitchen, he'd seemed preoccupied and hadn't done more than give her a quick single kiss.

She needed to be careful, to go slow, she reminded herself as she poured coffee for both of them and set the carafe down beside a plate of bacon. In the clear light of day she needed to become once more the sane, careful woman who lived inside her, the one who remembered how to stay in control.

"Nope," he said, sitting down opposite her and taking a sip of the steaming coffee. "One donation and that's it. Any other guesses, Faith?"

"Why don't you just spit it out?" She allowed a tiny smile. "I'm all ears."

"Good. Because I wanted to ask you if you'd be my date."

Her heart lifted. Okay, so maybe things *weren't* so different from last night. But then she remembered the last time he'd invited her to a dance in Thunder Creek and her chest tightened.

He must have read the thoughts dashing across her mind, because he spoke again, quickly, his eyes purposeful in the morning light.

"This time I'll show up."

Her first instinct was to smile, to reach across the table, touch his hand. But she managed not to move. *Go slow,* she lectured herself, as the question hung in the air between them. *Keep it light. It's bad enough you got carried away last night and made love to him until neither of you could see straight. Who knows what Zach really wants? Or where this is headed? Be careful.*

"All right." She spoke calmly. Calmly but pleasantly, she thought. No wearing of her heart on her sleeve, not this time. "I guess we have a date."

He didn't look pleased with her answer. He studied her, his eyes thoughtful. "Okay. Well . . . great."

"I have one question," she blurted as a thought struck her. "Are you asking me to the dance as my bodyguard . . . or as my . . . whatever we are," she finished awkwardly.

"I guess that's something you're going to have to figure out for yourself." He stood up abruptly. "I've got some business calls to return and I need to get in touch with Keene and find out if my crew can get back on site today. Let me know when you're ready to go back to the cabin. I'll drive you over."

"I don't need—" she began, but then saw the stubborn set to his mouth and decided she'd already annoyed him enough this morning.

She stabbed a forkful of eggs and shrugged. "I'll be ready whenever you are."

Zach scowled. Was this how it was always going to be between them? One minute she'd be tearing his clothes off, driving him crazy with sizzling kisses, and the next instant she'd turn cold as a glacier again? Would he have to keep winning her over, figuring her out, day after day?

The sounds of a truck roaring into the drive interrupted his thoughts. When he went to the kitchen window, his eyes narrowed.

"Company."

Faith was already hurrying up behind him, in time to see Wood Morgan clamber out of a shiny red Dodge truck. An instant later Rusty Gallagher emerged from the passenger seat, dressed in pressed jeans and a pinstriped shirt and carrying a briefcase.

"What the hell do they want?" she muttered, knowing it wasn't anything good.

Zach had already reached the back door. "Stay inside.

They don't need to know you're here," he said in a low tone. "This might get ugly and there's no reason for you to be involved—"

"Give it up, McCallum," she muttered, and walked past him out the door.

She paused outside, halfway across the wraparound porch, as Zach walked out behind her and strode down the steps to greet his guests.

Faith watched her presence register on Wood's face and on Rusty's. It was not yet eight o'clock. Most likely half the town would be buzzing within an hour that she'd spent the night with Zach McCallum.

But at the moment she didn't care. From the set expressions on the men's faces, she knew what was coming. Strong-arm tactics. Well, Zach wasn't going to have to face that all alone.

Besides, she thought, *Wood Morgan wouldn't dare get too ugly—not if he knows there's a witness present.*

"What are you doing here, Faith?" Wood stopped short a few feet from Zach, staring at her on the porch. "Or shouldn't I ask?" he smirked, then sobered quickly as Zach took a step toward him. "I hope you've been trying to talk sense into McCallum."

"What you're doing here is more to the point, Wood. What do you want?" she retorted.

"Hiding behind women now, eh, McCallum?" Rusty's mouth curled into a sneer. Beside him, Wood Morgan gave a short laugh.

Faith saw that the attorney's hands were clenched into fists, even the one holding the briefcase. He'd probably love nothing more than a chance to repay Zach for what had happened in the Tumbleweed, but she planned to make sure it didn't come to that.

"Wood, you can come inside and say whatever you have to say. I'll give you five minutes." Zach's tone was hard as baked clay. "But your hired thug doesn't set foot in my house."

"Rusty's not a thug—he's my lawyer," Wood retorted. "And he has something for you."

"Yeah, and what's that?" Zach's hard gaze shifted to Gallagher. Looking at him, Faith shivered. Zach's eyes were arctic—and dangerous. She wouldn't have wanted to be in Rusty's boots right now. He, however, didn't appear to be intimidated.

He snapped open the briefcase, yanked out a sheaf of papers, and thrust them at Zach. "Petition. Signed by one hundred forty-two residents of Thunder Creek and environs. All those opposing the construction of a charity camp on the land in question."

Rusty's lip curled as he stared warningly at Zach. "Lots of folks feel pretty strongly about this. It wouldn't be a good idea to ignore it."

Zach glanced indifferently at the petition. "The land in question just happens to be my land. I can do whatever the hell I want with it. Your petition isn't worth the paper it's printed on."

"So if that's all, gentlemen, you can be on your way now," Faith said crisply.

"You should be wearing a skirt . . . easier for him to hide behind," Rusty taunted.

Wood guffawed. "Faith, honey, I don't have a problem with you. Hell, I've known you since you were a pigtailed brat who wanted to do everything your brothers did. And you know I have great respect for all the Barclays, especially Ty. He's a helluva sheriff and when the time comes for him to run for reelection, I want to support him. I surely hope I'll be able to do that."

"Are you implying you won't if I represent Zach?"

Wood shrugged. "I'd have to reassess things. Including my opinion of all the Barclays. I want a sheriff who will actively support the citizens and best interests of Thunder Creek."

Fury surged through her. "Go to hell. What I do or don't do has nothing to do with how my brother does his job."

"All the Barclays stick together," Wood countered. "If you don't care about what happens to Thunder Creek, Ty probably doesn't either."

"Leave it to you to come up with that load of crap." Faith came down the porch steps fast. "Well, take it from me, my principles are not for sale and neither are my brother's."

"What's wrong with you, Faith? Why do you care what happens to this guy?" Rusty intervened. He moved in closer and snagged her wrist. "You hustling for him now? Are you his attorney? Or . . ."

Gallagher flicked a glance over her damp curling hair and wrinkled sweater, scorn flashing in his eyes. "Or maybe you're just his slut?"

Zach hit him. The thwack of his fist connecting with bone and flesh resounded in the chilly morning air as Rusty fell backward and hit the ground.

"Now you've done it, McCallum." Wood glared at him. "That's assault."

"Guess what, pal—you're next." Zach advanced on Wood. The other man instinctively took a step backward, then another.

Wood Morgan had played football at Thunder Creek High back when he met Tammie, and he'd won his share of fistfights since kindergarten, but something fierce and hard in Zach's face made him give ground.

"If you know what's good for you, you'll get the hell off my property. Now."

"Get out of here, Wood," Faith said quickly. "And take this cur along with you."

"You've gone too far, McCallum." Wood summoned his courage. "There's clearly a pattern of violence and instability here. If we bring you up on charges, things won't go your way. Think of your son—"

Zach grabbed Wood by the shirt. A muscle twitched in his jaw, but his voice was coldly controlled. "You stay the hell away from my son."

"He'll hear things. He'll get hurt . . . you don't want that—"

Zach's eyes darkened, but before he could hit the other man, Faith jumped in. "Don't, Zach. Don't do it. He's not worth it."

For a moment there was a horrible silence, then Zach shoved Wood away. On the ground, Rusty had managed to pull himself to his knees. Blood oozed from his lip.

Wood grimaced, compelled to try one more time. "Things don't have to be like this, McCallum. If you sell that land to me, we can get along just fine. One hand washes the other, you know?"

"Why are you still here?" Zach growled.

"I just want you to read that petition. See all the names of the people who oppose you. There are some important people there. Think about it—"

Zach picked up the petition from where it had fallen to the ground. "Here's what I think of your petition, Morgan."

He ripped the papers in half and let the pieces flutter to the grass. "This meeting is over."

Rusty Gallagher struggled to his feet. He looked like he

was about to try to launch himself at Zach, but Wood grabbed his arm.

"Enough. Let's get out of here. There's no reasoning with some people."

"I want him arrested. He assaulted me!"

Wood's lip curled. "Around here, Gallagher, we don't arrest someone for punching us out. We fight back. Besides, you had it coming," he muttered, with a glance at Faith. He started dragging the lawyer back toward the truck.

"But don't think this is over, McCallum," he called out. "We've got copies of the petition. People are talking. And they're angry."

Zach ignored him. He looked at Faith. "You didn't have to do that."

She went to him, touched his hand, the right one he'd used to hit Rusty. "Neither did you," she said quietly.

In the truck, Rusty glowered, staring straight ahead as Wood headed back toward town.

"We need to increase the pressure on McCallum," he grated. "He's too damned stubborn for his own good. Next time, instead of just a goddamned warning, we have to make good on the threat, do a little damage at his precious construction site. Show him we mean business."

"I don't want to hear about it," Wood said quickly. He cast a glance at the other man, who was gingerly touching his bloodied lip.

"Just remember, I don't want anyone getting hurt."

"No problem."

Wood's stomach churned. Acid reflux, he thought. It had been keeping him up nights for weeks. Maybe that's why his hands were so taut on the steering wheel, why his chest felt like a giant rock was wedged inside it.

Or maybe it was just because he had a plain uneasy feeling about the way this whole McCallum thing was going.

It didn't help that he was beginning to dislike Gallagher almost as much as he disliked Zach McCallum. The man might be a shrewd lawyer, but he was full of bluster and he drank too much. Besides that, he'd mainly gone after Zach this morning by baiting Faith. That didn't sit well with Wood.

And who knew what Gallagher would do under pressure? Wood wondered, thinking of Tammie and the kids, wondering how they'd feel if Gallagher bungled things and he ended up in jail. It could happen, if Ty Barclay came back and started really probing into the bomb threat at TexCorp's construction site. What if Gallagher had left some loose ends and got nailed—he'd babble like a magpie to save his own hide.

And there was also the fact that someone might have overheard that night when Gallagher had first broached the subject of something "happening" at the TexCorp site, something that would not only delay construction but get McCallum's attention. Jesus, the man had been a little too cocky, talking about it right in the office, especially since a few of the tech guys had been working late down the hall and even Tammie had been reviewing the books in the accountant's office. If anyone had heard *anything* . . .

Wood felt sweat soak his armpits as he realized all the ways this whole thing could go south.

"Don't forget, Rusty, under no circumstances are you or anyone who works for Morgan Enterprises to do anything illegal," Wood said, his tone firm. "We're working through legal channels to do what's best for Thunder Creek."

"Of course." Rusty smiled sourly, wincing as his cut lip

cracked. He knew a legal cover when he heard one. Wood Morgan was smart—he wanted to be able to testify to the fact that he'd had no knowledge of any bombs or bomb threats against McCallum's new headquarters, that he would never have approved such a thing.

Two could play that game. "I always abide by the strictest ethics, Wood. As an attorney, I'm sworn to uphold the law and even if I wasn't, I'd do it anyway."

"Just so we understand each other." Wood made the turnoff leading into town. "And one more thing that needs to be done today. I really admire the way Rick Keene is handling things while Sheriff Barclay is away. He's extremely fit to be our new sheriff. Make another ten-thousand-dollar donation to his election campaign. And be sure to let him know personally how much we appreciate all his hard work and that we'll do everything we can to help him get elected."

Gallagher nodded. "Consider it done. I'll take care of it as soon as I get back to the office."

Wood felt a little better. He'd treaded on thin ice before. You had to if you wanted to win. You had to do whatever it took, try a little harder than everyone else.

But he wasn't about to fall through any cracks. He hadn't come all this way, achieved his postion as a community leader and prime mover and shaker, just to see himself go under.

What Gallagher proceeded to do from here on out was up to him. *Whatever happens,* Wood thought, *my conscience will be clear.*

Chapter 20

FAITH STARED IN AWE AT THE THREE GORGEOUS cocktail dresses arrayed like shimmering jewels across Roy and Corinne's king-size bed.

"Corinne, they're all beautiful. Are you sure you don't mind?"

"Mind?" Roy's wife burst out laughing as she sat down on the upholstered bench at the foot of her bed. "I can only wear one dress at a time, you know. And it had better be this one."

She ran a hand along the stretchy silk fabric of a delicately sequined wine-colored cocktail dress. "I'm not really showing yet, but I've already gained seven pounds. I think I'd have a hard time pulling off those skintight numbers. Now you, on the other hand . . ." Corinne grinned at Faith.

"You'll look fabulous in either one. And I know Josy would be thrilled for you to wear one of her creations."

Faith knew she was right. Ty's wife was loving, warm, and generous, and the moment she'd heard about Faith and Kevin's engagement, she'd offered to design Faith's wedding gown.

That idea had died the moment Faith called off her

engagement, but now the opportunity to wear one of Josy's gowns was right in front of her. Before she and Ty had left town, Josy had brought some samples to Corinne so she could choose which one she'd wear to the dinner dance and auction.

Which was damned lucky for me, Faith thought, since she hadn't brought anything dressier to Thunder Creek than one knee-length black skirt and a few silk sweaters. She might have pulled it off, except she discovered this morning that the skirt had a wine stain on it that she'd forgotten all about.

And the dance was tonight . . .

In fact, Zach would be picking her up in just a few hours. She still had to run by the Crystal Horseshoe Dude Ranch and make sure all of the last-minute auction items were properly tagged and displayed before going home to shower and dress.

Thankfully, Patti was taking care of picking up the programs from the printer. She'd been feeling under the weather since yesterday with a sore throat and a low-grade fever, but had insisted she'd be fine by today and would have no trouble getting the programs. So Faith figured she should have just enough time to pull herself together before Zach arrived.

All of the committee members had agreed to arrive at the dude ranch two hours early to help set up flowers, place cards, and decorations and to deal with any on-the-spot situations. So she only had a few hours to spare.

No time to dillydally over dresses. But still . . . the choice between the lacy blue sheath and the amber silk was difficult. Both were lovely.

"This one," she told Corinne suddenly, lifting the strapless amber gown from the bed. The bodice glistened with hand-sewn sequins and the color was rich and vibrant. It would be great with her hair and eyes.

The flow, color, cut of this dress were at once sexy and elegant. That was the problem. "I love it, but . . . Corinne, it's not really me. If you only knew—I wear charcoal pin-stripes or button-down black every day. All the time. Black suits, black jackets, black heels. This is so . . ."

"Feminine? Fun? Drop-dead sexy?" Corinnne burst out laughing. "You're not an assistant DA tonight, honey. You're not even a lawyer. You're a gorgeous woman attending a glamorous charity event with one of the hottest men to walk the earth. Go for it."

Go for it. Why not? Faith couldn't help wondering about the expression on Zach's face when he saw her in something this seductive. Her lips curved. "Can I wear it with black heels?"

Corinne winked at her. "The higher the better."

An hour and a half later she was back at the cabin as the afternoon sun drifted across the calm blue western sky. All had been in perfect order in the main lobby and dining hall of the dude ranch, and the auction items were handsomely displayed. Everything looked ready to go.

She'd felt a twinge of satisfaction when she surveyed the array of donated items. With any luck, a great deal of money would be raised for the new wing of the hospital tonight.

But as she lifted the gown from the SUV, a shiver tingled down her spine. She glanced quickly around, not even knowing why.

She hadn't heard anything. Or seen anything. She just had an uneasy feeling, like that time in town . . .

It's only because it's so lonely out here, she thought

impatiently. *And because you haven't been back to the cabin much.*

She'd only come by intermittently during the past days, long enough to fetch fresh clothes, clean up, check on the place. She hated that whoever had killed Candy had managed to make her anxious about staying at this cabin, a home away from home that she'd loved all of her life.

But he had. Her neck muscles clenched as she scanned the area—the trees that ran behind the cabin, the slope winding down toward the ravine, the place where she'd tripped over Candy's body. The yellow police tape was down, but the spot was engraved in her memory forever.

And she couldn't shake the feeling that someone was watching her. Her heartbeat quickened as she studied the area yet again, every sense alert. There was no sound except for the rustle of the wind, the song of a meadowlark.

No one was in sight, and nothing looked unusual.

But she found herself hurrying toward the door. Even when she entered, though, and locked the door behind her, the feeling persisted. She hung the dress in the closet and then found herself returning to the window, gazing out all across the mesa, her heart racing.

She saw nothing, no one, except the wide blue sky, the sweep of rock and scrub grass, the lavender blue sagebrush sloping down the hills. A lone hawk swooped toward the mountains, effortless in the clean, crystal air.

But her sense of foreboding lingered. Strange—since she'd been sleeping with Zach, her nightmares had faded away, but now during her waking hours, especially when she was alone, uneasiness pricked at her.

She bit her lip and tried to shake her apprehension.

Time to get in the shower. It was getting late. She had to

find some jewelry that would look right with the dress, and do something with her hair . . .

Faith forced herself to leave the window, to stop feeling afraid. Since when did she believe in premonitions?

Yet she took a moment to give the cabin a good once-over—even looking in closets, in the tub, and under the bed before she turned on the water in the glass-enclosed shower and stripped off her clothes. Then she locked the door.

She let the tension and unease run off her in rivulets as the water struck her with tingling force. The scent of milk-and-honey shampoo and body wash clung to her damp skin as she dried off and wrapped a fluffy towel turban-style around her hair.

She had an hour to turn herself into a dinner-dance diva.

Good luck with that, she thought. Then she remembered the amber silk dress. She hadn't worn anything soft and beautiful in a long time. What would Zach say when he saw her in it? Even more important, what would she see in his eyes?

Stop mooning like a fourteen-year-old about to go on your first movie date, she told herself. *You've been sleeping with the man all week. And he's made it clear he can't keep his hands off you . . . and vice versa,* she thought with a grin.

Their lovemaking had been exquisite—passionate and exciting and wonderful. Sometimes gentle . . . other times so wild and fierce it was almost primal.

But he hadn't spoken a word about love.

And why should he? The teenage days of puppy love and pledges of forever were long gone. They were two adults who were starting from scratch, and whether they were building a new relationship or just indulging long-held passions—what difference did it make?

But the truth was . . . it *did* make a difference—to her. It made all the difference in the world. Because she was in love with him. She'd never stopped being in love with him.

Even when she'd been engaged to Kevin, she realized, he'd never had the hold on her heart that Zach did. Letting Kevin go had been painful, but she'd managed it without a tenth of the pain she'd felt when Zach had abandoned her. And she was as much of a fool when it came to Zach McCallum today as she'd ever been. But she'd be damned if she'd let him know it.

Grabbing a fresh pair of ivory satin panties and a matching bra from the chest of drawers across from her bed, Faith began to dress.

He smiled to himself deep within the trees north of the cabin.

She was spooked, he could tell. The binoculars had shown him the exact expression on her face, and it was delicious.

The bitch didn't look so confident anymore, did she now? She looked worried. Tense. Dare he say it? *Afraid!*

He almost laughed out loud with glee.

Wait until the night was over. She'd be beyond worry. She'd be over the edge. And that was just where he wanted her—for now.

Chapter 21

✦ ✦ ✦ ✦

🌙 ✦ PATTI CLOSED HER EYES AND SWALLOWED PAIN-
fully. Her throat hurt worse than it had yesterday. Her fever
was elevated to 102.

Damn it, after all this planning and work, she was going
to miss the dinner dance. The auction. The biggest night of
the year in Thunder Creek.

But as frustrated as she was by that fact, she was far
more worried about the baby. What if she needed to take an-
tibiotics? She didn't want to take anything that might affect
the baby. Even painkillers. She'd sucked on half a dozen
lozenges so far today, and had drunk a whole pot of tea.

But her throat was getting worse, not better.

Time to give it up, she told herself as she sat up in her
bed, one hand touching her throat. There was no choice but
to call Faith and break the news.

"Hello?" Faith sounded breathless when she answered
the phone, and Patti knew she was probably rushing to get
dressed.

"Bad news, girlfriend," Patti rasped, trying to sound
more upbeat than she felt.

"Patti? You sound horrible. Your voice . . . don't tell me
you're worse!"

"I'm worse. My fever started shooting up again about a half hour ago. Doc Evans is coming over later to check me out—he's worried about strep. And Bob's on his way home. The bad news is that you're going to have to tell me all about the dinner dance tomorrow because I'm not going to make it. And I have all the programs here. Bob can bring them to the auction later or—"

"No, Bob should stay with you," Faith interrupted. "Honey, don't worry about a thing. I'll swing by right now and get the programs, and I'll have Zach pick me up at your place."

"Are you sure?" Patti reached for another lozenge, but she'd left the package on her dresser. Too tired to get up for it, she fell back against the pillow. "If you don't mind, that would be great, Faith. I do feel sort of light-headed with this fever so it would be better for Bob to stick around."

"I won't have it any other way. Can I bring you anything?" Faith asked, sounding worried.

"How about some of those yummy desserts Katy and Bessie whipped up?" Patti sighed. "A slice of everything should do it. I'm eating for two, after all."

"You've got it. I'll come by tomorrow with a platter of goodies. And I'll fill you in on everything. I'm leaving in one minute, honey, so hang in there."

Setting the phone down, Patti reached for her cup and took another sip of lukewarm green tea.

So much for champagne and dancing in my new little sequined dress, she thought. She closed her eyes, willing herself to sleep, to get some strength in case Bob wasn't back before Faith arrived. Ever since Candy's murder, Bob had insisted they keep all the doors locked, so she'd have to go downstairs to let Faith in.

Right now that felt like a gargantuan task.

She must have drifted off to sleep. She wasn't sure how long it was before something woke her. A sound.

A door was squeaking. The front door—Bob kept meaning to fix it. Odd though that he would come in that way instead of through the kitchen like always . . .

"Bob? Honey?" Swallowing against the pain, she pushed herself up again and peered at the clock. Only a few minutes had passed—he must have made record time.

"Honey, are you coming up?"

There was no answer. Bob always answered her . . .

She heard a footfall at the bottom of the stairs. Soft. Stealthy. Not like Bob's loud clumping.

Patti's blood froze. It wasn't Bob and it wasn't Faith. They would have answered her . . . someone else was coming up the stairs . . .

She grabbed for the phone, clutching it like a lifeline as she pushed herself out of bed. Adrenaline got her to the door, but before she slammed and locked it, she leaned out into the hall, peering fearfully down the stairs.

And then she saw him and the color drained from her face.

He was halfway up, his face turned toward her. But she had no idea who he was. He wore a mask, like a child's Halloween mask, all black, with slits for the eyes, nose, and mouth—the slits outlined in gory red.

Terror shot through her, not for herself, but for her baby. Screaming, she jumped back and tried to slam the door, but he moved faster than anyone she'd ever seen and smashed it into her. She flew backward into the dresser and went down hard, the phone flying from her grasp.

Pain splintered through her and a silent scream raged in her throat as she tried to stand up. But she was moving too slowly and he was coming at her. There was a knife in his hand, but she wasn't even staring at that—she was staring in stupefied horror at the chilling soulless expression in his eyes.

And she knew in that instant she was going to die.

Faith seized the little silver makeup bag she was bringing to the dinner dance in place of an evening clutch. She dropped her lipstick, cell phone, and driver's license inside, then spun toward the mirror for one last quick glance, aware of the need for haste.

Not bad, she thought, smiling at the sight of the willowy woman in the mirror. The woman had a mass of gleaming curls, shimmering coral lips, and smokily defined eyes. She looked sexy, sensuous in that clinging fiery gown. She wore simple diamond stud earrings and the pearls her grandmother had given to her before she died. They were the same classic strand of pearls she wore in court every day, but tonight they looked different—*she* looked different.

All because of this sultry dream of a dress.

Okay, Zach's going to drool when he sees you, she thought with satisfaction, then whirled toward the door, moving fast for a woman in three-inch stiletto heels.

She didn't look like she belonged in an Explorer tonight—she looked more like the kind of woman who'd step out of a Jag—but she put the SUV into gear and roared off in a cloud of dust.

Faith didn't slow down until she braked in Patti and Bob's driveway and parked behind Patti's Bronco.

There was no sign of Zach's car yet, so she might have time to heat up some soup for Patti or at least make her a fresh pot of tea, she thought as she hurried toward the front door.

She'd intended to knock, but it was ajar. Pushing it open, she stepped inside, but as she opened her mouth to call out, she heard Patti scream.

High, piercing, and terrified, the sound cut through her and for one horrible instant she froze. She stared blindly up the steps toward the place where that unholy shriek had come from.

Then she was rushing up the stairs, nearly tripping in her stilettos, but hanging on to the stairwell as she ran at full speed. "Patti, Patti, where are you—"

She heard a sliding sound, a thumping, and sobs.

Weak, fading sobs . . .

Oh, God, no . . . no, no, no.

Faith tore around the corner, following the sounds— they were coming from Patti and Bob's bedroom.

She gasped in the doorway, stunned by what she saw.

Patti—on the floor near the dresser, her face white as death. Pain burned in her unfocused eyes. Blood was everywhere . . . covering Patti's nightgown, smearing her trembling hands, splashed across the hardwood floor.

"My . . . baby," Patti whimpered as Faith knelt frantically beside her. "Save . . . my baby . . ."

"I will, Patti. I promise. Stay with me, honey, just stay with me!" Faith was already punching the phone buttons. "I need an ambulance at the Maxwell ranch!" she shouted into the phone. "Patti's been stabbed. There are multiple wounds—hurry!"

The biggest stab wound was in Patti's thigh—a jagged, gaping wound still pouring blood.

Faith bolted into the bathroom, grabbed some towels from the rack, and dashed back. As she folded one against the wound Patti jerked convulsively, moaned, and then her eyes drifted shut.

She's going into shock. But she's not going to die. She'll wake up, she'll get a transfusion, she'll be fine, the baby will be fine.

Please God.

Single-mindedly, Faith kept pressure on the wound, terror sweeping her. Later she would see the wide open window, the curtain smeared with blood as whoever had done this had snatched it aside before climbing out and jumping to the ground.

All that would be for Rick Keene to look at.

She was looking at her friend, watching agony and grief and death creep into Patti's face.

Then, from inside her clutch, dropped and forgotten on the bedroom floor, her cell phone started to ring.

Chapter 22

ZACH ROUNDED THE HOSPITAL CORNER FAST, nearly colliding with an orderly pushing a gurney. He avoided the man at the last instant, swearing—and then he spotted her. She was slumped in a metal folding chair outside Room 247, her head in her hands. Even as he strode toward her, a nurse rushed into the room and Faith lifted her head, watching the woman hurry past. There were tears on her face, he saw, his gut clenching. And blood on her gown.

She saw him then and pushed herself shakily from her chair. Anguished tears filled her eyes. At the sight of them, and of the blood spattering her arms, her hands, her gown, his insides twisted into hard painful knots.

"It's Patti, Zach—she might lose the baby," she wept as he gathered her into his arms. He held her close as her sobs intensified. "He . . . he stabbed her . . . she lost so much blood . . . she hasn't regained consciousness—"

"She will. Do you hear me, Faith? She will. Patti's strong, she'll pull through this. And so will her baby."

He stroked her hair, cradling her against him as if he could somehow take some of her pain onto himself, ease the burden in her breaking heart. "Hang on, sweetheart. It'll be okay."

But he knew it might not be. The horror of it made him tighten his arms around her. He'd give anything for two minutes alone with whoever had done this.

It took a while before her sobs subsided. Zach controlled his need to find out what had happened, waiting until she was quieter and until she took a deep, shaky breath.

"I got your message," he said soothingly. "Bob's here with her?"

She nodded. "He . . . arrived right after I called . . . for the ambulance. He's in with . . . P-Patti . . . now."

"Can you tell me what happened, baby?" He had to fight to keep from bombarding her with questions. "Did you see who did it?"

"I'd be interested in hearing your answer to that myself."

They both started at the sound of Deputy Rick Keene's voice. Zach released Faith and turned toward him.

"Not now, Keene. Give her a few minutes—"

"No, it's all right, I want to talk to him!" Faith brushed at her tear-streaked face with the back of her bloody hands. "I'll do anything I can—to help you catch him. I-I know just who you have to look for. I should have told you before."

Keene stared at her. "You know who killed Candy Merck and who attacked Patti? You saw him?"

"No, I didn't . . . s-see him—he was gone by the time I got upstairs, but I know who did it—he left a message on my cell phone. It's all because of me. He's trying to scare me . . . to intimidate me." She turned to Zach and fresh tears burned her eyes. "It's my fault this happened," she whispered. "They have to find him now—tonight!"

"Bayman." Zach drew in a breath. "Bayman left a message on your cell?"

"Yes—right after I found Patti. I . . . I heard it ringing,

but I didn't listen to the message until after we were at the hospital . . . after they took Patti—"

"Who the hell is Bayman?" Keene broke in angrily. "If you've been withholding information from me, I want to know why. I don't care who your brother is—"

"Shut up, Keene. She wasn't holding anything back. She didn't know until tonight—"

"I didn't know for *sure*." Faith spoke rapidly. "But after this . . ." She dug into her clutch, handed the deputy her cell phone. "Listen to this. Just listen."

Keene took the phone, scowling. As Faith replayed the last message, he listened intently. Faith knew every word—she'd listened to the whispered message in shock three times while the doctors worked on Patti.

"Are you scared yet, bitch? You oughta be. Susan'll be scared too, after you tell me where to find her. How many have to die before you tell me?"

Keene's eyes turned cold and sharp. He replayed the message. "I'm going to need to take this as evidence," he said in a hard tone. "And I'll need a description. Who the hell is this guy?"

Faith swallowed. "He's a convicted felon from Philadelphia who has repeatedly stalked and assaulted his wife. His name is Hank Bayman."

Furiously, Keene pointed toward the glass-enclosed visitors' lounge as Zach stood tight-lipped beside Faith. "In there—right now. I want to know your connection to Bayman—I want a description, I want to know everything. And you'd better not leave anything out."

Several hours later, Faith slumped wearily in her chair as Keene and another deputy finally left the visitors' lounge, armed with every bit of information about Hank Bayman she had scoured from her brain.

"What time is it?" she asked Zach in a subdued tone.

Beside her, he glanced at his watch. "Eleven."

Suddenly she remembered the auction. The dinner dance. She stared down at her bloodstained gown. Crimson splashes mottled the soft amber fabric. She'd broken a heel racing up the stairs at Patti's house. She'd never noticed until now.

"Oh, God, Zach. Tammie! The auction. The programs—"

"Don't worry about it. I called Tammie while Keene was questioning you, gave her the basics, and told her to keep it to herself until the evening ended. I'm sure they managed just fine without the programs."

"Thank you." She shot him a grateful smile.

"For what?"

"For . . . being here for me—with me."

"I'd say it's a pleasure, except under the circumstances, it isn't." He glanced out into the corridor, toward the room where Patti lay hooked up to monitors and IVs. Bob was in there with her, no doubt holding her hand and saying a lot of prayers.

"You heard what the doctor said, Faith. The baby's holding its own. Chances are good it's going to be fine."

"I know." Her voice quavered. "But she lost so much blood."

"Yeah, but by some miracle, no vital organs were hit and neither was the placenta. You got there just in time."

He stood up. "There's nothing more we can do here tonight, Faith. Let me take you home."

She knew he was right. Patti was stable now. So was the baby, and Bob was right there with both of them.

"Okay," she said. "Just . . . give me a minute."

She tiptoed into the hospital room. Bob released Patti's hand and enclosed her in a bear hug, and she could feel his broad shoulders trembling.

"Thank God you got there when you did," he muttered thickly. "You saved her life, Faith."

"I wish I'd gotten there sooner."

Staring into his gray, somber face and bleak eyes, her heart broke all over again. "Can I get you anything? Do anything?" she asked.

"Yeah—go home, Faith. Get some rest. And . . ." He glanced over at Patti, hooked up to a dozen tubes and wires. Her usually rosy cheeks were as white as the hospital bedsheets, and her breathing was raspy.

"Say a prayer, Faith," he muttered huskily. "Please. For her and the baby."

She didn't remember walking out of the hospital or getting into Zach's car. She didn't remember getting back to the Last Trail ranch house. Suddenly she was walking like a zombie into Zach's bedroom, shivering with a chill that came from within.

He saw it and lit the fireplace as she fumbled her way out of the ruined amber gown and slipped into the bathroom.

So much blood. Patti's blood. She couldn't wait another instant before washing it off.

The hot streaming water from the showerhead poured over her. She scrubbed at her skin, wishing she could scrub the memory of Patti bleeding on the floor from her mind as easily.

When she stepped out at last into the steamy bathroom, Zach was there, holding a huge white terry-cloth bathrobe. Without a word, he wrapped her in it. Then he scooped her up and carried her to his bed.

"You know you're spoiling me," she mumbled as he set her down gently.

"Only the best for my girl."

She was fading fast but the words caught at her. She searched his eyes and stretched out a shaky hand, touching his cheek.

The night had taken a toll on him as well. His black suit jacket and string tie looked rumpled and there was dark stubble all along his jaw. His eyes were tense and worried . . . worried for her, she realized.

"Am I?" she asked softly, as exhaustion dragged at her and her defenses seemed to have faded in conjunction with her energy. "Am I your girl?"

"My one and only. Always." His tone was firm. He looked so calm, so steady, so reassuring. *Zach.* He gently took her hand from his face, wrapped his fingers around hers, then brought her hand to his lips and pressed a kiss to her palm. "Always have been, always will be."

A smile curved her lips and she closed her eyes. She thought she heard him whisper something more. It sounded like *my girl*.

Then she dropped like a stone into sleep.

He laughed to himself up on the mountain. She'd nearly walked in on him tonight while he was stabbing her friend. How exciting was that?

He had never played a game or fought a battle quite like this one. Nothing else could compare to it.

He wasn't sure anymore that he could ever go back to the way things were before . . . or if he even wanted to. This was much too much fun. It filled him, filled every part of him, thrilling him, even in his sleep.

It suited him more than he ever would have dreamed.

Of course, he hadn't been able to finish off her friend. He regretted that. But the effect was nearly the same. And now she was frightened, deliriously frightened.

He laughed gloriously and zipped the khaki jacket up to his chin. The wind was fucking freezing up here tonight, but he didn't want to leave the mountain, to go back to that dumpy apartment where he had a bed and a couch and a bathroom. He wanted to stay up here where he belonged—in the open, with the stars and the moon and the wind.

He felt high here, high above the small, insignificant world—and powerful, like a god. Gods didn't live in apartments or houses or motels. They lived on mountaintops, amid all the forces of nature.

He knew autumn was coming to the mountains, he smelled it in the icy tang of the air. But even if it snowed tonight, he wouldn't care.

Faith Barclay's fear would keep him warm.

It wouldn't be long now before he turned her fears to pain. Soon he would go to work on her and listen to her scream. Maybe he'd make her scream for hours before he let her tell him what he wanted to hear.

Only when the moment suited him would he end the game.

He'd bathe in her blood—and watch her die.

But first he had one little matter to attend to. A simple matter—for someone who knew what he was doing. A matter of an elementary timer any moron could assemble—and the planting of a modest little bomb.

Chapter 23

FAITH WOKE TO BRILLIANT SUNSHINE STREAMING into the bedroom, and Zach sitting on the edge of the bed, pulling on his boots.

"What time is it?" she mumbled in a voice thick with sleep.

He glanced over at her with a smile. "Time to rejoin the living, Faith. Almost ten."

"Oh, God. *Patti*." As the memories of last night flooded back, she shot up to a sitting position and swung her legs over the side of the bed. "I have to get to the hospital."

"I'll drive you in—as soon as we grab some breakfast. Patti's fine—she's stable. I checked at seven and again a half hour ago."

"The baby?" Faith asked, one hand at her throat.

"So far, so good. The doctors are encouraged."

Relief nearly made her dizzy. She rushed over to Zach's dresser and grabbed some of her clothes from the bottom drawer. She'd taken to leaving some things at the Last Trail ranch over the past week.

"Good thing I left these jeans here. Somehow I don't think a blood-splattered cocktail dress will work at the hospital today," she said, catching sight of the gown she'd worn last night, which Zach had draped over a chair.

"In case I forgot to mention it, that dress looked great on you last night." He came to her, cradled her face in his hands. "But you know what? You look even better this morning, waking up in my bed."

She was suddenly intensely aware that she was still wearing his robe. And nothing underneath.

Longing filled her as she saw the warmth in his eyes. He kissed her forehead, then his mouth lowered to her lips. A delicious heat swept through her as he gently kissed her.

"Except for one quick appointment this morning, I'm all yours today, Faith. Whatever you want, whatever you need, that's what we'll do. Together."

"Does that mean you're going to be glued to my side?" she asked, brushing her mouth over his again.

"If that's what it takes."

"To protect me, you mean." He didn't answer and she sighed, pulling back and meeting his eyes. "It's Bayman who ought to be afraid for his life right now. I'm sure my office has already faxed his photo and mug sheet to Keene. The entire sheriff's department will be hunting for him. I don't think I need a bodyguard, Zach."

"Tough. You've got one anyway."

As she started to protest, he silenced her with another long, hard kiss. "I lost you once, Barclay—it cost us ten years. This time it could be forever. I'm not willing to take that risk."

There was no mistaking the determination in his eyes. Her heart surged with emotions she hadn't allowed herself to feel for a very long time.

"We'll talk about it later," she said softly. Drawing his head down to her, she kissed him again.

Roy arrived just as they were finishing breakfast. Neely had extended her visit with her sister at Zach's request, so they'd had a fast meal of toast and jam and Cocoa Puffs—Dillon's favorite cereal.

"Are you all right?" her cousin demanded, barging into the kitchen as soon as Zach opened the back door.

"Don't I look all right?" Faith tried for a lighthearted tone, but Roy wasn't having any of it.

"Damn it, Faith, word around town is that the guy who killed Candy and attacked Patti last night in her own house is after *you*. I heard he's some maniac stalker. And you prosecuted this guy?"

"Not very successfully," she muttered, putting the jam back in the fridge. "What did Keene do? Broadcast it to the entire town?"

"Pretty much. He told Wood and Tammie at the hospital this morning when they showed up with a plant for Patti at eight A.M. Keene was already there—hot to question her and see what she could tell him."

"Was she able to give him a description?" Faith turned toward him quickly.

But Roy shook his head. "Not according to what I heard. Keene hit Bessie's Diner right after that and Ada and Bessie grilled him. Seems Patti told him the bastard was wearing a mask. Black . . . with slits for the eyes and stuff. She couldn't see his face at all."

Faith and Zach exchanged grim glances.

"But Keene's feeling pretty confident anyway. He's so busy running for Ty's job already that he's bragging the case is broken and it's only a matter of time until he bags his man."

"Let's damn well hope so," Zach growled.

Roy glanced at him, then turned back to Faith as she

took a last sip of coffee. "I couldn't reach you on your cell phone, so I drove up to the cabin," he said slowly. "It was quiet and there was no sign of Ty's car. Keene told Bessie you left the hospital with Zach last night so . . . I took a chance you might be here."

He looked at the two cups of coffee, the two bowls of cereal, with chocolate milk puddled in the bottom of each.

"Thanks for taking care of her, but I can take it from here," Roy told Zach evenly. "She's going to stay with me and Corinne until this is over or until Ty gets back—whichever comes first."

"That's up to Faith, isn't it?" Zach's tone was cool.

"Roy, don't worry about me—"

"Damn it, Faith, if anything happened to you, Ty and Adam would personally skin me alive and you know it." He grimaced. "And Corinne told me I'd better not come home without you. We're your family, honey. You belong with us."

She met his gaze. "Think, Roy. This man—Hank Bayman—has obviously snapped. He's already a stalker, a wife-beater, a bully of the first order. Now he's killing people—all to get to me. What if he comes after me when you're gone—while I'm there with Corinne? I'm not going to put Corinne or your baby in danger—look what he did to Patti."

Roy blanched. "I'll take a few days off—hang out with you and Corinne. Now that the cops know who they're looking for, they're bound to catch him soon. And," he said, his brows drawing together, "if he shows up at my place, I'd be more than happy to take care of him personally. And save the county the cost of a trial."

Faith looked him dead in the eye. "I won't make you a target, Roy—or Corinne either."

"Yeah, and what about Zach's son? Dillon? If that psycho finds out you're here, *he* could be in danger—"

"Dillon's out of town for a few weeks," Zach cut in. "He's with the Graysons at the Grand Canyon."

Roy stared at Zach. He was thinking it over. "But we're family," he repeated doggedly. "She belongs with us—"

He stopped abruptly. "Better yet, Faith, why don't you head back to Philly? Bayman won't escape the manhunt that's on for him now. So why do you have to stick around? I have a feeling your so-called relaxing vacation has come to an end anyway."

So did Faith. But she wasn't about to run. If Bayman had found her here, he could find her anywhere, manhunt or no. And maybe that wouldn't be a bad thing, she thought. If she had to deal with him herself, she was more than capable. And she had plenty of motivation.

"Look, I'll call you if I need anything, Roy—that's a promise. In the meantime, I have to go. I need to get to the hospital and see Patti."

In the end, Roy followed them to the hospital. Zach dropped her off at the door, explained that his appointment wouldn't take long, and told her to wait for him at the hospital. He'd be back within the hour.

Faith suspected that further arguing about bodyguard duty was a lost cause for now. Besides, until she had a chance to go back to the cabin and get her gun, she didn't mind having someone watch her back.

It seemed strange to be uneasy in broad daylight, but she couldn't help it. It had been daylight yesterday when Bayman broke into Patti's house. Daylight when he'd cornered her in her bedroom and carved her up with a knife . . .

Riding up in the elevator, she made up her mind that as

soon as she was finished at the hospital, she'd have Zach take her straight back to the cabin for her gun and some more clothes.

The second floor was crowded with people who'd already heard about Patti. Bessie was there—she told Faith that she'd convinced Bob to go home for a few hours of sleep and a shower, promising to stay with Patti until he returned. Ada Stone and Katy Brent were also there, as was Tammie Morgan. Before Faith could get to Pattie's door, Tammie took her aside.

"Don't ask me how, but I managed to pull off a fantastic evening!" She beamed. "Even without the programs, and without the two of you there to do your share of the work, I pulled it all off. I just pushed on and no one even *missed* you and Patti at all."

Behind Tammie, Faith saw Ada roll her eyes. She shifted her gaze back to Tammie's tanned and hollow-cheeked face.

"Did we meet our goal?" she asked, managing to free her arm of the other woman's braceleted grasp.

"Even better—we finished eight thousand dollars *over* our goal," Tammie said triumphantly.

"At least there's some good news."

"Don't you want to hear about how much the necklace I donated went for? The one I bought in Las Vegas? It was the hit of the night—"

"Tammie, can it wait? I'm glad the auction went well, but right now, I'm here for Patti."

Faith stepped around her and went into the hospital room before Tammie could respond, then held her breath, fearing the other woman would follow. Fortunately, Bessie jumped in and steered her away in time. Faith peered at Patti and approached the bed, her heart twisting painfully.

Patti was awake, looking pale and weak as a sick kitten, but she smiled tremulously.

"Bob told me . . . you were the one who . . . saved me." Her voice was so low, Faith had to bend closer to hear. "You . . . saved the baby too . . . the baby's going to be all right. It *has* to be all right," she whispered, clutching Faith's hand.

"Of course it will, sweetie. Your baby's going to be fine. The worst is over, you just have to rest." Faith pressed a kiss to Patti's cheek. "You don't have to talk now, it's more important to save your strength."

"Deputy Keene was here . . . a little while ago. He needed to question me."

Faith knew that already, but now, seeing how weak Patti was, her anger at Keene flared. No wonder Patti looked so wrung out—Keene had probably pressed her for answers. Couldn't he see how sapped she was?

She wasn't about to pester Patti with her own questions—not until she was stronger—but she couldn't resist one.

"I know the man who stabbed you wore a mask," she said softly, "but were you able to give Rick Keene any kind of description?"

Patti's eyes clouded. "He was medium height . . . I think. I could . . . only remember his eyes . . . they were brown."

Bayman had brown eyes. Faith's stomach clenched. "That's great, Patti. That helps. Don't think about it anymore now. Just get your strength back. For you and for the baby."

"I . . . know. I have to . . ." Patti's eyes closed. For a moment Faith just stood beside the bed, looking down at her and remembering the bloodied heap she'd found on the floor . . .

Suddenly, Patti opened her eyes. Tears filled them and streamed down her cheeks. "Faith. I'm . . . scared," she said, her voice breaking. "I . . . I can't lose my baby . . ."

"You won't, Patti." Faith took her hand and gently squeezed her fingers. "Your baby is strong. Like you, like Bob. Remember that. Your baby's going to be just fine."

But she knew those were only words. And Patti knew it too.

"Say a prayer for the baby," Patti whispered, clutching her hand. "Please."

Tears blurred Faith's eyes. She nodded, her throat aching. "I will. Right now. You just hang in there and try to sleep. Bob will be back soon and Bessie's right outside."

Patti nodded almost imperceptibly. Her eyes drifted closed again.

When Faith left the hospital room, her heart was trembling. The hallway felt too noisy and crowded. She had promised Patti—she had to say a prayer—and she wanted a quiet spot.

Drawing a breath and giving Bessie and Ada a wan smile, she slipped toward the elevator. But Roy stood up from a molded plastic chair in the hall and fell into step beside her.

"Go home, Roy. You should be with Corinne. Who knows what this lunatic is going to do next?"

"Yeah, well, it would be a lot easier to keep an eye on both of you at once, cuz."

"I'm just going down to the chapel. Zach will be back soon, and he made me promise not to leave the hospital without him. So there's nothing to worry about, okay?"

"No, it's not okay. I don't feel a whole helluva lot better about you and Zach McCallum than I do about you and some maniac with a homicidal grudge. You think I don't remember how much he hurt you?"

"You think I'm not old enough to take care of myself?" She stopped at the elevator and punched the button. "Roy, I'm twenty-nine, not twelve. Give it a rest."

"The guy's bad news, Faith, and you know it. Trouble's always followed him and that hasn't changed. He has a lot of enemies in this town. Wood Morgan is dead set against Zach leasing his land to that camp outfit, and he's got some power hitters lined up behind him. And a lot of folks here in town haven't forgotten what Zach did to Pete Harrison."

The elevator doors opened and Faith stepped in, keeping a tight-lipped silence as Roy followed her.

"You know as well as I do that you're on shaky ground if you hook yourself up with McCallum, Faith. I'm your family, and if Ty and Adam were here they'd both want me to protect you—from Bayman and from Zach—"

"Don't forget the bogeyman," she said, stepping off the elevator on the first floor and turning left toward the chapel near the lobby doors.

As Roy started to follow, she stopped in her tracks and faced him.

"Roy, I don't need a chaperon. Go home to Corinne and take care of her. If I need a babysitter, I'll give you a call."

She kissed him quickly on the cheek and opened the door of the chapel. For a moment she was afraid he would follow her inside, but to her relief, he shook his head and started toward the exit.

With relief she closed the chapel door and walked slowly into the small paneled chamber resonant with deep, peaceful silence.

She was only dimly aware of the altar, the candles, the quiet maroon carpeting, the pamphlets of prayers spread on a table, representing a variety of religions. Mostly she felt the stillness surround her, as warm and comforting as a lovingly crafted, handmade coat.

Faith sank down on a maroon padded bench and closed her eyes. Patti's pale face and weak voice filled her mind.

I'm scared . . . I can't lose my baby.

Her heart brimmed with pain.

Please, God. Please let Patti's baby survive.

Her cheeks were wet with tears. But there was still hope for this child. Still a chance.

Faith bent her head, closed her eyes.

And with every ounce of strength in her heart, she prayed.

Zach had never expected to find himself in Wood Morgan's office at the Circle M cattle ranch, ten miles from the Morgans' Crystal Horseshoe Dude Ranch. But around seven this morning, he'd decided it was time to make a move—even one as unprecedented as this one.

He didn't care for the ugly direction a lot of things were going in Thunder Creek, and it seemed a worthwhile risk to take a stab at turning some of that around.

True, compromise went against his nature—maybe that was something that ran in families—but experience had taught him that a bit of give-and-take can sometimes make all the difference.

For his own kid, and for those who'd benefit from a few weeks at summer camp in the West, he'd take a chance.

Of course, that didn't guarantee that Wood Morgan would have the brains to meet him halfway.

If not . . . to hell with him . . . they'd do this the hard way.

But it was worth a try, Zach thought as he stared Morgan

in the eye. Better for those kids if they were made welcome instead of to feel that they were unwanted and the target of hostility. Better for Dillon if he didn't have to deal with fallout from a fight that had nothing to do with him, if he could just be a kid and make his own friends—and enemies, if need be. Minus his father's baggage.

"In the interest of peace, I'm prepared to offer you a compromise," Zach told Wood evenly.

A grin spread across the other man's face. "I knew you'd come around."

"Call it whatever the hell you want. I've got more important things to worry about right now than you and your stooges. In case you haven't noticed there's a killer on the loose. I want this over."

Wood nodded. "You're worried about Faith, aren't you? She's right in the center of this, from what I heard. I guess for the two of you, the fire never died, huh?" He chuckled. "Who knew you'd turn out to be such a romantic, McCallum?"

"Shut up, Morgan. My personal life is none of your concern. You stick your nose in with Faith, with my son, with anyone who works for me, I'll bloody it." Zach's tone was calm, but there was no missing the flint in his eyes.

Wood was accustomed to saying what he pleased, to whomever he pleased, but something in those steely eyes gave him pause.

"Fine." He cleared his throat. "I got it. No need to get your dander up. So you're willing to forget about the camp and sell me the land after all?"

"What I'm offering you is a compromise, not a capitulation. I'm throwing you a bone, Morgan, and if you're smart, you'll take it."

"What the hell does that mean?"

Leaning back in the chair opposite Wood's desk, Zach

watched the other man thoughtfully. "I'm willing to sell you a quarter of the land you wanted. By my calculations, that's enough to build roughly a dozen condos, up to two thousand square feet apiece. If you go smaller, you can build closer to two dozen. It's beautiful country, prime real estate. Your rich guests will love it. But you'll have to forget about the fancy spa, or else build it within your current property. The camp will lease the other three-fourths of the land from me as planned. There'll be a mile of grassland separating the two. And those kids will be welcomed in town, with no obstacles or backhanded propaganda out of you. Take it or leave it."

Angrily, Wood shoved back his chair and stood up, bristling. "What the hell kind of offer is that? I want to build thirty condos and the spa—right where my architect planned them."

"Too bad. This is a one-time offer. Yes or no."

The other man flushed, anger suffusing his face. "I thought you wanted peace. I thought you wanted not to have to worry about my petition."

"Don't forget about bomb threats to my business."

Wood never blinked. "I don't know anything about that."

"Yeah. Sure." Zach snorted.

"Be reasonable, McCallum. We're two of a kind, both of us movers and shakers. We can coexist peacefully, or eat each other alive. It's your choice."

"Correction." Zach's eyes glinted silver. "TexCorp oil can buy and sell this ranch and your dude ranch *and* your real estate businesses ten times over. If I choose to play rough, you'll feel it. I'm not interested in throwing my weight around, but if I have to, I will. Now I've offered you a compromise to avoid all-out war. But I guarantee you,

Morgan, if you start one, I'll finish it." Zach's eyes were colder than any blizzard to hit Thunder Creek in the past century.

"For the last time," he said, his gaze nailing the other man's. "Take it or leave it. *Now.*"

The fierce, calm determination in Zach's face made Wood Morgan bite back the urge to order the man off his property. McCallum definitely wasn't the same hot-headed kid he'd once been. He was tough, he was hard, he was cunning. He didn't think with his fists, but with his head. And his stock holdings. And his bank account.

And from everything Wood had seen thus far, he was beginning to realize Zach McCallum would make a much better ally than enemy.

"Half and half," Wood countered abruptly.

Zach started toward the door. "One quarter of the land under question. Final offer." He paused with a hand on the doorknob.

"Damn it." Wood fingered his mustache, thinking furiously. His desk phone rang, but he ignored it, staring at McCallum, taking his measure one last time.

Hell, a dozen condos at three thousand a week, fifty-two weeks a year, were better than none. And he could always build the spa off the main complex of the Crystal Horseshoe. Tammie had preferred that option from the start.

He hated losing, though—at anything. Still, this fight with McCallum would be costly—in time and aggravation. And if he ended up losing anyway, all he'd have to show for it was a powerful new enemy.

"Done." He came around the desk, held out his hand. "How about a drink to seal it?"

"No, thanks. Too early for me." Zach shook his hand.

"I'll have my attorney draw up the papers. You call off your attack dogs, especially Gallagher and Harrison."

"Harrison's a loose cannon," Wood warned. "I'll do what I can, but . . ."

He was talking to dead air. McCallum had walked out.

Zach reached for his cell phone the moment he was in his pickup. He wanted to call Faith, let her know he was on his way back to the hospital, make sure she stayed put.

Only then did he remember that she didn't have a cell phone anymore. Keene had impounded it.

Damn. He hit the accelerator and the truck peeled up the Circle M drive.

Through the open window he heard a far-off boom.

It sounded like an explosion.

Chapter 24

FAITH DIDN'T KNOW HOW LONG SHE SAT praying in the chapel, tears sliding down her face. But as she began wiping at her eyes, the door opened suddenly and she turned her head to see Owen slip inside.

Walking slowly, he came to sit beside her. Her teary smile of welcome faded from her face as she became aware of his distraught expression.

"Owen, what's wrong?" Faith's heart lurched. "It's not . . . Patti? Not . . . the baby?"

"No, no, Faith. There's no news. I . . . I didn't mean to scare you." He swallowed hard. She'd never seen Owen look so bleak, and something in his eyes alarmed her.

"What is it then? You look like . . . like someone died."

"I just . . . need to tell you something. If I don't . . . I'm going to go crazy. With everything that's happened, with you and Zach, and what happened to Candy—"

His voice broke. "I should've gone outside with her," he muttered thickly, head bent. "You know that, right? Everyone probably knows it. If I'd stayed with her—"

"Owen, stop it. Stop it right now. It wasn't your fault. Thunder Creek isn't exactly Crime Central. You had no way of knowing it wasn't safe for her to walk outside—"

"Let's see if you feel so charitably toward me when I say what I came here to say," he interrupted, growing agitated. "Let me talk, Faith, before I lose my nerve!"

She stared at him, her mouth dropping. Desperation and pain burned in Owen's eyes.

"It was me, Faith. All those years ago . . . when Pete was in that coma. I did it, Faith. I hit him. *Not Zach.*"

Faith stared at him. *Owen had hit Pete, put him in that coma?* She struggled to take in the implications of what he was saying.

"Zach wasn't even there," Owen went on, dropping his head into his hands. "He didn't get there until later. He was the one who called the ambulance."

"But . . ." Faith shook her head. "I don't understand. Pete was your best friend—"

"We got into a fight." Owen dragged his head from his hands and stared at her, his mouth twisted in a grimace.

"Over Laurie Dubroski. A stupid fight because he was taking her to the dance that night, even though he knew I had wanted to ask her." A strangled laugh came from his lips, but to Faith, it sounded like a sob.

"I was furious. I went to my job that day at the gas station and all I could think about was what he'd done, about him and Laurie going to the dance together. Dumb, huh?" he asked bitterly, then went on in a grim tone. "I got madder and madder. And then Pete showed up right before the dance to fill his daddy's pickup with gas, and I . . . I lost it."

In the quiet chapel, Owen's eyes closed for a moment with the memory. "I lost it, Faith. I went crazy. Blame it on hormones or damned teenage stupidity or whatever the hell you want, but I hit him. I hit him as hard as I could." He shuddered.

"And that was it. He went down after one punch. He hit his head on the ground, and . . . and he didn't move."

All this time—it was Owen, she thought dazedly. *And he let Zach take the blame.*

"I shook him," Owen continued, his voice quavering. "I tried to wake him up. His head was bleeding—I didn't know what to do."

The words came faster. "I was scared to call an amubulance, scared Fred Harrison would fire my dad. We'd just found out the week before that my mom needed surgery, and my dad had to keep his job to pay the bills. And the last thing my parents needed right then was to have their kid arrested for assault, possibly for murder. I panicked, Faith. I just knelt over Pete, and I cried, and begged him to wake up—and then Zach drove up."

Owen surged to his feet, his hands clenched at his sides. "I hate myself, Faith, more than you hate me. More than Zach must hate me."

"I don't hate you and I'd bet Zach doesn't either. But it's time to do the right thing." She rose and stared directly into his eyes. "You owe it to Zach and you owe it to yourself."

"I know." His voice was thick. "I'm going to tell Harrison. I'll go today, right now." He closed his eyes for an instant and his face looked gray in the dim light of the chapel.

"And the whole town will know by tonight," he muttered to himself, rocking back on his heels.

Despite everything she'd heard, despite the lie he'd kept secret for all these years, Faith's heart went out to him.

"I think you should wait and take someone with you," she said slowly. "I'm worried about how Harrison might react. You shouldn't go alone—"

"No. No more waiting." Owen hugged her shoulders

quickly then lurched away, his tone determined. "I have to get it over with—and I need to do it myself, Faith!"

"Owen—"

But he sprinted toward the chapel door. Faith hurried after him. Owen was wracked with guilt—and Fred Harrison might very well be wild with anger. Not a good combination.

She called to him as he ran down the hallway, but he never slowed. She saw him push through the doors leading out to the street and followed him outside. He was already darting toward his car, parked across from the real estate office down the street.

She was debating whether to go after him, to try to persuade him to wait, when a deputy appeared out of nowhere and stepped right in front of her.

"Ms. Barclay, I've been looking for you. Acting Sheriff Keene wants to see you in his office."

"Fine—later. I have to catch someone—"

"No, ma'am." Politely, the deputy moved to block her path. He was tall, muscular, and determined for all of his quiet civility. "I have orders to bring you in right now. You'll have to come with me."

Faith started, her gaze swinging to his clean-shaven face. He wasn't one of the deputies that had come to the cabin after Candy's murder, but he looked vaguely familiar.

"Am I under arrest?" she demanded irritably. Her glance shifted back toward Owen, and she swore silently. He was already in his truck, gunning the engine, and as she watched, he roared away.

"Damn."

The officer ignored her muttered oath. "You're not under arrest, ma'am," he said patiently. "But you need to come with me right now. Acting Sheriff Keene will explain when you get there."

The deputy had neatly cut brown hair and earnest, ordinary brown eyes. He looked like a nice kid, and there was only a hint of sternness in his long jaw. Young, inexperienced, trying hard.

"I'll bring you right back here to the hospital when you're finished, Ms. Barclay."

"Fine, but I need to make a phone call as soon as we get there."

"No problem, ma'am."

He was parked at the end of the hospital parking lot. Faith hurried alongside him, anxious to call Zach and alert him to what was going to happen at the Harrison place any moment now—and also to let him know where she'd gone. If he came back to the hospital and she wasn't there, he'd think the worst.

Her mind clicked through everything Owen had told her as she walked. Zach hadn't done it. He'd never hit Pete Harrison. Yet, for all these years, he'd taken the blame, stayed silent.

Why?

To protect Owen, she realized, pain squeezing through her heart. He'd obviously realized what it would mean to Owen if everyone in town learned he'd injured his best friend, put the son of his father's boss into a coma. Everyone in Thunder Creek, including Zach, had known that Owen's mother was in poor health. So Zach had let Owen place the blame on him for all these years, keeping the secret even now when Harrison and Wood Morgan were trying to use it against him . . .

Suddenly she realized that the deputy had fallen behind

her. She paused as they reached the police cruiser. "I don't suppose you'd let me use your mobile phone—" she began.

But she got no further. Someone grabbed her from behind and shoved a damp aromatic cloth against her face. Faith struggled, trying to kick him, trying to scream, but she couldn't breathe. Strong arms had snaked securely around her and the cloth was pressing into her nose and mouth—she couldn't tear his hand away. Her muscles weren't working . . . her strength was ebbing . . . the light was fading.

Still she struggled and kicked and writhed—until darkness like a dank wind swept her up and carried her away.

Chapter 25

THERE WAS NO SIGN OF FAITH IN THE WAITING room or the hallway. In fact, Zach thought as he hurried toward Room 247, Patti's visitors seemed to have cleared out. Faith must be in with her, he guessed, and, reaching the room, he stepped quietly inside.

But Patti was asleep, with Bob seated beside her in a chair. And Faith wasn't there.

Bob stood up when he saw Zach and followed him out into the corridor.

"How are Patti and the baby doing?" he asked quickly, even as he scanned up and down the corridor once more.

"Doing better, thank God. The doctor thinks now that the baby's going to be okay." Bob's face was drawn, but there was a sheen of hope in his eyes. "You're looking for Faith?"

"Yeah, I dropped her off a while ago. She was supposed to wait for me. Have you seen her?"

"She left before I got back." Bob fought a yawn, and scraped a hand through his rumpled hair. "But Patti told me she was here earlier."

Zach tensed. He didn't like the feeling in his gut. Where the hell had she gone? Why didn't she wait for him? He couldn't even call her—Keene had her damned cell phone.

"I'm going to check the rest of the hospital—the chapel and the cafeteria," Zach said quickly.

Bob caught the edge of concern in his voice and his attention sharpened. "Bessie was here with Patti when I got back—maybe she knows something," he suggested.

Zach phoned the diner on his cell as he paced the length of the corridor, and checked out the visitors' lounge where Keene had questioned them the night before. But when Bessie came to the phone, she wasn't much help.

"Well, when Faith left Patti's room, she looked pretty shook up. I'm sure she was plenty worried, because I was too. But Roy was there," Bessie added suddenly. "He rode down in the elevator with her. What's going on, Zach? You sound worried."

"I just need to talk to her, Bessie. We missed connections and I thought she might have left me a message—with you or someone else."

But his thoughts were racing. Faith's car was back at his ranch. She didn't have a cell phone—and she wasn't where she'd promised him she'd be.

Faith, where the hell are you?

There was no message at the nurses' station, no sign of her in the chapel or the cafeteria, and he had a nurse's aide check the bathrooms. No Faith.

Finally he called Roy.

His gut clenched when Roy told him she'd gone into the chapel more than an hour ago, and that was all he knew.

"What's up? You lost her, McCallum? With a killer on the loose?"

"She was supposed to wait for me," Zach shot back. Every muscle in his body was tense and the pain in his head throbbed. "Start calling around. Find out if anyone's seen her."

"I'm on it," Roy said. "I'll check back with you in fifteen minutes."

She's all right, Zach told himself as he clipped his phone back to his belt. *She has to be all right.*

"Excuse me, I couldn't help overhearing." A young nurse with short dark hair came toward him from the nurse's station. "You're looking for Mrs. Maxwell's friend—Faith Barclay?" She smiled.

"I saw her a little while ago when I was coming on duty. I was just finishing my shift last night when she came in with Mrs. Maxwell," the young woman explained. "And I could see how upset she was. But she was fine when I saw her today," the nurse assured him.

"Where did you see her?" Zach demanded.

"Right outside. She was speaking to a deputy when I came into the hospital."

"Was it the acting sheriff—Rick Keene?"

"No. I didn't recognize him. I'm sorry." The nurse shook her head, then spread her palms. "I have to get back to my station, but . . . I wanted to reassure you that Ms. Barclay was perfectly fine when I saw her. You don't need to worry."

Zach nodded, tight-lipped. His thoughts were spinning as the young nurse picked up a chart and headed into Room 244.

Maybe Keene had sent a deputy for her. Maybe he'd wanted to question her again. Or return her cell phone. She might be at the sheriff's office right now.

There was one way to find out. He bypassed the elevator and sprinted down the stairs two steps at a time.

Chapter 26

HE HAD HER. AT LAST.

Excitement permeated his body like red-hot peppers injected under the skin. He could barely keep his jittery eyes on the road—he kept wanting to stop the car, get out, bang on the trunk. And listen to her plead.

Ha. That would be the best part. Hearing her voice begging him, begging him to let her out, let her go—that would be the first level of victory.

Then came level two. The blood and guts. He laughed to himself, almost giddy with excitement. Faith Barclay's blood and guts. That would be sweet.

After all this time, she was going to pay. Through the nose and through every other orifice.

Cry, plead, bleed, and pay.
It was going to be a red-letter day.

Faith awoke groggily and in darkness. Nausea filled her throat, bile choking her. Oh, God, she felt sick. So sick. And she was rolling, bumping . . . her body being battered and tossed . . . as if she were on a ship. A dark enclosed ship . . .

She heard a horn and realized suddenly through the throbbing in her head that she was in the trunk of a car.

A car, she thought dizzily. And then, as memory returned instantaneously, jarring her from the vestiges of sickly sleep, she felt a jolt of terror.

His car.

He'd grabbed her . . . pressed that cloyingly sweet cloth to her face . . . chloroform? What had happened to the deputy? How had Bayman gotten to him first?

Her heart was pounding and she felt like she couldn't breathe. She fought desperately in that small, dark space to keep from vomiting as the car bumped over the rough road.

She tried to move her hands, her legs. They felt weak as butter sticks, but at least he hadn't bound her.

There hadn't been time.

She had to get out of here, get help, get away . . .

Faith tried to think through the dizziness and the pulsing pain in her head. Then it came to her. The taillights. If she could kick them out . . . stick her hand out through the gap . . . someone might see . . .

But the roads around Thunder Creek were lonely, she knew as despair washed over her. What were the odds another car would be following behind?

But she had to try. Twisting her body in the cramped space, she began desperately to get her bearings and to grope for the taillights. She found one on the left side and twisted again, hope sliding through her.

Awkwardly she managed to shift into position. She mustn't move too much, she thought. She couldn't let him feel any movement in the trunk or he'd know she was awake.

Taking a deep breath of the suffocatingly close air, she

kicked at the light with the heel of her boot, softly at first, then harder, then with all her strength, praying he wouldn't hear, wouldn't know.

Tears welled in her eyes as she finally broke through. Air, sweet, fresh air flowed in and she took deep gulps. She managed to twist her body around once more and inched headfirst toward the broken taillight, then pushed her hand out through the opening.

Please let someone be there, she prayed as she waggled her fingers with all of her strength. *Let someone see.*

The car accelerated. They were climbing. Faith put her face to the opening, breathed in fresh air.

She had no jewelry to throw out, in the hopes someone would find it, see it, know she'd been there. Nothing in her pockets . . .

Suddenly the car swerved abruptly and came to a sudden jarring halt. She held her breath as the weight of the car shifted, and a door slammed.

He was out of the car.

He was coming. He was coming to get her now.

Chapter 27

"SORRY, MR. MCCALLUM."

Deputy Ken Marsden shrugged and turned the palms of his hands up. "Can't help you. Miz Barclay isn't here. Neither is Deputy Sheriff Keene. We have a situation going on right now."

"I don't give a damn about your situation. I want to speak to the deputy who talked with Faith Barclay today."

"As far as I know, no one from this department spoke with Miz Barclay today. The investigation is still ongoing, and we can't return her cell phone yet. She—"

"Where's Keene?"

"I told you he's not here—"

"Where is he?" Zach advanced until he was right in the deputy's face. "I want to talk to him *now.*"

Marsden bristled. "He happens to be a mite busy. And so am I. So I suggest you back off and I'll have him call you when he has a chance."

"Not good enough." Tension vibrated through Zach. Every second that he didn't know Faith was safe was tearing him apart. "Faith Barclay is missing."

Somehow just saying those words aloud made them seem terrifyingly, ominously real. Zach had tried to believe he'd find her here, that Keene had her once more going over the attack at Patti's house detail by detail. If she wasn't here . . . where the hell was she?

"Missing?" The deputy stared at him skeptically. "What exactly does that mean?"

"It means I can't locate her," Zach bit out. "And the last person to have seen her says she was talking to a deputy from this department—the department that's run by her brother, Ty Barclay. Remember him?" he added sarcastically. "I don't think Ty would look kindly on my getting the runaround when I'm trying to make sure his sister is safe."

Marsden looked startled. "Run that by me again," he said quickly. "About her speaking to a deputy from this department. Do you know who it was?"

"That's what I'm asking *you*."

Marsden sucked in his breath. "Okay, listen. I've been here all morning manning the office and I have no knowledge that anyone spoke with Miz Barclay today, much less that they were sent to find her. You got a description of the man who was talking to her?"

"No—you'd have to ask the nurse at the hospital who told me about it. She was coming on duty at the time."

Fresh alarm surged through Zach as he stared into Marsden's suddenly attentive face.

"Are you telling me that the man she was seen with wasn't really a deputy?" he asked in a low tone.

"I didn't say that—"

"Stop bullshitting me, Marsden," Zach yelled. "What the hell's going on?"

"We have a man down—Deputy Lee Sawyer. He's been hospitalized with a concussion. Someone coldcocked him no more than an hour ago while he was out on patrol— took his uniform, his vehicle, his gun, cuffs, everything.

When Sawyer came to, he was out in the middle of nowhere—turned out he was in a ravine two miles behind the Pine Hills apartments. We have an APB out now for the assailant but—"

"Bayman. It was Bayman. He has her," Zach said hoarsely, but an instant later, he realized his mistake.

"No . . . Shit. That can't be." He raked a hand through his hair as sick, numb fear overtook his body. "Faith never would have left with Bayman," he told Marsden. He fought a rising panic. "Who the hell was this guy?"

The deputy frowned. "An accomplice maybe."

All Zach knew was that Faith was in trouble, serious trouble.

"Get moving," he ordered. "Call Keene—I want every man you've got out there searching for her starting *now*."

The phone rang before Marsden could move toward it. He picked it up and listened, his glance flicking to Zach.

"Yeah, I got it." Setting down the phone, his mouth tightened. "More trouble. That was Big John Templeton. There's been an explosion at your construction site—he was passing by and called it in. All hell's breaking loose, I gotta get over there—"

"To hell with my site," Zach yelled, blocking his path to the door. "You don't go anywhere until you call Keene right now and get him focused on the search for Faith Barclay. Do it, Marsden, or I swear to God, I'll see you run out of town on a rail!"

"Your new offices are burning, McCallum—what's left of them. Templeton said the place is a shambles—"

"Call Keene!" Zach shouted, and grabbed up the phone, shoving it into the deputy's hand. "Faith Barclay is priority number one, do you hear me?"

He waited, his chest tight, until Marsden had placed the

call, until Keene issued orders for a search. Ty's would-be successor also ordered Zach to stay right where he was until Keene could come in personally and get more details from him.

"No way in hell," Zach muttered, wheeling toward the door. It slammed behind him before Marsden could do more than blink.

Jumping into his truck, Zach fought the terror pulsating through him. He was already calling Roy as he turned the ignition.

"Faith's in trouble. We need a search party combing the town, the foothills, Blue Moon Mesa. *Fast.*"

In the darkness, Faith braced herself as she heard a key scrape in the lock. She had to run or fight the moment an opportunity presented itself. She prayed her muscles and reflexes would work.

Bayman was a big man, burly, strong. As a cop he'd been trained to protect himself. But Ty and Adam had trained her too, she reminded herself, fighting the fear that clogged her throat. She'd do whatever it took . . .

The trunk swung open and light poured in, blinding her after the thick darkness. She blinked, peering at the dark shadow looming over her, the shadow staring in at her.

Her heart was hammering so hard her rib cage hurt. She bit back a scream as he leaned in toward her and suddenly she could see him—young and strong, with a merrily smiling face, ordinary even features, a pair of eyes the color of chocolate chips.

It wasn't Bayman.

It was the deputy—the one who'd escorted her away from the hospital.

"I hope you had an uncomfortable ride," he said in a clear, cold voice, as she pushed herself up to a sitting position, struggling against the dizziness that surged through her as she shifted position.

"Who . . . are you?"

"Your opponent. Your adversary. Your executioner." He grinned wickedly. "Correct answer—all of the above."

He took hold of her arm. "No more time-outs. The clock is running. It's time to finish the game."

As he dragged her from the trunk, Faith staggered, pretending to be more unsteady than she was, though she still felt light-headed and her limbs were heavy. When she stood on the ground, her legs shaking, she saw that they were on a mountain road, high up, overlooking Thunder Creek's cemetery in the distance.

This must be Snowflake Mountain, she realized suddenly. It was a lonely place, not nearly as popular or scenic as Cougar Mountain or Shadow Point.

She could see no signs of life anywhere—not even a squirrel or rabbit skittering through the dead gray brush.

But she saw the path . . . the path that led down, winding and twisting to the creek far below, which flowed along behind the graveyard.

"It's just the two of us," he assured her, and let go of her arm to slam the trunk. "No one here to spoil our fun."

He half turned away from her and, in that instant, Faith spun toward the path and began to run.

"Fucking bitch!" he yelled, and sprang after her. She hurtled forward so fast that her feet skidded on the rocks. She ran desperately, rounding the corner, not daring to look back, but suddenly he tackled her and, with a grunt of triumph, knocked her to the ground.

The trees and scrub brush whirled—she hit the ground

with a sickening thwack that whooshed the air from her lungs, and then he was on her, holding her down, trying to pin her hands.

She fought him, twisting beneath him, kicking and biting.

She had to get away—he was hurting her—she had to get him off . . . she had to *run* . . .

He smacked her across the face, and pain ricocheted through her head. She struck out with her fist and managed to nick his chin before he wrenched her arm down, twisting it until she screamed in pain. She kneed him, heard him grunt, then as he crushed his hand against her mouth and nose, she bit him as hard as she could.

He shrieked and punched her again. She slumped beneath him, caught in a daze of gray-and-black-spotted light.

Then the world began to fade again—it turned black and cold and empty, and she knew just as she slipped over the edge that she was going to die.

Chapter 28

RACING THROUGH FAITH'S CABIN, ZACH SCANNED the living room one last time before he bolted out the door. He'd done a quick search, and Faith wasn't here—and it didn't look as if anyone else had been here either. But he'd found her .357 Magnum on the nightstand next to her bed and tucked it in his waistband. There was no time to go home for his own gun. Faith had hers loaded, ready to go.

He slammed the door and sprinted for his car, knowing every second mattered. Every damned second.

Roy and Gabe and Jackson Brent and Big John Templeton, as well as a dozen other ranchers and ranch hands, were peeling over one road after another, looking for a Crown Victoria police cruiser, or any sign of Faith.

But there was a lot of territory to cover and a million places to hide. And he was no longer sure who even had her, who had killed Candy and attacked Patti Maxwell. Was it Bayman and an accomplice? Or someone else?

He only knew the odds of finding her alive diminished by the moment. He couldn't stop moving, couldn't slow down.

If he was too late . . .

He couldn't bear to think about that. He couldn't deal

with it. All he knew was that he'd wasted more than ten years living his life without her, and now he might not get that second chance.

He hadn't even told her he loved her . . . not once. Did she know it? Did she have any idea how much he loved having her in his life again, how much he needed her—in his bed, in his heart, in his future . . .

But Faith might not have a future. He slammed his foot down on the accelerator and headed toward Shadow Point. When his cell phone rang, he grabbed it with one hand, the other taut on the steering wheel, but it was only Rick Keene.

"McCallum, I need you to get in here right now and answer some—"

"Go to hell, Keene. I'm not going anywhere until Faith is found."

"My men are searching for her and for the man who impersonated my deputy. I've just finished questioning Sawyer. I managed to catch up with him at the hospital right after he came out of X-ray—"

"And?" Zach demanded, braking at the path that led to Shadow Point.

"He didn't see a thing—he was hit from behind, so he can't ID his attacker. I also questioned that black-haired nurse, but all she really noticed was the uniform. She *thinks* he was young, in his twenties, average build. Now how about you leave the search to us and get in here so I can—"

Zach hit the disconnect button. A moment later, as he got out of his car to take a look around Shadow Point, the phone rang again.

"It's Roy. I've got something. Just spoke to Ada at the diner. She was parking near the hospital on her way to visit Patti this morning and saw Faith outside with the fake deputy."

God bless Ada. Hope pounded through Zach. "Was she able to describe him?"

"Not really. She couldn't see his face from where she parked, but he was young, tallish, average build. But here's the most important part," Roy rushed on grimly. "She saw the cruiser pull away just as she was going inside—and it was headed east."

East. Zach was already running back to his truck, flinging open the door. *East.*

"There's no guarantee they kept going that way," he muttered to Roy as he backed out of the clearing. "But it's all we've got."

"I'm headed that way too," Roy told him. "I'll check out the county picnic area alongside the creek—then head over to the cemetery."

"I'll take Cowell's Peak and Snowflake Mountain." Zach dropped his phone onto the passenger seat and stomped on the gas.

His muscles were so tense they ached. He stared straight ahead at the road as he drove, fear filling his blood as he thought of Faith out there, hurt, scared, in trouble.

She's still alive, he told himself. *She has to be.*

Rounding a curve, he saw the tall green pines atop Cowell's Peak looming straight ahead. And beyond them, the grander, more austere sight of Snowflake Mountain.

His gaze narrowed on each towering site, then the other.

On pure instinct, and a prayer, he took Moose Foot Road, not really a road at all, more like a well-worn trail. It was a shortcut that led to the aspen- and evergreen-covered slopes of Snowflake Mountain.

•   •   •

"You don't look so good, Faith," he said amiably as she at last opened her eyes.

He'd been sitting there, watching her on this long, pretty stone ledge practically since he'd carried her up here.

Aside from the blood she'd drawn when she'd nearly bitten off a chunk of his hand, he felt fine. Strong. Powerful. Excited.

Did she think she could hurt him? Stop him? That showed how stupid she really was.

The injury was nothing. Nothing at all. The bleeding had stopped. He'd poured some of what the locals called red-eye on the bite while Little Miss Assistant District Attorney snoozed, and he'd tied one of those stupid cowboy bandannas around it. Now everything was hunky-dory.

Today was the day. Nothing could stop him now.

He grinned as she stared up at him from the ground. He saw the fear in her eyes, and it reminded him of why he was doing this. Rage swept through him, the familiar glowing-red hurricane blast of rage.

"Yes," he whispered, his voice trembling with the power of this moment. "You should be afraid. Just like he was."

Faith saw the change come over him. The flood of emotions . . . amusement turning to anger . . . then to fury— and last, to a chilling satisfaction.

A little dab of spittle, the size of a tear, formed at the corner of his mouth, and his eyes went hot and blank as copper coins glinting in the sun.

"Just like who was?" she managed to ask as she tried to move her arms, her legs, and felt every muscle scream. "Who . . . was afraid?"

"You don't know . . . haven't guessed?"

"No . . . I don't even know who you are . . . I thought you were someone else."

"You thought I was Bayman." Some of the rage faded. Delight sparkled in his eyes. "That was convenient for me. Those phone calls he made? Very helpful. I really should have thanked him, I suppose."

"You . . . know him? Were you . . . working together?" Faith knew she had to move. Had to at least sit up, manage not to fall over. She had to see where she was, get her bearings—for when she got another chance to run.

Could she run? God only knew. She felt like she'd been mown down by a tractor. But some of the wooziness was fading.

At least her thinking was becoming more clear.

She placed her palms on the ground and pulled her knees toward her chest, trying to lift herself to a sitting position. It seemed to take forever, and she heard him snicker, but she managed it.

She was sitting on a ledge, with flowers—of all things—around her. Flowers and rocks. Good, she thought, taking hope where she could find it. *Rocks*. Some grass, and a mound of dirt and more rocks over near an aspen. To her right was the trail—and a sheer drop not more than fifteen feet away.

She'd like to drop-kick him over it.

She turned her head, saw Cowell's Peak with its distinctive hump to the right. So they were still on Snowflake Mountain—only higher up. A remote ledge, near the top, she guessed, tilting her head to the summit.

She'd been here before, she'd been everywhere in Thunder Creek before. And she had to know Snowflake Mountain better than he did. That would give her an advantage, she told herself. If she could get away.

But right now, they might as well have been alone at the top of the world. There were no roads here—only a dirt track. The road only went so far, then you had to hike or ride.

His car must be parked below, she thought, struggling against the fear that threatened to choke her. Had he carried her all the way up here? He must be incredibly strong.

She studied him again, her throat dry. He looked . . . familiar. But her mind was too foggy to place him. All she knew was that she had to fight him—and win—if she was going to survive.

He'd sweated through the gray shirt of the deputy's uniform. And though he was young and on the thin side, there was no mistaking the muscularity of his sloping shoulders. Yes, he was strong—stronger than he looked.

But so was she. She flexed her back, her leg muscles, trying to marshal her thoughts.

She had to try again to run.

Only . . . God, her head hurt. So did her face.

But she was still alive.

She couldn't figure out why. He wanted her that way, for now. He wanted her to know the reason he'd done this . . . whoever the hell he was.

That works for me, she thought desperately. The longer she could keep him talking, the more chance she'd find a way to turn the tables on him.

Or that someone would find them. Zach . . .

Zach would be looking for her, wouldn't he?

She peered down the track, trying to see the winding road below. Tears threatened when she thought of Zach. Last night she'd slept in his arms. What if she never saw him again? There were things she'd never told him . . . things she might die without saying.

"Why did you kill Candy? And attack Patti?" She heard the breathless questions as if from a distance. She was wondering if she could spring up and make another run for it before he reached her. But he was only a few feet away.

He shrugged. "To practice. To scare you. All of the above." He grinned at her.

"Why do you want to scare me?"

"You're so smart, you figure it out."

"Because *he* was scared," she said. "I don't understand. I don't know who you're talking about."

"Look closer," he mocked. "Don't you recognize me? Don't you know who I am? Or were you so intent on getting your verdict, your death penalty, that you didn't even notice anything else? Like the fact that my brother was *innocent*?"

His brother? She'd gotten a guilty verdict against his brother . . . she'd gotten hundreds of guilty verdicts, against hundreds of people who claimed to be innocent . . . he could be anyone . . .

And then it came to her—a fragment of memory, seared deep inside her brain. The courtroom taut with grief and anger, the murderer's gaze fixed on the judge, the victim's family holding each other and sobbing . . .

And the murderer's close-faced mother and stunned younger brother huddled behind the defendant's chair, looking small and defeated. The mother had been a hard short stick of a woman with hunched shoulders—the brother a teenager, a skinny, lost-looking kid with a mop of stringy brown hair, a soul patch, and eyes that seemed too big and angry for his face. He'd looked at her with those eyes and she'd been startled by the hatred in them.

"You're Dougie Clement," she whispered. Why hadn't she seen it before?

Because the past two years have changed him, she thought, a cold rock of terror hardening in the pit of her stomach. He looked older, he'd filled out, and he'd cut his hair. No more long, stringy mop—his was so short it was nearly a crew cut and his jawline had a man's hard edge. The soul patch was gone too. He was clean-shaven. And clean-cut. He looked nice and—except for his eyes—normal.

"Bingo—you win the prize." He snickered again. " 'Young Dougie Clement' is what the newspapers used to call me. Younger brother of convicted murderer Jimmy Clement. But now I'm all grown up, you see. And some around here know me by a different name. Boles. Walter Boles." He laughed.

She started. *That name—Boles.* She remembered it. And suddenly she remembered the face too.

He was one of the young men with Rusty Gallagher, walking with him to the diner the day she'd collided with Rusty on the street. The one carrying the laptop.

Run that new spreadsheet, Boles . . .

"You've been . . . working here . . . in Thunder Creek," she whispered, as fresh shock rippled through her.

"Bingo again." His eyes shone. "Want to see your prize?"

No.

He reached down into the backpack on the ground beside him and slowly pulled out a knife. It was the mother of all knives—a butcher knife with a ten-inch blade that glittered in the sunlight shimmering across Snowflake Mountain. He hefted it like a young Arthur sliding Excalibur gloriously free of the stone.

"What do you think of your destiny, Miss Faith Barclay?"

"I think you really don't want to do this, Doug." Trembling, she tried to keep her voice even, calm. But her heart was slamming against her chest.

"They're going to catch you and arrest you, you know. And when they do, you're going to need someone in the legal system to speak up for you . . . to recommend treatment for you—not prison or the death penalty, but a hospital where they can take care of you. If you give yourself up to me, I'll help you—I'll do everything I can—"

"Like you helped my brother?" His sneer was full of hatred. Holding the knife, he moved closer and began to circle around her. "Jimmy wasn't a murderer and you murdered *him*. What does that make you, Faith?"

"I'm sorry about your brother. Truly sorry, Doug. I was wrong—"

"Not only you," he snapped. "That other district attorney, Sylvester, the one who bossed you, he was wrong too! You were in it together!"

"Yes, that's . . . that's right. Ted and I were both wrong . . . and so was the jury. I never had a doubt your brother was guilty . . . I wish I had—"

"You're lying, bitch. You didn't care. Just so long as you won your case and got your picture in the paper!"

He was circling more quickly now. Faith felt that at any moment he would lunge at her. Her heartbeat was so fast she thought she might faint. She had to get up, be ready to dodge, to fight, run . . .

She started to stand, but Doug screamed at her. "Sit down! Don't move!"

She froze. Fury had transformed his face. The clean, even features looked distorted, almost like a mask. *He's crazy, there's no reasoning with him. Get up, get out . . .*

But he was watching her, looking as if he'd slash that knife across her throat if she so much as breathed wrong.

She stayed put—for the time being. "I'm not going anywhere, Doug," she said, fighting to keep her voice calm, though she was icy with terror.

Was that a car engine she heard in the distance? No, it was gone now. An eagle spread its wings high above and flew straight toward the sky. Aside from Doug's uneven breathing, the ledge was as lonely as the single cloud floating across that perfect blue sky.

"I want to help you," she said in a low tone. "To make you understand how sorry I am."

"Even though I killed your friend, and hurt your best friend. Poor pregnant Patti." He chuckled, and white-hot fury lit inside her.

What happened to his brother wasn't an excuse for what he was doing now. It wasn't an excuse for mutilating Candy, and for almost killing both Patti and her baby. Or for what he'd do to her if she didn't figure out a way to distract him pretty damned quick.

Fight or flee, Barclay, she thought. *Make up your mind—what's it going to be?*

"Admit it, you really don't feel sorry for me, Faith. You're just trying to save your own pretty little butt. Well, it won't work. I've been planning this since that day in court when Jimmy lost his appeal. After all those years on death row, you got what you wanted—the death penalty. And now I've got what I wanted. Revenge. I've spent years visualizing it, making it real in my head. Only now it's going to be *really* real. You know? You get it?"

"There's one thing I don't get." She swallowed as he finally stopped circling her and stood only two feet away. "How did you find me?"

Faith leaned back, facing him, her knees drawn up, leaning on her hands behind her. She felt around for a rock or a stick. Nothing. She shifted, moving an inch sideways,

ever so slightly. Slid her hand across the hard ground . . .
she felt something . . . a rock.

It was uneven . . . roughly the size of a plum. Her fingers curled around it but her expression never changed,
never wavered from Doug's oddly ecstatic face.

"I mean, how did you find me here in Thunder Creek?"
she added quickly. "I can't see how you could have tracked
me down."

"It was easy, let me tell you. I'd been tracking you for
years."

He nodded as her eyes widened.

"Yep, I knew the instant you booked your flight for Salt
Lake City and then the connecting flight to Casper. And
that's when I had my brainstorm. Do it there, in the boonies,
where the police are even slower and dumber than in the big
city. I'd have lots of room to hide and cover my tracks. And
I was right. I've been living in the Pine Hills apartments as
Walter Boles and right up here on Snowflake Mountain as
myself." He smiled widely. "I've been a very busy boy."

"Did you have . . . an informant? Someone in my office?" Faith's fingers clenched the rock. She had to keep
him talking as long as she could, until she could get an opportunity—even just a moment's distraction where she
could spring up before he could move. "I can't understand
how you knew I booked my flight."

He looked pleased. "There's nothing I can't find on a
computer," he boasted. "You know what my profession is?
Hacker. I'm a wizard with a keyboard, a database, and a
mouse." He chuckled and, for an instant, lowered the knife.

"I do all kinds of jobs for people—rich college kids
who want their grades changed, companies that want to
spy on the competition, even a few mob guys who want the
411 on informants, witnesses. I even hacked into the Jus-

tice Department last year—screwed up their files pretty good—and guess what—they never caught me."

A sly smile spread across his face. "Since I'm a free-lancer, I can work anywhere . . . for anyone . . . and get the job done. This past month, I've been working for none other than Mr. Wood Morgan."

"Wood hired you to . . . to hack into someone's computer?"

He regarded her as if she were an annoying child. "Silly Faith," he chided. "He doesn't know who I really am—or what I really do, of course." Doug shifted the knife again until it caught the light, and the silver of the blade seemed to dance along the edges. He was fascinated by it, Faith noticed. As fascinated as he was with his own cleverness.

"Wood Morgan thinks I'm Walter Boles, straight-A computer geek who just graduated from Cal Tech." He gave a giggle of laughter. "I showed him the perfect résumé—the knock-'em-dead grades, the recommendations from professors—all of them manufactured, of course. I got the job after only one interview. As a matter of fact, I've been set up here since right after you booked your little vacation a month ago—earning decent money too. Mr. Wood Morgan thinks I'm setting up a new accounting software system for his company, but actually, he's been paying me to use his mainframe computer to keep you in my sights."

Faith swallowed. "You set all this in motion after you found out about my vacation plans?"

"It didn't take much effort—only about ten minutes to break into the Philadelphia district attorney's system—I did that six months ago. I've been keeping really close tabs on you ever since. I know all of your cases, your court dates, the judges assigned to your trials." He licked his lips with satisfaction. "Even your credit card number," he added with gusto.

He let the knife drop to his side, seeming to forget about it momentarily. "You booked your plane ticket from your desk," he reminded her. "I had the information before the airlines even e-mailed your confirmation."

He warmed to his subject and Faith steeled her nerves.

"I'd already researched your family—and I knew they had roots in Wyoming. I knew that when you won your thirtieth straight case at the DA's office there was a nice little story in the local paper. I have that article, Faith—and everything else that's ever been written about the Barclays."

As she drew in her breath, he laughed again.

All this time, she'd thought it was Bayman. Bayman stalking Susan. But she'd had her own stalker—Jimmy Clement's kid brother. Only he wasn't a kid anymore. He was all grown up—and he was a killer.

"So, it was *you* making those calls to me?" she asked suddenly. "To my cell phone. And not saying a word?"

"Ah, you're not as stupid as I thought." His lip curled. "Bayman started it. To scare you. I liked the idea, so I kept it up. It was actually a lucky chance—my spotting him in Thunder Creek early on."

The rock was scoring into her palm, but Faith barely felt it. She could see he was getting restless. His gaze kept shifting to the knife, as if he were hypnotized by it.

"I don't understand . . . how did you know who Bayman was, or what he was doing?"

He walked right up to her, paused, looming over her, the knife down at his side as he stared at her in amusement. "You still don't get it, do you? I know everything about you. I know everyone who's connected to you. Bayman's picture was in the newspaper after he threatened you in court. There was an entire article about him when he was on trial for beating up his wife. You tried to put him away, only you failed. I saved the article, and Bayman's picture. I have pictures of everyone you know. They're all in my collection."

As Faith shuddered, he smiled almost gaily. "I followed him up to his camp one night right after I spotted him. I hid in the shrubs until it was night, until he'd had a few beers and wasn't as alert as he might have been—or should have been. And then—" He glanced at her speculatively. "Do you want to know what I did to him, Faith?"

"No." She moistened her lips uneasily. "I don't care . . . about Bayman."

"But I want you to see. Get up, come with me."

"I—"

"Get up, I said!" he roared. Her heart jumped into her throat as he grabbed her arm and yanked her to her feet, then dragged her toward the mound of dirt. "Look, you stupid bitch. Look!" he screamed. "This is what you're going to look like when I'm done with you."

He shoved her toward the mound of dirt and Faith stumbled against it, then stared down in horror at what lay just behind it—all that was left of Hank Bayman.

Oh, God, no. No, no, no.

He'd been dismembered, like Candy. But this time she *saw.* She saw the thing lying in the shallow grave on the other side of that mound, the pieces of his corpse loosely covered in dirt, gravel, and rocks. He lay in earth tinted with dried blood and a sea of ants crawling over him—his eyes were open, worms swarmed over his eyeballs, his fingers were splayed, unattached, the same with his arms, his legs—bloody stumps flung in all directions . . .

Faith's knees trembled, she closed her eyes. She was going to be sick . . .

Behind her she heard Dougie laughing.

"Practice makes perfect. That's what they say." His words were singsong. "And you know what, Faith? I think I've finally had enough practice."

Her throat closed. His tone had changed subtly. She trembled at the excitement blazing in his eyes. They were the eyes of a madman.

Slowly, he lifted the knife, raised it over his head, as if it were a spear he was poised to throw.

"Are you afraid, Faith? I want you to tell me you're afraid."

"You're the one who should be afraid." Behind her was the horror of Bayman in his grave. Before her the madman. Faith had no choice. She had to use the only weapons she had.

Her fingers digging into the rock, she smiled at him. A cold, mocking smile.

"I killed your brother, Dougie, and I can kill you too. Are you prepared to die?"

His mouth dropped open. Twitched. Rage flared in his eyes. "You're the one who's going to die, Faith. I have the knife."

"But I'm brave, Dougie. You're a coward. You sneak and kill unsuspecting people, people who can't protect themselves. I've already taken a chunk out of you today. The next time, I might bite off more than a finger."

"I'm going to cut you to ribbons," he choked, his voice rising. She saw his knuckles whiten around the knife. "You can't talk to me that way. I'm in charge now . . . this is my courtroom. I'm carrying out the death penalty."

"You're a raving lunatic." She laughed at him—

laughed, though her throat was dry as dust and she wanted to scream. She curled her lip, slanted him a scornful glance.

And watched his eyes grow wide, dark—the pupils dilated like the enlarging eye of a storm . . .

"You're going to get the death penalty yourself," she said.

"Shut up!" he shouted. "You shut up!"

"I'll send you to death row, like your brother—I'll stand there and watch them strap you down, and hook you up—"

"You bitch," he screamed, and lunged at her.

The knife plunged toward her chest—Faith pitched sideways and rolled, the way Ty had taught her, coming up to her knees as Clement drove the knife through empty air. Off-balance, he tried to change direction, but before he could, she hurled the rock like a baseball straight at his face and it struck with a thud in the center of his forehead.

He screamed in outrage, a scream cut off as she punched him hard in the gut. She heard him wheeze but she was already running, running desperately on pure adrenaline. She spared a precious second to glance over her shoulder and saw him coming after her, the knife in his hand, blood rolling down his face. His eyes were wild, hot with fury, and he was flying. Faith flew faster, her heart pumping, her legs trembling from the exertion of running over rocks and weeds down the slope of Snowflake Mountain.

She knew this mountain, like she knew all of Thunder Creek, and she knew there was a place to hide, if she could only get there . . .

He was pounding after her, she heard his boots striking rock and earth, his raspy breathing. Tripping over a boulder, she nearly fell, but steadied herself just in time by grasping at an aspen. She ran on . . . skidding and slipping, nearly twisting her ankle.

Then, *there it was*. Nearly weeping with joy, she ran toward the outcropping of rock and ducked into the crevice she'd found when she was ten.

Faith's breath came fast and shallow as she crouched down so that the rocks hid her, squeezing her body into the small space. It was just off the trail—if he went by fast enough, and she was still enough, he might not see her . . .

She held her breath, hoping the wild beating in her chest wouldn't give her away. Either she'd be safe or she'd be trapped . . .

She tried to hold her breath, to make herself small and silent and invisible, but she heard her own heartbeat roaring in her ears, and she was shaking, shaking hard as she hunched between the rocks.

Seconds crawled past. Agonizing seconds. Then Clement hurtled onto the trail. She closed her eyes tight, sucking in air, listening to his boots skidding on rock, listening to his harsh breathing, and picturing those hot brown eyes that were as dark and soulless as a pair of tarnished coins.

The sounds of his pursuit passed—and faded. The sun beat down on her shoulders, the mountain wall glittered pure and ancient all around her. Faith leaned her head against the sun-warmed rock and inhaled the clean perfume of the pines.

He was gone.

Zach climbed swiftly. Squinting beneath the brim of his hat, he surveyed the twisting trail, deserted except for a long black snake slithering under a rock and the tufts of purple lupine and Indian paintbrush growing alongside the scrub brush.

He quickened his pace, his long strides covering the ground swiftly, his gaze scanning, endlessly scanning, every nook and cranny of the trail. His mind was still spinning, trying to take in the fact that not Bayman, but some young nondescript fake deputy had kidnapped Faith.

Was Bayman even involved in this—or had they been wrong about his involvement from the beginning?

He was sweating in the warm sun, perspiration beading on his face, dripping down his neck. But not only from the heat—from fear. A cold, deadly fear of what was happening right now—fear of what that psycho might be doing to Faith.

Where the hell are they? he wondered for the hundredth time.

Maybe they weren't here at all. Maybe they'd gone to Cowell's Peak . . . or maybe Ada had been wrong . . . or they'd doubled back, changed direction . . .

Maybe Faith was already dead . . .

No. Don't think that way. She can't be . . she won't be . . . keep going . . .

He heard something up ahead. Every muscle tightened, his nerve endings snapped to attention. Someone was running down the trail, straight toward him. He heard the clatter of boots, rocks, the gasps of heavy breathing. *Faith?*

"Faith!" he shouted. The sound of running stopped. He heard nothing.

Shit.

"Faith!" he shouted again and sprang forward, sprinting up the trail and around the curve, but what he saw there brought him to a cold skidding halt.

The brown-haired man in the deputy's uniform was

crouched right in his path, grinning. There was a gash the size of an egg in the center of his forehead. Blood dripped down his face, staining his gray shirt, but it wasn't the blood or the gash or the grin that Zach focused on.

It was the knife in his hand. The butcher knife that glittered like a lustrous sword . . .

His blood curdled. "Where is she?" he demanded hoarsely. "She'd better be alive."

The man with the knife shook his head. "Dead. Dead, dead, dead."

"You're lying."

"Dead," the man repeated. He raised his voice suddenly, shrieking, "Why aren't you at your construction site, crying over the rubble? You're wasting your time here looking for a dead woman! The district attorney bitch is dead!"

Zach's control snapped, the world blurred to red. "Then so are you."

He moved fast as any gunfighter, yanking Faith's gun from his belt. As the killer clutched the knife and bared his teeth in a grotesque imitation of a smile, Zach shot him through the hand, and watched the butcher knife clatter to the ground.

Zach ignored the monster's shrieks and raced forward.

"Dead?" he muttered, and drove his fist into the killer's jaw, which broke with a loud crack.

The brown-haired man screamed in agony as Zach knocked him to the ground like a bowling pin.

Faith took a shuddering breath.

He's gone, she told herself, scarcely able to believe it. *Gone.*

For now.

But he was out there, searching for her. Oh, God, he could double back and run straight into her if she tried to go down this damned mountain . . .

She fought against the sobs rising in her chest.

More than anything in the world, she longed to stay where she was, hidden and safe, to never go back in the open. But she had to. She had to get down off the mountain. There was no real safety here—she had to get to Zach, call the sheriff, tell them so they could find Clement and stop him before he killed someone else.

Pushing herself up on unsteady legs, she blinked against the pain in her head and her jaw. She had to be careful, to listen for him. She'd hide if she heard the slightest sound . . .

Edging warily onto the trail, she peered in both directions, then started forward, listening intently. She started downward, moving slowly, so as not to dislodge any stones or make any sounds. But she'd only gone a short way when she suddenly heard voices . . . yelling voices. Her heart leaped into her throat.

Zach—was that Zach? Dry-mouthed, she scrabbled down the trail and then heard his voice again—it was definitely Zach, shouting, though she couldn't make out the words. She rushed forward, then froze when a gunshot thundered. Her hands flew to her throat and her blood turned to ice.

An instant later a scream of agony split the air and she abandoned all caution, rushing headlong toward the sound.

Running, slipping, her heart in her throat, she tore down the mountainside, and then she heard him.

"Where is she, you bastard? Where the hell is she?"

Zach. With a sob of joy, she dashed around the curve in the trail and then she saw . . .

He had Clement flat on the ground. The madman's face was bloodied, and Zach's knuckles were raw. The knife sparkled amid the rocks, five feet from where Clement lay helpless.

Zach had ceased punching him. He now had his arm pressed hard against the windpipe of the man on the ground, and he was leaning all his weight into it.

Dougie Clement was fighting for air, uselessly flailing his arms, trying to tear the larger man's arm from his throat.

"Zach! Zach, stop! I'm all right. I got away . . ." She stumbled forward, staring at him. His skin was gray and drawn—he looked like death warmed over himself.

Oh, my God, Zach—she thought, but aloud she gasped, "Don't kill him!"

"He deserves it." Zach never let up the pressure on the man beneath him, but his gaze burned into her face. Relief heavy as a downpour of rain washed over him, even as he took in the bruises, the pain in her eyes. He saw the cuts on her hands, the shaky steps she was taking toward him, and white-hot anger pumped through him.

"He hurt you." Zach looked down at the man beneath him and leaned in on his windpipe some more, his mouth tightening. "He nearly killed you, didn't he?"

"It doesn't matter now. Zach, don't. Don't do this . . ."

Fear and desperation brought her to his side, kneeling beside him, her hand on his arm. "Zach, let go. *Now*. It's wrong, this isn't the way—he has to face justice. Zach, *please*."

"*Justice*." He gritted his teeth as her pleading words slid over him, but they had the desired effect. They rinsed away the ugly jagged edges of his fury and a cold, disgusted calm returned. He stared down at the madman writhing in agony beneath him and slowly relaxed his death grip.

At that moment, they heard a faint shout from below. "Zach . . . that you? Did you find her?"

It was Roy. And when Zach shouted back to him to get up there fast, it was another voice—Rick Keene's voice— who answered.

Faith barely heard. She sank down on the ground beside Zach and Clement, trying to catch her breath, slow her heart. She was safe . . . Zach was safe. It was over.

Dimly she was aware that Zach had pushed himself off Dougie, that two deputies were now kneeling beside the beaten man. Dougie was whimpering, crying like a child as they drew their guns and called for an ambulance.

As more deputies swarmed up the mountain, and Keene warned them not to touch the knife, Roy appeared and knelt down, wrapping his arms around her. She shivered, too tired to stand.

"You two—you all right?" Keene barked at her and Zach. "I need statements before you go to the hospital—"

"Wait . . . listen to me." Faith roused herself from a daze of shock and relief. She turned her head, gazing at the lawman as Roy stepped back. "Hank Bayman . . . he's up there . . . up the mountain. He's . . . dead," she whispered. "He . . . killed him."

Keene stared at her. She heard Zach swear.

"How far up?" Keene asked grimly.

"A ways. You . . . you can't miss it. There's a ledge, a mound of d-dirt." She started trembling, and suddenly Zach dropped down on the ground again beside her.

As shudder after shudder shook her, Faith heard Keene giving orders to his men. Some were to head up Snowflake

Mountain and find Bayman's body. Others were to wait until forensics got there to take charge of the knife.

Faith leaned against Zach's chest and blocked out everything but the warmth of his arms around her.

Then the voices and the men were gone, Dougie Clement was gone, carried on a stretcher down to the ambulance. Even Keene had gone, summoned by a deputy to view Bayman's body.

She and Zach were alone, except for the deputies left to wait and stand guard over the butcher knife.

"Come on, baby, let's get you checked out. I think you're in shock."

She looked at him, lost it, and began to sob in his arms.

"Shh, Faith, it's okay," he soothed her. His arms tightened. "It's over, baby. It's all over."

"You don't understand," she sobbed, as the full impact of what had happened rolled over her like an avalanche. "He did all this because of me . . . b-because his brother was executed. Jimmy Clement was that madman's brother. Candy died because of him, and Patti nearly did, and her baby—"

"Patti and the baby are doing better," Zach interrupted her. "Bob says they're going to be fine. And it's not your fault, Faith . . . none of it." He frowned, studying the bruises on her face, the intensity of her sobs. "I'm getting you to the hospital. You could have a concussion . . ."

"Keene said we have to give our statements—"

"Screw Keene. I'm taking care of my girl."

My girl. Her heart gave a bump. "I'm all right, Zach. I'll be fine—"

"Damn straight you will." Gently, he kissed the top of her head. His silver eyes burned into hers and when he spoke again, his voice was husky.

"Because now that I've got you back, I'll never let anyone or anything hurt you again."

She felt a tingle run through her. It drowned out the pain and the guilt and the fear of the past hours. It made her feel clean and whole and alive in a way she hadn't in a very long time.

"You . . . have me back?" she repeated in a low tone, and her hand crept up to touch his face. "I'm not sure I was ever gone."

She gave a small, choked laugh. "Or that you were ever either . . . at least from my heart." Finally, she was being honest with him, more honest than she'd been with herself for the past ten years.

Zach felt warmth leap through him, and a kind of settled peace he hadn't felt in a long while.

"You were always in mine, Faith." His mouth caught hers, and he spoke against her lips. "My, God, if you only knew. Always."

As the wind rose and danced all around them, chasing tumbleweed down the slopes of Snowflake Mountain, he kissed her again.

"I love you," Faith whispered.

Zach looked into her eyes and thanked his lucky stars. He'd been granted a second chance.

"You don't know how glad I am to hear that, Faith. Because I just happen to love you too."

Chapter 29

"YOU'RE SPOILING ME," FAITH PROTESTED.

"That's the idea." Zach set the tray down on his bedside table and shoved his hands in his pockets.

Sitting up in his big king-size bed, wearing only a T-shirt and panties, Faith wasn't even looking at the mug of hot tea or the luscious slice of strawberry rhubarb pie he'd brought her from the whole one Bessie had dropped off a short while ago.

She was gazing at him, an expression in her eyes he didn't quite fathom.

It was twilight in Thunder Creek, nearly five hours after they'd made their way down Snowflake Mountain. The sky was a spectacular blend of soft rose and lavender and gold, and there was a chill in the air that made them glad for the fire Zach had built in the bedroom's huge stone hearth.

It had been an incredibly long day.

They'd spent nearly two hours at the sheriff's office being grilled by Rick Keene—with orders to come back the next day for a follow-up interview. Faith had been checked out at the ER and sent home with orders to rest.

Zach had made sure she did just that. But he couldn't settle down, at least not yet. He had a different agenda. He was afraid that if he shut his eyes, when he woke up things would be different between him and Faith—she'd have pulled away again, rethought what she'd told him on the mountain—and backed off.

There was no way he was going to relax until everything was set between them, until he was sure that she wasn't going to change her mind again and withdraw from his life.

So he'd watched her sleep in his bed, tucking the blanket over her shoulders when she tossed and turned, brushing a kiss against her cheek. He'd taken comfort watching her breathing ease and slow, seeing the faintest of smiles touch her lips as peacefulness settled over her.

Dillon was coming home in only a few days, and Zach was finding it difficult to believe there was a chance he'd have both of the people he loved right here with him.

After what he'd thought today when that madman told him Faith was dead, when he himself had been searching for her with dwindling hope and growing fear, having her here now was a miracle in itself. Having both of them in his life was almost too much to hope for.

He wanted to believe it, but he wasn't sure he could.

So he'd watched Faith sleep. He'd stretched out beside her and cradled her against him and thought of the life he wanted to give her, right here at the Last Trail ranch, wondering if there was any way in hell it could possibly come true.

The way she was looking at him now stirred his foreboding. He had no idea what she was thinking, but she looked troubled. Hesitant.

Sometimes you had to take the bull by the horns. "Okay, Barclay. Out with it. Hit me with your best shot, I can take it."

"I . . . hope so." Faith bit her lip. She held out a hand, inviting him closer, and he caught her fingers in his and sat down beside her on the bed.

He wanted to throw off all the blankets and make love to her. Long, slow, intimate love. She looked delicious in nothing but that white T-shirt and pink lace panties, those endless golden legs, her hair spilling wildly about her shoulders.

But she had something to say. His stomach tightened. "Go ahead, whatever it is, Faith, I'm listening," he said grimly.

She squeezed his hand tighter. "Owen told me the truth in the chapel at the hospital. I know, Zach. I know that he was the one who hit Pete, not you."

There was a long silence. Then Zach shrugged. "It looks like everyone in Thunder Creek will know what really happened pretty soon. When Bessie brought the pie, she mentioned that Owen had come in to the diner this afternoon and told her the truth about that night. She said he'd just come from confessing to Fred Harrison—and he looked pretty shaken up. But he seemed to want everyone to know, now that he had told Harrison. He even called Hal Miller at the *Thunder Creek Daily* and asked him to write a story clearing everything up."

"Is he doing it?"

"Yeah." Zach seemed surprised. "Even though it's old news, and not that many people even remember or care, Miller's writing the piece himself—something about a long mystery finally solved. It's all going to come out."

"It needs to come out, Zach, once and for all. Not only for your sake, but for Owen's. He's eating himself alive with guilt—both for what he did and for keeping it a secret."

"I guess I didn't do him such a big favor," he muttered.

"You did in some ways. Zach, I know why you took the blame, and why you allowed everyone to think you hit Pete for all these years—even now, when Wood Morgan and Fred Harrison were trying to turn the town against you. I understand why you did it and why you kept quiet."

He slanted a questioning glance at her.

"You thought you had nothing to lose," Faith said slowly. "You were going home to marry Alicia anyway, and you didn't plan on coming back to Thunder Creek."

"That was a big part of it. I was also stupid and hurt and shortsighted as hell. I figured my life as I wanted to live it was pretty much over. It really didn't matter to me what anyone thought of me—except for you. And at that point, I knew you were going to hate me anyway, Faith, so why the hell not give you even more of a reason? Make it easier for you to move on."

Her heart ached. Yet she persisted. "There was something else too. Wasn't there? You were thinking about Owen . . . and his family."

His wide shoulders lifted in a shrug. "Yeah. I knew old man Harrison would fire his father's ass if he found out Owen had been the one to put Pete in the hospital. I knew Owen's father needed that job, that his mom was going in for surgery. And it was an accident," he said quietly. "It didn't seem right that a whole family should have to suffer because a couple of boys got in a fistfight and something went very wrong."

She snuggled closer, snaking her arms around his neck. "You big jerk," she muttered against his throat. "Who ever would have guessed you were such a softie?"

"Don't spread it around."

"I should have known. I should have always known."

Zach's arms went around her, and he breathed deeply of the warm honey and milk scent of her skin. "I thought you'd be mad as hell that I never told you, that I kept quiet even these past few weeks when we've . . . gotten close again."

"Well." She smiled, and pushed back her hair. "I'm all done with anger. Too tired, probably." Her gaze was tender as she met his eyes. "I don't know about you, Zach, but I could really go for a slice of that pie now."

Twilight had bloomed over the land. The fire had died down and the room was full of shadows. Faith suddenly got up from the bed, turned on all the lights, drew the curtains against the night, and came back to sit beside him, her long legs tucked beneath her.

She was tired of shadows. Of darkness. And she was hungry. She nibbled at the pie, then stopped suddenly, lost in thought.

Zach reached out a hand, gently touched her cheek. "I wish I could change things, Faith. *Everything.*"

"Don't say that." She shook her head and slowly smiled, and this time it reached her eyes. "You don't want to change everything. You have Dillon. He's a wonderful boy."

His eyes lit. The corners of his mouth quirked. "He's a good kid," he said modestly.

"He's a great kid and you know it. You're crazy about him."

Zach chuckled and traced a hand over her bare, golden thigh. "I'm crazy about *you.*"

She grinned and took another bite of pie. "He wants a mother," she said thoughtfully, slanting a glance at him from beneath her lashes.

Zach watched her, his gaze suddenly keen and intent. "Yes, he does. And interestingly enough, he already has a potential candidate in mind."

She licked the fork. Slowly her tongue caressed the tines, gooey with pie filling. Zach felt his blood start to roar.

"What does his father think about that?" she asked casually.

Zach took the plate from her, set it aside. "His father thinks the love of his life would be a fantastic mother."

"Even if she's had no experience?"

"She's a quick learner. I've known her a long time and she caught on to French kissing in a flash. Same for strip poker."

Playfully she punched him in the arm, and he captured both her hands in his.

"She's also briliant. I hear she's a wizard in a courtroom," he went on. "Mothers have to be able to win lots of arguments with their kids. She's very qualified in that department."

"They need to love their children. Sometimes, in a second marriage . . . that can take a bit of time. Do you really think your candidate is up to it?"

"Absolutely. She has the biggest heart I know. And she'd have the rest of her life to get the hang of it."

"It's beginning to sound like a slam dunk to me," she murmured, her eyes closing as he nibbled the edge of her ear.

"There's only one thing." Zach pulled back, looked straight into those shimmering dream-blue eyes. "Dillon and his dad both want him to have brothers and sisters. Lots of 'em."

"How many is 'lots'?"

"At least two of each."

"Five children, Zach? You want to have five children?"

"For starters. How else am I going to fill up this big old house?"

How indeed. Faith laughed.

"Of course, it doesn't have to be this house," he added quickly, suddenly cradling her face in his hands. "I can work from anywhere. We could buy a house in Philly . . . in the suburbs . . . anywhere. It'll mean a bit of travel, but I can run my company from wherever you want to live—"

"I've been thinking about staying on in Thunder Creek," she said softly. "Hanging out a shingle. Private practice."

"Well then." Zach's gaze gleamed into hers and Faith realized it had been a long time since she'd seen that light of hope in his eyes. "I'm going to need a sharp attorney with a good head and a big heart to work out all the details with the camp and the various organizations recommending the first batch of campers. Think you might be interested in working for a corporate client?"

"Not particularly." Her eyes danced. "But in your case, I might make an exception."

Zach took her in his arms. His kiss told her everything he hadn't yet said in words. Faith felt her heart soaring. There had never been such tenderness between them.

Perhaps it was because death had come calling, and life had prevailed. But they made love with slow, precious passion, each touch, each stroke and kiss sending charged sensations through them. When they lay naked together on the bed and she opened herself to him, for the first time she opened more than her body. She opened her whole heart.

Zach made love to her as if it were their first time. As tenderly, lovingly, and completely as he had that very first night on Cougar Mountain. His need for her roared through him, but he loved her slowly, deliciously, with infinite gentleness, covering her eyelids, her lips, and her throat with kisses as he entered her and felt them become one.

Their movements became more urgent, fevered need took over, and Faith cried out as he plunged deep into her core. They bucked and rocked together, fusing their hearts, souls, and bodies until they were soaked with sweat, trembling and blissfully sated.

Outside, darkness settled over the mountains and Thunder Creek grew quiet as a cave. Faith and Zach lay curled together, and finally, in the cocoon of darkness and each other's arms, they slept.

•   •   •

First thing the next morning, before she even had coffee, Faith called Susan.

"I want you to go out to dinner at a nice restaurant tonight on me—and crack open a bottle of champagne. The kids get Shirley Temples and all the dessert they can eat."

"*What?* Oh my God, what's going on?" Susan gasped and then hushed the kids. "Turn down the TV, quiet a minute, okay, guys?

"Faith," she continued, "what are you talking about?"

"I'm talking about good news, Susan. I'm talking about the rest of your life. You never have to worry about Hank again."

"Don't tell me—he's been arrested? He's in jail?" Susan whispered, hope throbbing in her voice.

"Better. He's dead." It gave her only pleasure to say those words. But for a moment Faith heard nothing but silence.

Then, "Oh my God. You're sure?"

"Positive." Her lips were taut. "I saw the body myself."

Only then did Susan start to cry. And Faith knew she wasn't crying with sorrow.

"It's over, Susan," she told the sobbing woman, who was going to need some time to adjust to living life free of terror.

"Go out and celebrate. Look the world in the eye. Hank will never hurt you or scare you again." She was smiling into the phone as Susan wept with joy. "Go ahead, cry over him for the last time. It's all over."

Chapter 30

THREE DAYS LATER FAITH DRANK HER MORNING coffee alone on the porch of the cabin, gazing out over Blue Moon Mesa.

She had never seen it look quite so peaceful as it did today. The mountains rose, faintly lavender in the morning light, and the sky was smooth and pure as a sapphire.

Two young hawks circled overhead, then winged off toward Snowflake Mountain. The air was still and crisp, carrying the scent of cool stands of pine.

Only when she glanced over toward the place where Candy Merck's body had fallen did Faith feel a chill. Candy's death had been senseless. Dougie Clement had been after *her*. Candy never should have been hurt. But neither should Patti, or her baby, both of whom, thankfully, were fine.

At least Dougie was going to pay for his crimes. In the past few days Keene had gathered enough evidence to convict him ten times over. The apartment he'd been renting at the Pine Hills apartments yielded a wealth of evidence. Two strands of Candy's blond hair had been found on the cuff of a pair of gloves he must have worn the night of her murder. Her driver's license and purse were under his pillow. And the mask he'd worn when he'd attacked Patti had been nailed to the bathroom wall.

That was only the beginning. Clement had made little effort to conceal anything incriminating, no doubt believing he was too smart to ever get caught. A wallet and credit cards belonging to Hank Bayman were found tucked in a metal box under the bed, along with bomb-making and timer instructions downloaded from the Internet.

Keene told Zach they clearly linked Dougie to the explosion at the construction site, an explosion he'd apparently rigged to keep Zach busy while Faith was being kidnapped.

But so far, he hadn't been able to connect Clement to the note warning of the original bomb threat.

Probably because he didn't do it, Faith thought, taking a sip of her coffee. She and Zach were both convinced that Wood Morgan and Rusty Gallagher were responsible for that note—Dougie had only taken advantage of it, using their threat as a cover for his bomb.

But she highly doubted Keene would bother to pursue it. He'd gain nothing from going after them when Morgan was so generously supporting his campaign for sheriff.

At least, Faith reflected, watching a fox slink through the trees, there was now no reason to worry about Wood Morgan making any more trouble for Zach or the camp. He and Zach had made an arrangement, called a truce, and Morgan had recalled his petition drive.

Peace on earth, she thought grimly. *Or at least, in Thunder Creek.*

Especially since Dougie Clement was going away for good. He might not get the death penalty, but he'd be committed to either prison or a maximum-security mental hospital for the rest of his life.

Yesterday morning he'd been charged with two counts of murder, two counts of assault with intent to commit murder, one count of kidnapping, and one count of detonation of an explosive device with the intent to terrorize, maim, or kill. He'd then been taken under heavy guard to the Natrona County jail in Casper to await trial.

It was over.

Faith lifted her gaze to the rich turquoise sky and let herself bask in the peace that seemed to flow like a late summer breeze through the trees of Thunder Creek.

Only when her phone rang did she stir from her chair on the porch and go in search of it.

"Guess who's home?" Zach chuckled in her ear. "The kid hasn't stopped talking a mile a minute for the past half hour. The high point of his trip was riding all the way down the canyon and almost getting bit by a snake."

"Oh my God. Is he all right?"

"Are you kidding? He wants to go back and do it all over again. So are you ready to come over and spring the big surprise?"

"Are you sure you want to do it this way? Both of us telling him together? He doesn't know me that well yet, Zach. Maybe you should tell him first and I'll come by later—"

"Hey, since when did you turn into a chicken? Come on over here. We're going to do this together as a family."

As a family. She and Zach and Dillon, a family. Her heart lifted.

"I hope you know what you're doing, McCallum. I'm on my way."

Zach's pickup was over near the corrals, but other than that, the Last Trail ranch looked unusually quiet as she parked in the driveway.

Zach came out on the porch as she walked up the steps and kissed her.

"Dillon's out back in Ardelle's garden, playing with Batman. Are you ready?"

"You don't think he'll start to cry or anything, do you? I mean, he'll know I'm not going to try to replace his mom, right?"

"Believe me, replacing Alicia would be the kindest thing you could do for him." Zach smoothed her hair, kissed her deeply, and took her hand. "My little boy's going to feel almost as lucky as I do."

It was serenely quiet as they strolled through the house, the gracious, warm house Ardelle Harvey had loved all of her days and that had fascinated Faith from the first moment she entered it.

Faith's heartbeat quickened as she saw Dillon and Batman sitting in the grass beyond the deck. The boy tossed a ball a short distance, and Batman raced after it, trotting back proudly with it in his mouth. But they both stopped and looked over as she and Zach came out onto the wide planked deck.

Dillon jumped up, his quicksilver eyes alight. But instead of coming over to say hello, he opened his mouth wide and shouted, "Surprise!"

From every corner of the trees and shrubs and from behind her at the sides of the house, others yelled the same.

"Surprise!"

A flood of grinning people swarmed toward her, laughing and clapping. Bessie and Ada, wearing matching grins, Roy and Corinne, Gabe, Owen, the Templetons . . . *Patti and Bob*. And . . . from the side of the ranch house came her family—her mother and father—all the way from

Philadelphia—her brother Adam, and bringing up the rear, arm in arm, Ty and Josy—back from New York.

"What the hell is going on?" Faith croaked in disbelief as her family enfolded her in a giant Barclay embrace.

"You didn't think we'd let you get engaged without all of us being here, did you?" Her mother smiled.

"How . . . did you know? . . ."

"How do you think?" her brother Ty shot back. "Clue number one stands about six foot three and is right behind you. Kind of hard to miss. Even if he did summon us by phone."

A glowing Josy squeezed Faith's arm. "It looks like he's got something to say," she murmured, glancing behind Faith at Zach.

As her family stepped back and the crowd grew silent, Faith slowly, dazedly, turned around.

Zach was grinning at her, looking pretty damned pleased with himself.

"You might have noticed that the other night I never formally asked you to be my wife. Not in the usual way—with a proposal."

"You don't ever do things the usual way," she laughed.

"That was intentional." His tone grew more serious and he raised his voice so that it carried throughout the crowd of friends and family gathered around them in the garden.

"Years ago I ran off and left you high and dry, and the whole town knew about it. Now I'm going to ask you to marry me, and they're all going to know that too. They're going to be our witnesses. Every one of you," Zach addressed the crowd to cheers and whistles. "Pay attention now," he instructed them.

Oh my God. He's crazy. Faith felt a blush stealing up her

throat, flooding into her cheeks. When Zach did something, he didn't ever do it by half measures, did he?

Right now he was kneeling down before her, and as he did, he reached out and took her hand in his.

From the corner of her eye, she saw Dillon pressing forward, his mouth gaping open in delight.

Then she couldn't see anything but the expression on Zach's face as he gazed up at her.

"Marry me, Faith. I love you. You're my heart. My light. My life. I'm asking you before all our friends and family, and I'll keep asking you until you say yes. Will you do me the very great honor of agreeing to become my wife?"

There was no amusement in his eyes now. They were intent on hers, gleaming and purposeful. The hushed crowd around them—friends and family—might not have existed. Faith saw only Zach, her Zach, with that sexy smile on his lips and the tension in his jaw as he waited for her answer.

"If you say yes," he added softly, his fingers warm and strong around hers, "you'll give me the chance to make up to you for all the years we've been apart."

Silence thundered through the garden as Faith stared into his eyes.

"Then I guess I'd better say yes," she whispered.

"Couldn't hear you," Bessie called out, and Faith's brother Adam chuckled.

"Me either," he said.

Corinne piped up, "Louder."

"Yes!" Faith shouted, laughing too. "Yes, Zach, I *will* marry you and I'll hold you to that promise for the rest of our lives!"

Applause and cheers and whistles broke out, but Faith scarcely heard them.

Zach stood, wrapped his arms around her, and kissed her thoroughly. Deeply. Possessively.

They were the only two people in the garden, in Thunder Creek, in all of Wyoming. No, in all of the world.

Heat rushed, blood raced. Their mouths clung, hungry, needy, and finally fulfilled.

When they broke apart, Zach yanked a small white velvet box from his pocket. He flipped it open. Faith stared at the diamond ring nestled in smooth pink velvet.

It was emerald-cut, set in platinum, and it dazzled brighter than a July sun.

"Put it on." Dillon tapped her arm as she gazed wordlessly at Zach. "Dad, help her put it on."

More laughter and applause as Zach slid the ring on her finger.

Then Faith knelt and gathered Dillon close. "We're all getting married, Dillon. Our whole new family."

"Cool." The boy's grin almost outshone the diamond. "But I don't want a ring or anything. A baby brother—now that would be awesome."

"We'll start working on it right away," Zach promised. As he saw the laughter burst across Faith's face, a strange new feeling descended upon him. Contentment.

So that's what it felt like.

"Bring out the food and let's get this party rolling," Bessie chirped, and all around them people began to scatter. Batman barked, and Corinne and Patti rushed to take charge of setting up the buffet tables.

Faith felt her mother kiss her cheek, her father hug her. She embraced them and her brothers, and stepping back, still dazed, met Zach's eyes in the sunlight.

They smiled at each other, but there was no time, and no need for words.

They both knew what the other was thinking, feeling, as the party swept into full swing around them, as great platters of fried chicken, sliced ham, crusty rolls, and potato salad filled the buffet tables covered in red-and-white-checked cloths. Roy and Owen dragged a cooler from the bushes, and everyone hurried to grab plates and flatware, beer and colas.

But Faith and Zach weren't even aware of the food—only of each other and the unbreakable bond between them.

This was their time, now, at last. Their time to laugh, to celebrate, to marry. And beneath the enduring sun and mountains, moon and stars, clouds and sagebrush, and all the passing seasons of Thunder Creek—their time, at last, to love.

About the Author

JILL GREGORY IS THE *NEW YORK TIMES* best-selling author of thirty novels. Her novels have been translated and published in Japan, Russia, France, Norway, Taiwan, Sweden, and Italy. Jill grew up in Chicago and received her bachelor of arts degree in English from the University of Illinois. She currently resides in Michigan with her husband.

Jill invites her readers to visit her website at www.jillgregory.net.